The Gathering Storm

Mary Tant in [a] Christie-
small group of polite char
and rui
owned   DORSE
Christi
ment

GW00701805

400

THE ROSSINGTON SERIES

The Rossington Inheritance

Death at the Priory

Friends ... and a Foe

Players and Betrayers

The Watcher on the Cliff

Don't Come Back

MARY TANT'S WEBSITE

http://www.marytant.com

MARY TANT

The Gathering Storm

Threshold Press

© Mary Tant 2013

First published 2013 by Threshold Press Ltd,
Norfolk House
75 Bartholomew Street,
Newbury Berks RG14 5DU
Phone 01635-230272 and fax 01635-44804
email: publish@threshold-press.co.uk
www.threshold-press.co.uk

British Library Cataloguing in Publication Data
A catalogue record for this book is available from the British
Library ISBN 978–1–903152–31–7

Designed by Jim Weaver Design

Printed in Great Britain by Berfort Information Press, Stevenage

FOR ALISON AND JIM
DEAR FRIENDS AT
ALL TIMES

ONE

Lucy Rossington stopped waving and let her hand fall to her side as the car disappeared from sight along the drive with a fading rattle. Her brother Will had insisted on tying cans to the back bumper, where they made a satisfyingly loud noise as the groom had driven his bride away. Lucy stood still, staring unseeingly after the car as a hum of voices around her rose and fell, exhilarated and happy.

'Well,' Anna Evesleigh said lightly beside her, 'that's all done. I really think Daddy was afraid Fran might back out of it at the last moment. As it is, I've got myself a stepmamma. And quite a different person to my own dear mother.'

Lucy came out of her thoughts with an effort and turned to the woman who had spoken, whose nicely curved figure was expertly set off by the fashionably high-waisted dress she wore. In an attempt not to outshine the bride Anna had eschewed her favourite scarlet and opted for a deep pink. Almost absentmindedly, Lucy noticed how well the colour suited her friend's rose and cream complexion and long dark curls.

'It did go nicely, Anna,' Lucy replied. 'I don't think I've ever seen Fran look so happy. And your father was obviously proud of her.'

'Mmm,' Anna agreed, picking hydrangea-petal confetti out of her hair. 'It has been a bit of a struggle, though. I really think she'd have gone quite happily to the church in her jeans and without doing her hair.'

Lucy's gamine smile lit her small pointed face. 'You did a sterling job. That cream dress and jacket were just right for Fran. Not too fussy.'

'She's got a good figure,' Anna said judiciously, rubbing the petals between her fingers. 'It must be all the hard work she does on her farm, because it certainly isn't her diet.' Anna shuddered delicately. 'She's got nice thick hair too. The short angular style suits it well. But,' she gave a little sigh, 'I don't expect she'll look after it when she gets home.'

'For God's sake,' a man said loudly, 'what does it matter? She's got Richard, hasn't she? She won't need to worry about how she looks now.'

Anna gave an exaggerated start and turned to face the man who stood scowling at her, his arms akimbo, his red hair wildly tousled. She smiled sweetly. 'Why, Mike, that's clever of you. Daddy doesn't mind in the slightest how Fran looks. I don't expect he even knew why she looked different today.'

Her eyes ran over Mike Shannon. He had discarded his jacket and tie, revealing a rumpled white shirt that had odd washed-out brown stains down its front. 'Mike,' she exclaimed, 'surely you don't wear that shirt when you're working on a dig?'

He glanced down, a puzzled expression on his square freckled face. 'Of course I don't,' he muttered. 'But I can't always pick and choose when I might find something interesting. Anyway,' he growled, his eyes narrowing, 'you don't have to worry about my clothes.' He glanced at Lucy. 'If you want to hang around out here in girl chat that's fine, but Hugh's starting work on the barbecue. If you want to eat you'd better come and help him.'

He turned on his heel and strode back into the house. Anna stared after him, then threw an amused look at Lucy, who was gazing abstractedly at Withern, the house that she and her husband Hugh Carey had bought just over a year ago. It was worth looking at, Anna thought. It always had been, even in the state of extraordinary dilapidation it was in when Hugh found it.

The two women were standing before the double-fronted house that, in the late Georgian era, had been tacked onto the end of a sixteenth century farmhouse. The original building, not visible from here, had been left over the centuries in pretty much its original form, and used generally as domestic quarters.

'Who'd have thought so much would happen when you bought this house,' Anna commented. 'Especially Daddy finding your farming neighbour was an old friend of his and marrying her. And you and Hugh have done a fantastic recovery job with this place. I can't believe you got so much sorted out in such a short time. It looks as though you've been settled here for ages.'

'It feels like it sometimes,' Lucy agreed, her low voice quite flat.

Anna glanced at her quickly. 'I suppose it seems odd, making such a big effort on the renovation and decoration, and now having everything finished. You must feel at a bit of a loose end,' she said. 'I only hope Daddy and Fran can agree on where they're going to live. I don't really know why she won't come to our house. I'm hardly ever there, and if I'm in the way when I come down I can always plant myself on you. After all, it isn't as if Mother ever lived there, and I'm sure Daddy can buy fields for Fran's animals. It isn't as if she's got loads, her place is only a small farm.' Anna lifted an elegant shoulder. 'But perhaps it might be better if they found somewhere of their own. It just seems such an effort. Now is probably the time to do it too,' she smiled brilliantly, 'while they're both so happy with each other.'

'Yes,' Lucy said soberly, 'before the rose-coloured glow fades.'

'Lucy,' Anna was seriously perturbed, 'everything is alright, isn't it? Between you and Hugh, I mean.'

Lucy brushed back a strand of chestnut hair from her face, tucking it into place in her long bob. 'Oh yes,' she said. 'We're fine.' She called Ben, the tricolour collie who had been sniffing along the hedge that lined the drive leading round to the farmyard, and walked towards the front of the house.

As Ben came up eagerly Anna fell into step beside her friend, saying bluntly, 'Come on, Lucy. You seem to be in a world of your own these days. And not a happy one, either.'

Lucy flicked a quick look at her, her hazel eyes sombre. 'I've just got some decisions to make, that's all,' she said quietly. 'We all have to from time to time.'

She went through the open front door into the wide hallway. When she had first seen this it had been partially obscured by the filthy glass in the sash windows and the sheets of cobwebs that hung from the high ceiling. Now the replastered walls were pristine, the cornices repaired, and all painted a light grey. A glass storm lantern hung from the centre of the ceiling, reflected in the floor length mirror in a gilded frame that almost covered one wall.

This was the formal entrance to the house, where the pale stone floor tiles were almost always uncluttered. It was the entrances in the older part of the building that were cluttered with the boots and coats of everyday country use.

Lucy did not pause to appreciate the change in the room. She stopped beside the console table on one side of the hall, leafing quickly through the letters that had been put there. Almost impatiently she pushed them to one side, dropping a thick white envelope that she hastily retrieved, dropping it carelessly onto the pile again. She walked quickly past the painted treads of the sweeping staircase to the door that led through to the back of the house, Ben pattering at her heels.

Anna cast a quick glance at the large picture that hung over the console table opposite the mirror. Hugh's choice, she knew, as her eyes passed approvingly over the curves of the snipe caught in flight, a bird of brown shades against the warmth of a heather moor. She tore her gaze away and followed Lucy, more anxious than before, and without the usual thrill of surprise that the change from Georgian gentility to Elizabethan farmhouse normally gave her.

As they walked down the long corridor that ran along the old front of the sixteenth century farmhouse, with Ben's claws clicking on the granite slabs, Anna did not even glance through the original front door of the farmhouse, which stood open onto a small garden. This door had been reopened during the renovations, after Lucy had carefully pruned the tangled mass of roses that had concealed it. The caterers had used it today as the shortest route between the kitchen and the orchard, where a gazebo had been erected under the ancient fruit trees for the small wedding reception Anna's father had insisted upon.

For a second Anna's spirits lightened, remembering how in turn Fran had insisted the reception should be out of doors. It was fortunate that Fran's weather prediction had been accurate, Anna thought, slowing her step to cast a quick look out of one of the small windows at the sunlight, whose warmth had already brought a tinge of pink and crimson to the early rosebuds.

The sound of men's voices caught her attention, and she looked down to the end of the corridor where Lucy was disappearing into the kitchen. Mike's voice was loud and indignant, covering the clear laugh of a younger man that Anna knew as Will, Lucy's brother, and a lower voice that was Hugh's, Lucy's husband.

Anna paused in the kitchen doorway, watching Mike push away the dogs that milled around his legs. From the fuss he was making, Anna thought, you'd think it was a whole pack falling on him. Really it was just Ben, Lucy's collie, and Will's large black curly-haired mongrel, Hades, whose long tail was lashing furiously with pleasure at the game he thought Mike was playing.

It was Mike's own fault, Anna decided, that the dogs always leaped on him, because he always made it such fun. But Ben, Anna noted, had already slipped into position near Hugh, who was preparing steaks for the barbecue, drizzling herbed oil over them as he laid them across a tray. The collie lay quietly, his black head on his speckled paws, his golden eyes alert, waiting for any spillage.

As Hades flung himself down next to Ben, long pink tongue lolling out of his grinning mouth, Anna glanced round the room, appreciating the cream walls and deeper cream kitchen cupboards. It seemed to be full of light, especially now that it had been opened into the other rooms at the back of the house.

The connecting doors in the new archway were pushed back, revealing the dining room that had been created when two large storerooms were knocked into the old parlour. The table in the centre had been opened out to its full extent, and Anna guessed that it had been made ready, just in case Fran's weather forecast had been wrong and the unseasonal hot and sunny weather had not lasted.

Anna's eyes turned towards Lucy who had opened the doors of a modern dresser, which was a deep shade of cream like the other kitchen units. Lucy's simple cotton plaid shift in shades of green looked very good on her slight, boyishly slender figure, especially with the sequin and bead embroidery across the bodice. Anna made a mental note to ask Lucy where she had found it, while her eyebrows contracted slightly as she noticed how thin Lucy had become.

'Of course I'm hungry,' Mike said loudly, startling Anna, as he leaned back on a kitchen chair, balancing it on two legs. 'Will is too.'

The young man leaning against one of the wooden work surfaces grinned. He was taller than his sister Lucy, and had dark hair, but there was a noticeable family resemblance in their build and features. 'Too right,' he said. 'See, I keep telling Lucy to keep chips and burgers in the freezer, especially as we're on study leave. We'd be okay now.'

His friend nearby shuddered as she chopped tomatoes with a deft hand. 'Not really, Will,' she said. 'Anyway, I'll soon have these salads done, and Hugh's nearly got everything ready for the barbecue.'

'Are you sure, Niri?' Lucy asked quietly, putting plates onto a wicker tray. 'We can always go into Coombhaven for a meal.'

'Of course I'm sure,' Niri said calmly. 'You know how much I like cooking, and it's a shame not to enjoy this weather. Who knows how long it's going to last.'

'It was clever of you to change,' Anna commented. 'That was a nice dress you were wearing.' She glanced down at her own. 'Perhaps I'd better slip into jeans as well.'

'I had to,' Niri said. 'I don't run to dresses, so I borrowed one of my mother's. I daren't mess it up.' She turned to the two men lounging on the far side of the table. 'Will, if you and Mike remove the pergola and take the cloths off the table in the orchard we'll probably be more comfortable. And you can light the barbecue too, then we'll be able to eat fairly soon.'

Mike let his chair land heavily on all four legs and stood up reluctantly. 'Alright,' he said, 'we'll make ourselves useful. Just as well I don't mind messing my clothes up.' He shot a meaningful look at Anna as he passed her, with Will at his heels. Hades leaped up to follow his master, but Ben stayed in place, his eyes just flickering across to Lucy to check what she was doing.

'I don't know how you can all face food again so soon,' Lucy said, as she added a heap of cutlery to the wide wicker tray. 'Anna,' she said as she moved towards the doorway, where the collie came to join her with a little reluctance, 'would you bring the glasses after you've changed. They're all ready on a tray in the dining room. I'll just take this lot out and then I'll come up too and get out of this dress. It was far too expensive to risk at a barbecue.'

'Of course,' Anna said, relieved that her friend sounded herself again. 'I won't be more than a few minutes. Hugh,' she asked over her shoulder as she went back towards the long corridor, 'did you chill the champagne I brought?'

The man who was now efficiently chopping onions and peppers into large segments paused, knife in hand, as he looked towards Anna. 'Naturally,' he drawled. 'But do you really think we're going to get through three bottles?'

Anna paused, turning to smile fondly at him. He was a man of medium height and medium brown colouring, not somebody who stood out at first glance. But first glances were so often deceptive, Anna thought, remembering Hugh's brilliant reputation as a barrister, the result of his resounding success in the first big trial where he had acted for the prosecution. He had surprised many people soon afterwards when he had suddenly left the legal world, and the meteoric career predicted for him, to completely change direction and lifestyle.

Anna wondered, for the first time, why he had done it. They had been friends for several years, meeting on the London social circuit long before Hugh had met Lucy, Anna's old school friend. But Hugh rarely spoke about himself or his own feelings, so in many ways she did not know him well. Yet Anna was sure that Hugh was already achieving a good reputation and growing success with the publishing venture he had started a couple of years ago, just at the time he had first met Lucy.

'Naturally we'll get through three bottles,' she said aloud, suddenly aware of his quizzically raised eyebrow as he waited for a reply to his question. 'This is a real party. I've got my father happily settled and off my hands. We have to celebrate that. And I wanted to thank you and Lucy for having the reception here.' She hesitated for a second, but then carried on, 'It's not just that the orchard is so pretty with all the blossom coming out, but Fran didn't want to have it at our house and we couldn't have had it on her farm.'

'We're fond of Fran and Richard,' Hugh said lightly. 'We were glad to help them.'

There was a slight frown between Anna's beautifully shaped eyebrows as she stood back to let Niri with her brimming bowls of salad go past her into the corridor. 'Hugh, do you know why Fran should be so set against living in our house? I really can't see how she could dislike it.'

'Of course she doesn't dislike it,' Hugh said, beginning to thread vegetable chunks onto bamboo skewers with alternate pieces of white fish. 'It's a beautiful house, but I expect she doesn't want to start married life in a place that has so much history for your father and none for her.'

Anna considered this. 'You did,' she said bluntly. 'Lucy's family have lived at Rossington Manor for centuries. Is that why you both came to Withern in the end?'

'Partly,' he replied, as he laid the kebabs onto a foil-lined dish. 'But it was different for us, because the manor is Will's. Lucy and I couldn't live there with him now he's come of age. He has his own plans for the place, and won't want us cramping his style.'

Anna was silent, remembering that Lucy had not wanted to move away from her family home at first. Before she could ask any more Hugh said, 'Off you go, those glasses will be in demand soon. I'll bring the food out in a few minutes and we can get the cooking started. The steaks should marinade for a little longer, but Mike won't want to wait. Neither will Will,' he added resignedly. 'And don't worry about Fran and your father. These things sort themselves out. If,' he added, almost as an afterthought, 'people want to stay together enough.'

The kitchen was empty when Anna returned a short time later, still elegant in her red cut-off jeans and loose white shirt. She paused to glance around the room, appreciating the modern simplicity of the wooden kitchen table with its recycled steel legs. With a jolt of surprise Anna suddenly realised she was thinking of what she would have done to the room. Smiling ruefully, she walked swiftly into the dining room to pick up the tray of glasses before she went back into the corridor and a short way along it to the old front door. The garden here was almost a courtyard, edged by the house on three sides, with a low wall separating it from the drive on the fourth side. Lucy had trimmed back the overgrown bushes and cut into the rough turf to form beds against the walls of the house and beside the path. As Anna picked her way carefully along the path, she saw that these beds were already planted with lavender and rosemary. And there were what she guessed to be other herbs. Certainly she recognised sage and thyme.

Anna went through the gate in the garden wall onto the lane

that served as the drive that led to Withern, both the house and
the old farmyard behind it, and then went further on to Fran's
farm. Ancient apple trees were already faintly hazed with pink
blossom beyond the hedge on the far side of the drive. As Anna
walked through the wicket gate into the orchard, she noticed that
Lucy had been busy here too. These trees had all been pruned
neatly, and, looking around more carefully now that the gazebo
was down, she could see the newly planted apple trees between
the survivors of the original orchard. No wonder Lucy was thin,
she must have been working flat out, Anna thought.

Movement to one side caught her eye. 'Mind out, Mike,' she
said sharply, swerving out of his way, the glasses rattling on the
tray in her hands.

'Don't stand there dreaming,' he snapped. 'This is bloody
heavy.'

He stomped past her, the folded canopy of the gazebo
clutched awkwardly in his arms, Hades worrying happily at a
dangling end. She noticed with annoyance that the long ribbons
she and Lucy had tied onto it were littering the ground beyond
them.

Will grinned at Anna, his dark eyes lit with amusement as he
passed her, the gazebo poles over his shoulder. 'Never get in Mike's
way, Anna,' he said. 'You should know by now it's not safe.'

'I certainly know he can't watch where he's going,' she replied
crossly. She looked around, seeing that the long table by the far
fence had been stripped of its cloths. They had been dumped on
one of the unused chairs, which Will or Mike had dragged up to
the side of the orchard, below the barbecue.

Lucy had offloaded her tray and laid out the plates and cutlery,
while Niri had placed her bowls of salad along the centre of the
table. Smoke drifted towards Anna from the brick barbecue in the
upper corner of the orchard, and she moved down the slope to
the table, suddenly aware of how heavy her tray was.

'Thanks, Anna, just put them by the plates and tuck the tray
out of the way against the fence,' Lucy instructed. She glanced

over her shoulder, then back at her friend. 'Do you think I can let the hens out now? They aren't used to being penned up.' She smiled mischievously. 'I knew Fran wouldn't have minded them, but I thought it would be trying your father a bit much to have them clucking around him while he ate.'

'I can't see why it would be a problem now,' Anna said, as she put out the glasses, 'as long as you're sure Mike won't tread on them.'

Lucy pulled a face, but walked over to the heavily wired enclosure at the other end of the orchard, Ben at her heels. The hens rushed towards the door in the fencing with a frenzied clucking, their bodies rolling from side to side in their haste to reach it. The collie watched them with interest but kept his distance as Lucy unpinned the door and released a flood of birds.

Anna propped her tray beside the others, a niggle of concern growing again in her mind. Lucy had obviously been back into the house to change too, for she was now wearing cotton trousers and a blue and green shirt. There was no reason, of course, Anna reasoned, why Lucy should have looked into the spare room for a chat about the wedding, but still it was odd, unusual, that she hadn't. Anna shrugged mentally. She was getting a bee in her bonnet. Better to leave that to Mike.

Leaning against the small gate that led out of the bottom of the orchard, Anna looked at the meadow that sloped down to the river Corre below. It was as if a sheet of indigo blue had been laid across the turf, pinned into place by bushes of foaming white blackthorn. Anna's eyes lingered on the bluebells, flowering in such profusion in the grass. Her gaze moved on down to the riverbank, where the willows were coloured with the green of new leaves. A patch of bright white caught her attention, and she stared.

'I didn't know you'd got another boat, Lucy,' she said in surprise. 'It's pretty big, isn't it?'

'Oh, it's not ours. We've still got the rowing boat, although Hugh's added a motor,' Lucy said, coming to stand beside her.

'That one belongs to some bloke who asked if he could moor there for a bit.'

'Do you know him?' Anna asked.

Lucy shook her head, her chestnut hair swinging around her shoulders. 'No, but he's a writer, one of those very serious novelists, so of course Hugh thought it would be okay.'

'Do you mind?'

'Why should I?' Lucy shrugged. 'He asked Hugh, and Hugh said yes. He goes down there most evenings to see him. It sounds as though they get on very well. In fact, I won't be surprised if Hugh offers to publish his book. Apparently the extracts Hugh's seen are very good.'

'What's his name?' Anna demanded. 'I might know him.' She smiled suddenly. 'Although serious novelists don't sound quite my style.'

'I don't know. Hugh said, but I can't remember who he is. I'm not even sure if he writes in his own name. I think,' she ended vaguely, 'that Hugh mentioned a pseudonym.'

'Have you met this man?' Anna persisted.

'No, I've been busy,' Lucy said, rather defensively. 'I haven't been back from London long.'

'Of course not,' Anna said. She was aware that Lucy was not happy with the subject, so she sought a change of topic. 'Now we're all here I'd like to check dates for the Rossington Play this summer, and run through the ideas I've got for it. We'll just have to hope the weather's going to be good again in August.'

'Okay,' Lucy sounded unenthusiastic.

Anna turned, resting her back against the gate, and stared at her friend. 'Don't you want to do it again?'

'It's up to Will, really, as it's a manor affair,' Lucy said. 'I know he's keen to make it a regular event. These outdoor plays seem generally to be popular.'

'Don't you want to be involved then?' Anna demanded. 'I suppose,' she tried more tentatively, 'you're very busy.'

'It's not that,' Lucy said slowly, 'but I may have to go to

London again soon, and I'm not sure yet what I'll be doing this summer.'

Anna's heart sank, but she managed to say lightly, 'That all sounds very mysterious and exciting.'

'Not really,' Lucy said flatly.

'Hey, you two,' Will called, 'come and get your champagne.'

'Don't say anything,' Lucy said quickly, 'but come for a walk tomorrow. I'll tell you then.'

There was a loud pop as Will released the cork from a bottle. Lucy and Anna turned towards him in time to see Niri deftly catch the spurting champagne in a glass.

'Really, Will,' Anna said as she reached the table and picked up another glass, 'I must show you how to open a champagne bottle without all that fanfare.'

'No doubt you're an expert,' Mike commented sarcastically.

'Definitely,' Anna said sweetly, holding up the glass in her hand to watch the bubbles dancing through the golden wine. 'I have so many skills, Mike, you've no idea.'

He snorted, jerking the glass in his hand and almost spilling the contents. He put it down impatiently on the table and stalked past her to join Hugh at the barbecue, saying gruffly, 'But I'm sure they don't include barbecuing.'

'Actually,' Anna confided quietly to Niri, 'they do, but I wouldn't dream of telling Mike. It's so nice for him to feel useful occasionally.'

Niri smiled. 'Men do seem to enjoy barbecuing,' she said, watching Will as he began to prod the steaks Hugh had placed on the grill.

'At least the others had the sense to get into jeans,' Anna commented. 'Mike seems to still be in his best trousers. Not,' she added lightly, 'that it's ever possible to be sure with him.'

Mike was fitting sausages rather haphazardly around the steaks. Picking up the last one, he cursed loudly as it dropped from the fork onto the grass. With a foot he held off the chickens that rushed over, and bent to pick it up. Holding it in one hand he glanced round, met Anna's eyes and ostentatiously placed the sausage back in its wrappings. The two dogs were nearby, watching him alertly from their carefully casual positions beside the table.

'What are you having?' Anna asked, remembering that Niri was a vegetarian.

'Hugh's done fish kebabs with mushrooms and peppers, and some plain vegetable ones too,' Niri replied, 'but they don't take as long to cook as the meat.'

'Oh yes, I saw them in the kitchen. They looked good,' Anna said. 'If there are enough I might have those. Steak seems rather hearty at this time of the day.'

'And in this heat,' Niri said, looking at the bright sunshine that still flooded the meadow below the orchard. 'I hope it lasts for a bit. I'm staying at the manor with Will to do our revision, and it's great to be outside when it's like this.'

'Of course,' Anna said, remembering, 'you must be just getting into the exam season. When do you finish school?'

'Not until the end of next month, even though the exams will be finished before that,' Will said in Anna's ear, making her start. 'Lucy said you want a meeting about the manor play,' he went on, holding out a large bowl. 'That's good, I need to check the days with you because I've got to set a date for my birthday party.'

Anna looked puzzled as she took a handful of crisps from the bowl he held out to her. 'But you've just had your birthday,' she pointed out. 'I sent you a card.'

'Yeah, I got it. And the GPS receiver's really cool, thanks. I've written to you,' Will said with conscious virtue, plonking the bowl down on the table near his sister, 'but I don't expect you've got it yet. I sent it to your flat in London, but you've been down here. Anyway,' he went on, 'I had a party at school for the actual date. The August one's going to be THE big eighteenth bash, where everyone's invited. You too,' he added generously. 'It's a kind of going away thing as well, because I'm off to India at the beginning of September.'

'India,' Anna exclaimed in surprise. She glanced at Niri. 'Are you going too?'

Niri nodded, sipping at her glass of water. 'Yes, we're going out together, but then we're doing different things. I'm going to work on a women's community scheme in Jaipur, but Will is going to be in various places.'

'Yeah,' Will agreed. 'You remember Safiya, Niri's aunt. Well, she's arranged for me to spend time on an internship with the Wildlife Service, then as a volunteer in a bear sanctuary near Agra and a wildlife sanctuary down in Kerala. That's in the mountains, the Cardamom Hills, doesn't it sound cool?' He grinned happily. 'It's rainforest there, and there'll be tigers and elephants and wild dogs.' His grin widened. 'Gran really approves. She knows Kerala, of course. I half think she'll come out to see me when I'm there.'

'It all sounds amazing,' Anna said, half enviously. 'I've always wanted to go to India.'

'You can follow my blog,' Will said. 'Niri and I are going to meet up from time to time. We want to see as much as we can of the country,' he continued. 'Her family out there sound cool, they've invited us to all sorts of places.'

'But what about the manor?' Anna asked. 'Is Lucy going to run things while you're away?'

'No need,' Will said, taking a large gulp of his champagne and pulling a face. 'I really don't know why people think this stuff is so wonderful,' he complained.

Niri nudged him with her elbow. 'The manor, Will,' she prompted him, glancing over his shoulder to where Lucy was picking up the discarded tablecloths and folding them neatly.

'Oh yeah,' he said, putting the glass down on the table. 'Well, it's all sorted. David, the estate manager, you know,' he glanced interrogatively at Anna.

She nodded. 'Yes,' she said, restraining her impatience, 'I have met David. Several times.'

Will grinned at her. 'I didn't know how good your memory was,' he said.

She ignored the provocation, and he went on, 'Well, David and I have agreed what needs to be done on the estate, and he and Jack Leygar at Home Farm get on really well, so they'll be able to sort out any problems. And Jack's daughter, Philly, is running the holiday cottages without any hassle.'

'Yes, I know how competent she is,' Anna said, frowning slightly. 'After all, she was my deputy for the first Rossington play last year. I was rather hoping she'd do the same again this year, and perhaps take on more of the admin.' Anna's frown deepened. 'But I suppose she's fully occupied with the lettings.'

Will laughed. 'Mike's infecting you with his approach. Always look on the black side of things.'

Anna opened her mouth indignantly, but Will hurried on, 'Philly's looking forward to doing another play. I told her,' he said firmly, 'we'd pay her this year.' He glanced at Anna. 'After all, we did make a profit last time.'

She nodded, thinking how much Will had matured in the last year. 'Of course we'll pay her. And you too, Niri, if you can do the research again,' she said, glancing at the younger woman.

'That would be useful,' Niri admitted. 'I need to earn money this summer to pay my way in India. My parents are covering the travel and living expenses, but I've got to get my own spending money.'

'How about next year, Will?' Anna demanded. 'Do you want to establish an annual programme for the Rossington Plays? Because if you do, how are we going to plan more if you're away?'

'No sweat,' Will said airily. 'We'll fix the dates when we're discussing this year's play, and then you can sort out what you need with Philly. If she helps Niri with some of the research this time, she'll know what to do next time.'

Anna glanced questioningly at Niri, who was smiling. 'I think it would work,' Niri said.

'You've got it all worked out, haven't you, Will?' Anna said, with a note of amusement in her voice.

The young man shrugged, a look of determination on his thin

face. 'I'm not giving the manor up,' he said quietly, 'but I'm going to live my life the way I want.'

Anna glanced over to where Lucy sat at the table, sipping at her champagne, looking down towards the river, her back to the activities in the orchard. Ben sat beside her, his head on her knees, as she absentmindedly stroked him.

Anna remembered how Lucy had given up her own opportunity to develop a more exotic life as a botanist, studying rainforest plants in Peru. When their father had died she had desperately wanted to keep the manor going for her younger brother.

Anna shuddered, remembering some of the events of the last couple of years, when one or other of the Rossington circle seemed to have fallen into dangerous situations. But, she reminded herself, the manor was now definitely a going concern. Lucy had succeeded in her aim. I wonder, a little voice murmured in Anna's mind, how Lucy feels about Will's plans.

'If you want to eat,' Mike said loudly beside her, 'take a plate and help yourself. Waiting isn't included in today's service.'

Anna started, and glared crossly at him.

'Lucy,' he shouted, ignoring Anna, 'come and get yours. Quick, before the vultures land.' He gave Anna a meaningful glance as he turned back towards the barbecue.

Will snorted with laughter. 'After you, ladies,' he said with extreme politeness, making an exaggerated sweep of his arm.

Anna ostentatiously ignored Mike, and smiled at Will as he and Niri moved after the other man. 'You're certainly going to miss Mike's manners while you're in India,' she said pointedly.

'What's this?' Mike demanded, stopping abruptly and swinging round. 'What are you going to India for, Will?' He scowled. 'Nobody tells me anything around here.'

Anna heard Will beginning to repeat his story as she picked up a plate from the table and fell into step beside Lucy as they strolled up to the barbecue. 'Will's plans sound exciting,' she commented, smiling at Hugh as he passed them on his way to the table with his own laden plate.

Lucy's expression brightened with interest. 'He's full of them,' she said. 'He's really deciding now what he wants to do in the future. He's applied to various places to read wildlife conservation. I think he's hoping to get a place at Plymouth.'

'Are you pleased?' Anna demanded. 'It doesn't sound as though he's going to be here very much.'

'Of course I'm pleased,' Lucy said in surprise. 'He's very keen to do something useful about the environment and animal welfare, and this should be a good opportunity for him to see what working in those areas is like.'

Anna was eyeing the steaks and sausages. 'Hugh's done these very nicely. Usually they're all over charcoal. I think I'll have some of everything.' She began to load her plate, asking cautiously, 'What about the manor?'

'Will seems to have got everything sorted out there,' Lucy said evenly.

Anna glanced sideways as she reached for one of the fish kebabs. But Lucy was leaning forward, helping herself to food, her hair falling over her face and concealing her expression.

'Get a move on, Anna,' Mike said sharply, reaching past her to pick up a sausage with his fingers. 'Oww,' he grunted. 'It's bloody hot.'

Before she could reply he said over his shoulder, 'I'll give you a list of sites, Will, and mark the ones you mustn't miss.'

Lucy moved away towards the table and Anna followed. 'I've never understood,' she said casually, 'how Mike and Hugh came to be friends. They're so different.'

Lucy glanced at her in surprise. 'But friends often are. Look at us. We're not much alike.'

Anna was taken aback. 'But we've got a lot in common,' she said. 'Attitudes, and all that,' she finished lamely.

'I know,' Lucy agreed, 'but if you think about it, Mike and Hugh do too.'

Anna lapsed into silence as they reached the table.

Hugh looked up from his conversation with Niri, who was seated beside him. 'Do I gather Mike's setting Will up to report back on archaeological sites?'

'It sounds like it,' Lucy said lightly, as she put her plate on the table and sat down opposite him. Ben flung himself to the ground beside her chair, scattering chickens in all directions.

'Pass me some salad, please, Hugh. It looks very good.' She helped herself out of the bowls, taking watercress with herbs, selecting a few lettuce and chicory leaves sprinkled with radishes and capers, and a handful of differently coloured chopped tomatoes mixed into couscous with yet more herbs. 'You always do unusual salads, Niri, they're so much more interesting than mine.' She sighed ruefully. 'I suppose I ought to make more effort.'

'I enjoy making meals,' Niri said, 'and I've probably got more time than you anyway.'

'Make the most of it,' Lucy said, lifting some early new potatoes onto her plate.

'Isn't there any plain lettuce?' Mike demanded, staring in disbelief at the bowls as he sat down beside Lucy. 'Not that I like salad anyway,' he muttered, as Hugh passed a bowl of mixed green leaves across the table to him.

'Well, Anna,' Hugh said as she took the other seat next to him. 'Are we making toasts, or do we just work our way through the champagne?'

Mike growled, not quite under his breath, 'And where's the beer? Champagne at a barbecue, I ask you.' He snorted in disgust, watching Hades slip under the table to lie across his feet.

Anna let Hugh fill her glass again, and watched as the others passed theirs over to be topped up. All except for Will, opposite her, whose virtually untouched glass stood in front of him. Anna smiled at him. 'Never mind, Will, just have a sip.' She turned to Hugh. 'I'll leave the obvious toast to you,' she said to him. 'Mine,' she raised her glass as she spoke, 'is "Lucy and Hugh, with my thanks for hosting the reception".'

Everyone sipped their champagne, except Niri, who lifted her glass of juice. They all glanced expectantly at Hugh.

'And of course,' he said, 'we must drink to Fran and Richard. "Long may the pleasures of marriage survive".'

After the next sip Will raised his glass with an air of bravado. 'To Gran,' he said, 'who came back from Italy specially for the wedding.'

'She's yo-yoing backwards and forwards all the time,' Mike commented. 'I thought she was going to stay there for half the year.'

'She is really,' Lucy said, 'but first there was Christmas in our new house, then this wedding. She couldn't miss either of those. But normally there'll be nothing happening for her to come back for.'

Mike carved a huge piece of meat from his steak. 'It looked odd, didn't it?' He began to grin as he lifted his fork. 'Fran and Richard setting off on honeymoon with your grandmother in the back of the car. And Fran's son. What a crew.'

Hugh smiled slowly. 'It's not everybody who takes extra company with them, but they're dropping Charlie at the station and Isobel's only going as far as the airport. Then she's off back to Italy while Richard and Fran have settled for France.'

'What's happening about Fran's animals?' Niri asked suddenly. 'I know Charlie can't be helping. He's gone to stay with his dad, he's hoping to persuade him to fund a summer course at RADA to make sure he really wants to do a BA there.' She smiled. 'Charlie knows he does, of course, it's just a scam to give him some more acting time.'

'I know,' Anna said. 'I spoke to a friend of mine there, after Charlie promised me he'd be around for the Rossington Play in the summer. I've made sure our dates don't clash with his summer course.'

'Fran's got somebody to stay at the farm and look after the animals,' Lucy said, pushing her plate away and answering Niri's original question. 'It's a busy time, with lambs and calves appearing at all hours of the day and night. I don't really know,' she added, 'why she and your father arranged the wedding for this time of year, Anna.'

'Daddy wanted to have it as soon as possible,' Anna said, cutting her last sausage into pieces. 'I think he was afraid she might change her mind. And the person she's got to farm sit seems very good.'

'Who is it?' Will demanded, swallowing a mouthful of steak.

'A woman called Josefina,' Anna said. 'Bulgarian, I think. Fran had an advert in the farming papers, but I think she got her from some kind of agency. She'd rather have had somebody local, but of course everyone else is very busy right now.'

'Fran seems happy enough about her,' Hugh commented.

'I'll go down and have a chat with her,' Will said authoritatively. 'Just to make sure she's managing okay.'

Anna smothered a smile. 'That would be kind, Will,' she said. 'I don't know anything about farming, but Fran's left her my number in case there are problems when Hugh and Lucy aren't around.'

'Just ring me. I really wouldn't mind,' he assured her. He glanced at Hugh and his sister. 'You two as well. After all, none of you would really know what to do in a farming emergency.'

'Here,' Mike interrupted, pushing a crumpled envelope across the table. 'I've written down those Indian sites for you. Make sure you get to them.'

'Why don't you come out and see them yourself?' Niri suggested. 'Any or all of you,' she glanced around the table, 'would be very welcome to stay with my family. I've got aunts and uncles and cousins all over the country, and they love having visitors. My parents are coming over too, at Christmas.'

Mike looked thoughtful as he wiped his plate with a piece of bread. 'Well, I might just do that,' he said.

Anna glanced at him quickly, remembering how taken he had been with Niri's aunt Safiya when she had stayed with the Chaudhrys the previous year.

Hugh laughed. 'I'll believe it when you do it, Mike. I've never known you have a holiday since you were a student.'

'With my workload that's not surprising,' Mike said gruffly. 'But maybe it's about time I did.'

'What are you working on now?' Anna asked.

He glanced at her suspiciously. 'Why?'

'I just wondered. You seemed to be around here a lot over the last couple of days,' she remarked.

He nodded. 'I'm mainly at the dig at Ravenstow Abbey, but I'm setting up a survey up there,' he gestured towards the house, 'in the field above the farmyard. I may do some preliminary explorations too. There's a pair of storerooms that have got some interesting features. Odd,' he said vaguely.

'What's odd?' Will demanded.

Mike scowled. 'I'm not telling you anything yet. I want to see what we find first. And,' he lifted a warning finger, 'don't you go causing trouble with the students.'

'As if!' Will exclaimed indignantly. 'I've probably had more experience than they have.'

Mike snorted, as Hugh intervened. 'Mike's playing a lone hand on this,' he commented. 'Even I don't have any idea what he's expecting to find.'

'I certainly haven't,' Lucy said stiffly. 'When did you decide this, Hugh?'

'While you were away,' he said, looking across the table at her. 'We haven't really had chance to catch up with things since you got back, have we?'

There was an awkward silence as the colour rose in Lucy's cheeks. Mike shifted his chair, narrowly missing a chicken that was pecking round his feet. The bird ran squawking away as Mike cursed. 'For God's sake, Lucy, surely you've got even more of these damned birds. You didn't have the white ones before.'

'No,' she agreed. 'They're Silkies. I got them because I like them. And they get on well with the adopted hens.' She turned, considering the bigger brown birds, who were busily exploring the ground under the trees, edging round the clumps of primroses that studded the grass. 'The ex-battery ones have recovered very well, they've all got feathers now.'

Silence fell again and Anna was racking her brain to think of something to say when the sound of tyres on the drive caught her attention. 'Listen,' she said gratefully, 'you've got visitors.'

Hugh looked across the orchard, to where the house was just visible above the hedge that edged the lane. 'Probably Josefina going back to Fran's place,' he said. 'Fran's given her the use of the old Fiesta.'

'It sounds like a bigger car,' Will said, craning his neck round.

'I expect the driver's lost,' Lucy remarked as the sound of the car died away. 'Our drive looks a bit like a lane and people do occasionally think they can get somewhere on it.'

'I suppose we'll have to put up a notice if it gets too bad,' Hugh commented. He looked round the table. 'There's lots more champagne. Unless anybody wants to move on to coffee.'

Among the general outcry, Mike's voice carried clearly. 'What about a decent beer?'

'There are some bottles in the larder,' Lucy said. 'You can get a couple if you like.'

Anna leaned across to the second bottle of champagne. 'Here, Hugh,' she said, 'show Will how to open it without fuss.' She smiled brilliantly at Hugh. 'An essential part of growing up.'

'I don't really like it either,' Will confessed. 'Can I have a beer too?'

'After your lesson,' Anna said firmly.

Mike let his cutlery clatter onto his plate and pushed back his chair. 'I'll get the beer.' As he got to his feet and turned he stopped, uttering an exclamation. 'Looks like you've got visitors, Hugh,' he said.

They all swung round to stare up the orchard to the gate onto the lane. A man, very blond, very bronzed, dressed in immaculate light trousers, with a pink shirt, and a bright blue scarf tied round his neck, was opening the gate. He stood back, allowing a woman to pass him.

She had improbable red hair, Anna thought immediately, wondering who she was. Beside her Hugh swore vehemently and she turned in surprise to see him staring at the intruders, the champagne bottle still held in his hand.

Hugh put it down carefully on the table and got up without another word, edging past Niri's chair to stride up the orchard. He was overtaken by the dogs, both Ben and Hades barking furiously as they raced forward to intercept the intruders.

'Who are they?' Anna demanded urgently. 'Why is Hugh so angry?'

'That's his stepmother,' Lucy said quietly. 'But I don't know who the man is.'

'I do,' Mike said grimly. 'That's Hugh's dear little brother Alex. His half-brother, rather. No wonder Hugh's narked. A visit from Alex means nothing but trouble.'

'Bel, this is a surprise,' Hugh said unenthusiastically. 'I had no idea you and Alex were in the area.'

TWO

'We've been trying to reach you,' his stepmother said, without any preamble, 'but as you haven't been answering the phone we've been forced to trek down here to find you.'

'Dear me,' Hugh drawled, 'this sounds rather desperate. After all, you don't like the country, do you?'

'Not in the least,' Bel snapped. 'And you must know it's urgent.'

Hugh's eyebrows rose in amazement. 'I can't see how,' he said dryly.

'Don't be disingenuous, Hugh,' Bel said. 'You must have known we'd want to talk to you as soon as you read the solicitor's letter. And I must say, it's taken him long enough to write, your uncle Edward has been dead more than two weeks.'

'Ah,' Hugh sounded enlightened. 'That explains it. I haven't seen the post, not my personal post anyway, for the last couple of days. What have I missed?'

'Hugh, I think something came for you today,' Lucy said quietly. 'There was an official-looking envelope on the hall table when I sifted through the letters.' She had her hand on Ben's collar, reassuring the collie whose stiff posture reflected the charged atmosphere. Beside her Will was pulling Hades away as the large dog sniffed curiously at Bel's crumpled linen trousers.

Bel glanced at her incredulously. 'Why didn't you tell him it was there?' she demanded.

'Lucy's not my secretary,' Hugh said, his voice soft and oddly penetrating.

Lucy's eyes widened as she remembered that Bel had once been Hugh's father's secretary. She saw the older woman's eyes narrow unpleasantly.

'We've better things to do than check the post every five minutes,' Hugh continued. He gestured to the orchard behind him. 'As you can see, you're interrupting a party. I'd ask you to join us, but I know you're careful about who you fraternise with.'

Behind them Will started to cough as he stifled a laugh, but Anna sat frozen at the table, listening to every word in amazement.

'Actually, Hugh,' his brother said, 'a drink wouldn't be such a bad idea. I've had a bit of a shock, you know. And I haven't met your wife properly. I should celebrate that.' He smiled broadly at Lucy, exposing a set of very even teeth, exceptionally white against his deep tan.

'Not now, Alex,' his mother said curtly. 'Hugh will just have to leave his partying for a bit, not encourage you to join in.'

'I'm not interrupting my arrangements on your whim, Bel. You can come and sit down over here if you want to talk to me.' Hugh waved his hand towards the spare chairs beyond the barbecue. 'I can give you ten minutes.'

'Really, Hugh, your manners haven't improved with your marriage,' Bel said. She saw his expression harden, and added hastily, 'Very well. This shouldn't take long anyway.'

She stalked over to the chairs, ignoring the group at the nearby table and sending a crowd of chickens squawking into the air as she disturbed them. Hugh strolled in a leisurely fashion after her, enjoying the sight of her flapping away the loose feathers that floated around her.

But Alex lingered, eyeing Lucy. 'Sorry about this,' he said cheerfully. 'Mums never could bear to wait for anything. But it's nice to meet you. I haven't even seen your picture, Hugh's kept you very quiet. And I can see why.' His gaze wandered appreciatively over her slender figure, coming to rest on her small pointed face and long chestnut bob.

Ben stirred, a growl forming in his throat. Lucy said quickly, 'I've only met your mother, and your uncles. Hugh doesn't speak about any of you much.'

'Not a family man, our Hugh,' Alex said. 'But then neither am I. It must run in the genes.'

Lucy's face tightened, but she spoke again quickly, aware of Bel's hectoring voice in the corner of the orchard. 'You've been abroad, haven't you?'

Alex nodded. 'All over the place. I'm a bit of an adventurer really.' He grimaced. 'Hugh's never approved, of course. He's always the big brother, thinking I should settle down and get a steady job.' His forehead creased in a frown. 'And look at him. Preaching to me, then doing exactly the opposite himself. Giving up his job and drifting off to the back of beyond with some tinpot little company.'

He recollected himself. 'Sorry, I shouldn't sound off. I've had a bad day.' He glanced at Will, who stood nearby with Hades. 'Your brother? No need to ask,' he said, without waiting for a reply. 'He's got the family looks. Not,' he added complacently, 'like Hugh and me. I favour our father, he took after his mother.'

Lucy could not find a reply to this, but Alex was not expecting one. He moved closer to Will, one eye on the big dog who was watching him intently.

'You've been in the news, haven't you?' Alex asked jocularly. 'All these discoveries you've made at your place. Cups and things, wasn't it?'

'A chalice,' Will corrected. 'Yes, we've found a few things at the manor.'

'Bringing in the dosh,' Alex said approvingly. 'Just the ticket.' He leaned forward confidingly, and the hair began to rise on Hades' neck. 'I've got a good proposition coming up, and I could cut you in. I'm looking for investors and this is right up your street.

You're a seafaring family, aren't you? Well, this is a nice little boat, doing holiday trips. Just what people want these days.'

'Oh, we've no money,' Will said, one hand tapping Hades warningly on the head. 'Just the house and that eats up cash.'

Alex looked shocked. 'No, no, no,' he expostulated. 'This chalice, and whatever else you've found, they must be worth a fair penny. You've got to convert them to cash. It's the only way.'

At the table Anna stirred, turning to Mike. 'He's not real,' she said, in a low astonished voice. 'He sounds just like a bad film star. And it must have taken some care to find a scarf that matches his eyes so well. I wouldn't be surprised,' she added thoughtfully, 'if he wears coloured contact lenses. But I think his hair really is sun-streaked. Unless, of course, the tan is fake, in which case he's probably got highlights too.'

Mike snorted with laughter. 'Oh, he thinks he's a star alright. Nothing will convince him that he isn't stunning in the role of male lead.' He groaned. His voice had attracted Alex's attention and the man moved past Will, his hand held out, a wide smile stretching his lips.

'Mike, I'd know your voice anywhere,' he said cheerfully. 'How are you? Long time no see.' He grasped Mike's unwilling hand and pumped it up and down. 'And you're doing well for yourself,' he said, 'with two lovely ladies for company.' He spread his smile equally between Anna and Niri, but his gaze came back to Anna and he winked slightly.

Mike pulled his hand away abruptly, but before he could speak Bel's shrill voice rang across the orchard. 'Alex, what are you doing? Come here at once. It's your inheritance we're talking about. And Hugh's being just as unreasonable as I expected. See if you can talk some sense into him.'

Alex rolled his eyes theatrically, but turned obediently towards his mother. Before he could move any further, Hugh got smoothly to his feet, turning to face his brother. 'There's nothing more to be discussed,' he said coldly. 'I haven't seen the solicitor's letter yet, as you know, so I don't have all the details. If what Bel says is right…'

'Of course it is,' she interrupted, standing up and taking a step towards him. 'Your uncle Edward has left his estate to both of you. But while you get yours outright, and most of it too, the old fool has left Alex's share in trust until he's thirty. As if he isn't a responsible person,' she said indignantly. Her voice rose sharply. 'And you're one of his trustees. Your uncle James is the other one, and he's already refused to listen to me. It's ridiculous. Alex's perfectly able to handle his own affairs. If you tell James that the trust is nonsense he'd pay attention. You were always as thick as thieves with your uncles.'

'That's hardly surprising, Bel,' Hugh said, 'as they practically brought me up.'

'And that's it, isn't it?' she demanded belligerently. 'You're punishing us because you think I took your dear Daddy away from you. Well, he didn't want you around, Hugh, it was nothing to do with me. Not that I wanted you either,' she added. 'You were always an irritating little beast, and you certainly haven't got any better.'

'Really, Mums,' Alex expostulated feebly. 'You mustn't get into this. It's no good raking up the past.'

'But it's so frustrating, darling,' Bel said, banging her hands together. 'Just when you've got this marvellous opportunity, and at last the money to take advantage of it.'

'Another opportunity, Alex?' Hugh said, one eyebrow cocked quizzically.

Alex nodded, oblivious to the sardonic tone in his brother's voice. 'It's just what I've always wanted,' he said enthusiastically. 'I've been telling young whatshisname here. There's a nice little boat for sale, already used for sailing holidays, with a good customer base and all that.'

'I don't want to know,' Hugh said. 'You and Bel have had my answer. I must look at the details of the will and talk to James, but I'd have to have a very good reason indeed to overset Edward's testamentary wishes. You haven't yet given me one. And

I can't imagine you could.'

'Ooooh,' Bel's voice rose in a furious wail. She swung an arm in temper, knocking the tablecloths to the ground. The dogs began to bark in short warning bursts.

'Now, Mums,' Alex said in alarm, 'don't upset yourself. We've just taken Hugh by surprise. Everything will be alright when he's had time to think. You'll see.'

He tried to put his arm round his mother's shoulders as she stood up. She thrust him off and turned on Hugh. 'You, it's all you. You made Edward do this...' She was screaming, her words almost unintelligible.

Mike seized the jug of water on the table in front of him and strode over to her, emptying it over her carefully waved hair.

The noise ceased instantly. For a fraction of a second nobody moved. The dogs stopped barking abruptly. Even the chickens seemed to have paused to stare.

'That's always the best thing to do,' Mike commented, walking back to the table. He grinned at Anna. 'So I've been told. I've never had the opportunity to try it before.'

Her brilliant smile flashed out at him. 'There's another jug here, if you need it,' she called over to Alex.

He was ineffectually dabbing at his mother's face with his handkerchief, trying to dry the streaks of water that were dripping off her chin onto her silk shirt. 'No, no, not really,' he said quickly. 'Perhaps,' he glanced at Hugh, who had turned away, his shoulders shaking, 'perhaps if she could just lie down for a bit. Surely you've got room for us, Hugh.'

Hugh overcame his bout of mirth and turned a set face on his brother. 'No, there isn't,' he said bluntly. 'We've got guests, invited ones.'

Will pulled on his arm. 'Niri and I can always go back to the manor,' he offered quietly.

'No,' Hugh said. 'Thanks, Will, but we've been looking forward to seeing something of you and Niri before you go off to India.'

At the table Anna opened her mouth, but Mike leaned over and caught her hand. Surprised, she turned to stare enquiringly at him.

'Don't offer,' he muttered. 'Hugh doesn't want them here.' He jerked his head at Bel and Alex. 'Why would he? They've never been anything but trouble and stress to him.'

'I didn't know,' she said quietly as he released her hand and sprawled back in his chair.

'There's no reason why you should,' Mike said. 'He doesn't broadcast it. I only know because I saw something of the situation when we were students.'

'I didn't know families could be like this,' Niri said, watching Hugh escort Bel and Alex along the lane towards their car. 'Poor Hugh.'

'Nonsense,' Mike said robustly. 'He had two uncles who cared for him and brought him up, he's made his own way, done his own thing. And look at Alex, doted on by his father and his mother, every whim indulged.'

'Yes,' Anna said thoughtfully. 'I see what you mean.'

Lucy came to join them, with an expression of shock in her eyes. 'Hugh's sending them to a hotel in Coombhaven,' she said as she sank into her chair. Her hand went up to brush a strand of hair off her face as Ben sat down beside her, his attention fixed on the people at the gate. 'I suggested they stay in Gran's house, but Hugh wouldn't hear of it.'

'Just as well,' Mike said, watching Will persuade Hades to lie down near the table. 'Alex would be sure to cause chaos there with some scheme or other.'

'Hugh really can't stand them, can he?' Lucy murmured. 'I didn't realise that.'

'They've done nothing to make him like them,' Mike told her gruffly. 'And everything to make him hate and despise them. He doesn't. But he should. I would.'

The conversation broke off as Hugh came strolling across the grass, his hands in his pockets. Behind him, Alex drove his car away down the lane, the tyres screeching as he accelerated. Even so, Lucy was sure she could hear Bel's high voice haranguing her son.

'Sorry about that,' Hugh said with an effort at his usual ease of manner. 'I shouldn't have taken my eye off the ball, or in this case,' he smiled wryly, 'the post.'

He looked across at his wife as he settled back into his seat opposite her. 'I'll try not to let them pester you, Lucy, but they're bound to hang around until they finally believe I'm not going to do what they want.'

She smiled. 'It doesn't matter. It's hardly as if I've seen much of them before this.'

'You won't now,' he replied grimly. 'Although it looks as though dear old Edward has passed on a poisoned chalice.'

'Do you want to go and read the solicitor's letter?' she asked.

He shook his head, reaching for his glass and draining it before he spoke. 'No, it can wait. But I'm pretty sure Edward paid Alex's debts from time to time, and now I guess Alex thinks that duty's passed to James and me.' He put the empty glass down on the table rather heavily.

'Here,' Mike said gruffly, 'have some more champagne. Drown your sorrows.' He gestured to the unopened bottle on the table.

Before Hugh could take it Will intervened, stretching out a hand for the bottle. 'Time for my lesson,' he commented. 'Otherwise Anna will never forgive me.'

Hugh's twisted smile touched his lips. 'Of course,' he said, his eyes flicking to Anna, 'an essential part of a young man's training.'

'Get on with it then,' Mike said. 'I thought the main idea was to drink the stuff. I'll go and get those bottles of beer while you're playing around.'

He pushed his chair back and got to his feet. Both the dogs lifted their heads hopefully, but only Hades got up to follow Mike. Ben's silky head lowered again, his golden eyes still alert as he watched the big black dog trail Mike up to the wicket gate.

'I'll go and get the pudding,' Anna said suddenly, leaning over to pick up one of the trays. 'There was lots left after the reception so I put some trifle and one of the chocolate meringues in the fridge.'

She edged round the table, startling a coterie of chickens who were pecking industriously along the edge of the fence. As they rushed away, cackling indignantly, Anna hurried after Mike, catching up with him at the gate.

'What are you doing?' he demanded, absentmindedly patting Hades on the head as the big dog sat down. 'Discovered a sudden plebeian taste for beer?'

'I like beer, especially chilled,' she said sweetly, 'but I prefer champagne for celebrations. And for consolation.'

She caught his arm as he began to stride across the lane. 'Mike, not so fast.'

He slowed down reluctantly, and let her pass through the garden gate. As he followed her down the path he said abruptly, 'Well?'

Anna waited until they were in the kitchen before she replied. Mike held a couple of beer bottles in each hand, and leaned against the table watching her as she took the puddings out of the fridge.

As she straightened up, putting the meringue down on the table, she looked up at him, her blue eyes unusually serious. 'What's the issue between Hugh and his stepmother?' She added hastily, as Mike began to scowl, 'I'm not being nosey, I just don't want to put my foot in it. And I'd like to help if I can.' She glared at him. 'He and Lucy are my very good friends.'

To her surprise, Mike's scowl faded. 'Okay.' He swung round and put the bottles noisily down onto the table. As he turned back to Anna he leaned against the table again, folding his arms across his chest.

'Hugh's mum died when he was seven. His father was an engineer, roads or bridges, something like that,' Mike explained, waving a vague hand, 'somewhere in South America. While Hugh's mum was alive, she and Hugh travelled with his father. A year after she died the old man married again, his secretary, and a few months later darling Alex was born. And Hugh was sent to boarding school back in England.'

Anna calculated swiftly. 'He must have been eight or nine, so surely that's not so very early to send him away? After all, schooling was probably not so easy out in the wilds.'

'If you believe in sending your kids away, I guess it doesn't matter how old they are. But you don't usually tell them they're going because they aren't wanted, even,' Mike growled, 'if it's true. You don't usually tell a kid that age that Daddy's got a new family now and you're not required any more.'

Anna stared at him in horror. 'Surely she can't have done anything so wicked?'

Mike shrugged. 'Maybe his old man didn't know. But he didn't have Hugh to stay in the holidays. I doubt if Hugh saw him more than a dozen times after his marriage. He died when Hugh was eighteen. Leaving,' Mike said between gritted teeth, 'his entire estate to his dearest Bel. Hugh wasn't even mentioned. I'd just met him then, and he was gutted. Not because of the money either.'

'No, I can't imagine it would be,' Anna said quietly.

'Anyway,' Mike said impatiently, 'don't start being sorry for him. He had his uncles, his father's brothers, and they took care of him.' Unexpectedly, Mike grinned. 'Edward was a civil servant, something in the Home Office, I think, a big hearty man with an amazing collection of men-only stories. James was the more sober one, a London solicitor, as solid and trustworthy as they come, but after a few pints he was always good for old folk songs. The rollicking sea-shanty types.'

'I didn't realise you'd met them,' Anna said, putting the puddings onto the tray.

'Oh yes,' Mike said, gathering up the bottles of beer, 'I used to go with Hugh to one or other of them during the vacations. There was one Christmas,' he said reminiscently, 'the best I've ever had…'

'You must tell me about it later,' Anna said, breaking in firmly, 'but we'd better get back to the others now. They'll be wondering where we've got to.'

She led the way down the corridor and out into the garden. There she hesitated, looking over her shoulder at Mike, who almost bumped into her.

'Don't stop like that,' he said crossly. 'I don't want to drop these.'

'Sorry, but I've just thought of something,' Anna said. 'You've met Bel and Alex before, haven't you?'

'Bel,' Mike snorted. 'Short for Belinda. She thinks it's more fashionable. And she used to call dear Alex Cameron, until he ignored her enough to stop her.'

As Anna looked puzzled, Mike explained, 'His second name, her maiden name. If you listen carefully when she isn't hectoring Hugh, you may catch a trace of the Scottish accent she uses to emphasise how proud she is of her Highland heritage. She wanted the boy to have her surname as his first name. It must be the only time Hugh's dad put his foot down. To some extent, anyway.' Mike snorted. 'At least she didn't call the poor brat Lochiel. I wouldn't have been surprised. Her account of the Camerons and the Jacobite rebellion can give you a completely different view of history.'

'But how did you meet them?' Anna persisted, refusing to be distracted.

'They were at Edward's funeral last week. Alex was there playing the concerned nephew, and Bel gave the performance of her life as the pious hypocrite, lace-trimmed hankie pressed to her eyes.' Mike's square face reddened with anger at the memory.

'It was kind of you to go,' Anna said.

Mike glowered at her. 'Hugh didn't want Lucy to face it, he was expecting trouble, I guess. And I wanted to be there. I liked old Edward. And I guessed they'd be there too, like vultures.'

'Had you seen them before then?'

'Sometimes. When they came harassing Hugh at college,' Mike snapped. 'Dear Bel took the line that Hugh should look out for his little brother, once Alex began getting into scrapes after their dad died. And Alex always had the view that Hugh should pay his debts.'

'Why didn't Bel? I thought she inherited everything from his father,' Anna asked in surprise.

'Either darling Alex's had it all, or she hangs on to what she's got. I wouldn't know,' Mike said gruffly. He nudged Anna. 'Go on. Will's coming to meet us.'

She glanced up to see the young man at the garden gate. 'Great,' he said, eyeing their loads. 'We were beginning to think there was a problem. I'll have a quick drink and some of those puddings, then I want to go down and visit Josefina.'

'Josefina?' Anna queried, puzzled, as she edged through the wicket gate into the orchard, skirting the waiting dogs.

'At Fran's farm,' Will said reproachfully.

'Oh yes.' Anna gathered her wits. 'I'd forgotten her name for a moment.'

'Too much champagne,' Will said in a deliberate aside to Mike. 'Hey, Anna, you were right, that's a cool way to open champagne bottles. No waste at all.'

Mike snorted, letting his own bottles down onto the table. 'Try your new skill on these,' he advised. 'You're more likely to come across beer than champagne.' He pulled a bottle opener out of his pocket, flicked the top off one of the beers and lifted the bottle to his mouth.

'The puddings look good. They all did at the reception,' Niri said. 'Where did Fran get them?'

'I made them,' Anna said lightly. 'Chocolate meringue is one of my specialities.' She registered Mike's look of surprise with an unexpected start of pleasure. Glancing at Niri, she said regretfully, 'But I suppose you can't eat any of it. You don't do dairy either, do you?'

'I do eggs if they're free range and organic,' Niri said, 'but I'll have some of the fruit, anyway.'

'The meringue's okay, then, I used Fran's eggs, but the fruit's only frozen,' Anna said. 'It's too early for fresh berries and currants. Daddy's got masses of raspberry canes at home, and I'd have used a lot of fruit from them if he'd got married later.'

'Mmm, this is really good,' Will said in surprise. 'I didn't know you could cook, Anna.'

Her brilliant smile lit her face. 'I have all sorts of unsuspected skills, Will,' she said lightly.

The young man snorted. 'Yeah, right. I remember how you dealt with those guys involved in all that stuff at the priory a couple of years ago.'

Niri looked at her with interest. 'Will told me about that, and how he found the priory chalice. You did self-defence classes, didn't you?'

'Yes.' Anna's eyes sparkled. 'Special ones for women, taught by an ex-army bloke. They were great fun. I never expected to use it for real though.' She brushed fragments of meringue from her jeans and gestured generously around her at Mike and Hugh. 'And of course, I didn't really need to, my heroes were rushing to the rescue.'

'Including Inspector Elliot, riding in on a speedboat,' Will said with relish.

Mike was not scowling as much as he usually did when this story was told. 'The bastards deserved what they got.' A reluctant smile tugged at his mouth. 'You surprised them as much as you did us.'

Lucy had taken small amounts of trifle and meringue, but pushed her plate away with most of the food uneaten. She stiffened, looking across the western end of the orchard, past the chicken house. 'Who's that in the meadow?' she demanded.

They all turned to stare at the figure that had just come through the field gate. They saw a man in his forties, compact and wiry, dressed in jeans and a t-shirt. Each hand held a bulging carrier bag, and he began to walk down the meadow, his shoulders sagging slightly under their weight.

'Looks like you've got a tramp,' Mike said. 'Take the dogs and see him off, Will.'

Will laughed. 'That's Hugh's recluse from the boat, isn't it?' He glanced enquiringly at Hugh.

'Yes,' Hugh agreed. 'He normally uses the river path, but I told him he could come across the meadow when he'd been shopping. It cuts off about a quarter of a mile.' Hugh looked at Lucy as he spoke. 'He has to catch the bus in and out of Coombhaven.'

'I hope you told him to watch where he puts his feet,' she said crossly. 'The orchids will be coming through, and the skylarks are already nesting.'

'Of course I did,' Hugh said mildly. 'Look, why don't I ask him to join us for a drink? Then you can meet him.'

'Not now, Hugh,' Lucy said. 'This is just for friends, not extras you've picked up.'

'Writer, isn't he?' It was Mike who saved the moment. 'Anything good?'

Hugh's expression lightened as he looked away from his wife. 'Not archaeology, Mike,' he said. 'Not normally novels either,' he added as Anna opened her mouth. 'Although that's what he's trying his hand at now. He's best known for writing satirical social commentary under the name of Flim.'

'Never heard of him,' Mike muttered. 'Flim,' he said in an aside to Will, 'what kind of name is that?'

'It's a pen name, Mike,' Hugh said patiently. 'His real name is Hector Trone.'

Will had just raised his beer to his lips. He held the bottle still, choking with laughter.

Hugh's mouth twitched as he saw the others staring at him in disbelief. 'Truly,' he murmured.

'I can see why he goes in for a pen name,' Mike commented.

'Look, I'd better be going,' Will said. 'Literary discussion is a bit too much like school. I'll go down to Fran's farm and talk about the real world.' He got to his feet and Hades sprang up joyfully. 'Are you coming, Niri?'

'Yes, alright,' Niri replied. 'Don't do the washing up until we get back, Lucy. We're not trying to get out of it.'

'Nonsense,' Anna said robustly. 'You made the salads. We'll save some of the dishes for Will to wash, but I'll do the rest. I haven't done anything else.'

Will pulled a face at her over his shoulder as he walked up the orchard with Niri, Hades running ahead to wait at the gate.

'I'll start on it. Most of it can go in the dishwasher,' Lucy said, getting to her feet. 'I'll get some coffee on as well.' She waved a restraining hand at Anna, who was only halfway through her portion of chocolate meringue. 'Don't hurry, just come in when you're ready.'

Lucy began to load the stacked dinner plates and glasses onto a tray. As she straightened up and turned away from the table, grasping the tray handles, she paused, a look of annoyed disbelief on her face. Ben began to bark again. 'For goodness' sake, it seems we've got another visitor.'

Hugh looked up to the drive, frowning. His expression lightened almost at once as he saw the dark Jaguar inching its way past the house. 'I should have guessed,' he said ruefully, getting to his feet and soothing the dog. 'Uncle James has come down too. The phone lines must really have been red-hot today.' He glanced at his wife. 'Give me the tray, Lucy. I'll take it up.'

She shook her head. 'No, I'll meet him and bring him down here. You can talk business later.'

'Yes, go on,' Mike urged. 'James'll like some champagne and pudding.' His eyes switched to Hugh, who was looking irritated. 'Come on, Hugh. You know James won't talk business until the social niceties are out of the way. And he'd be gutted to think he was interrupting a party. Let him join in.' Hugh began to smile reluctantly, and Mike went on, 'Don't send the old bloke down to Coombhaven too. He won't want to fraternise with the enemy. I'll let him have my room, just give me a chance to shift my stuff.'

'I'll help you, Mike,' Anna said. 'You can talk with your uncle while we're sorting out the room, Hugh.'

'You seem to have got it all arranged between you,' Hugh said. 'Fine. There's a decent couch in my study, Mike. We can make that up for you.'

'Sure,' Mike agreed. 'I've got a sleeping bag in the back of my car. There's a tent too, so if you get overcrowded I can always use it. I might stay over a night at the Ravenstow excavation when I've got things moving on yours.'

Hugh groaned. 'I'd forgotten about that. When do the students arrive?'

'Tomorrow. That gives them a day to mooch around, then they're ready to start on Wednesday for a week,' Mike said. 'The ones here won't bother you. There are only a couple of them, Laura and Adam, mature students wished on me from an evening class by old Mersett. He's started doing these courses "to meet a need",' Mike mimicked the pompous tones of his professorial colleague at Oxford. 'But he's always offloading his students on me for practical work. And he sends me reams of details about them. Even their travel arrangements don't escape him. Travelling separately, visiting friends, bird-watching.' He snorted dismissively. 'I'll have to go up to the abbey from time to time to keep an eye on what my own students are doing, but it should be pretty straightforward and I've got one of my postgraduates supervising things.'

'Shouldn't you be there when they start?' Hugh asked, surprised. 'Brother Ambrose was telling me about it when I saw him in the week. It sounds like a major project. Our storerooms can wait. They can't be particularly important.'

Mike shifted in his seat, his gaze drifting over the orchard, watching the chickens as they pottered underneath one of the trees, clucking gently. 'I've already marked the trenches, so they can get started in good time. They don't need me there for that. Anyway, it doesn't hurt to have several things on the go,' he said, adding vaguely, 'keeps the budget up, you know.' His eyes brightened, focusing on the wicket gate. 'Here comes James.' He leaped to his feet and strode up the orchard.

Anna watched him go, turning to Hugh who was edging round the end of the table. 'Don't you think Mike seems rather evasive about his activities?'

She realised at once that Hugh had not heard her. He was already moving to greet the man who was coming down the orchard between Lucy and Mike, with Ben leading the way. He was very similar in appearance to Hugh, of medium height and build, but his colouring was faded to a washed out grey, both in face and in hair, and he moved as if he was very weary.

Anna saw Hugh and his uncle meet, shaking hands with restraint. She stood up as they reached the table, seeing the affection in the older man's eyes as he walked beside his nephew, talking softly, Ben now leaping along beside them, keen to entertain the new visitor.

'Anna, I want you to meet my uncle James,' Hugh said.

James smiled at her with pleasure, his tired face crinkling into deep lines. 'I'm very glad to meet you, Anna,' he said. 'Lucy told me you were here. I saw you in Paris, you know, in The Queen's Necklace. That was a marvellous performance you put on.'

'It was a lovely part,' she said, taking her place at the table again.

Lucy gestured James into Will's vacated place beside her, and the collie came to sit on the grass between them. The dog laid his head on James' knee and the man stroked him gently as he leaned forward to carry on his conversation with Anna. 'What are you doing now?'

'I've got a part in a Jacobean drama at Stratford this autumn,' she said, 'but I'm getting more and more requests to put together local dramatic pageants and plays.'

'Ah yes,' James said, accepting a glass of champagne from Hugh, 'like the one at Lucy's old home. She invited me for the Rossington Play last year, but sadly I couldn't make it.'

'Come this year,' Lucy urged, as she passed him a bowl of chocolate meringue and raspberries. 'Anna and Will are going to make it a regular annual event.'

'I'd like that,' James said. 'You must give me the dates and I'll see if I can keep them free.'

Mike leaned forward, elbows on the table. 'What imaginative perversion of history are you giving us this year, Anna?'

Lucy drew in her breath, but Anna looked brightly at Mike. 'A local take on the passing of the Spanish armada, and how the Irish mule chest came to the manor.'

Mike's eyes narrowed, but before he could say anything Anna took the wind out of his sails. 'Actually, Mike, if you can spare the time, I could do with some advice.'

She took a sip of her own champagne, watching Mike's expression with a small bubble of amusement rising in her chest. The amusement surfaced in a gurgle of laughter.

James, watching the exchange as he ate his pudding, thought how beautiful she was, with her sparkling dark blue eyes, rose-tinted cheeks and the long curling black hair that tumbled down her back. He glanced sideways at Mike, wondering how he felt, and saw only the look of deep suspicion that had fallen over the archaeologist's freckled face as he sprawled back in his chair.

'Really, Mike, it's nothing difficult,' Anna said reassuringly. 'I'd just like to be sure I'm not getting anything really wrong. I don't,' she added quickly, 'want you to write anything.'

'What do you want then?' he demanded, cradling his bottle between his fingers.

'Well, Berhane, you remember her?' Anna paused.

'I'm hardly likely to have forgotten already,' he snapped irritably. 'Even if the events of last damned New Year weren't burned into my brain.'

'Berhane,' Lucy said in a quick aside to James, 'is an old school friend of mine and Anna's. We had a bit of a problem when we stayed with her this winter.'

James put down his spoon and smiled at her. 'From what I hear, problems seem inevitable when you all get together.'

'Yes, well,' Anna said hastily, as Mike's mouth opened,

'Berhane wants to put together a community play for the autumn, and she's asked me to write some scenes for it.'

'How do I come into it?' Mike demanded.

'You don't really,' Anna said, struggling to sound patient, 'but I want to include something about the early settlers on the moor, and about the Victorian archaeologists. Nothing very detailed,' she added, 'but I'd like it to be accurate.'

Mike muttered something inaudible, but Anna decided she would not ask him to repeat it. She waited as he struggled with himself.

'Alright,' he said ungraciously, 'but don't go putting my name to it. I don't want anybody to know I'm involved.'

'Well, Mike, given the success of Anna's last productions,' Hugh interposed, 'you might want to think about it. You could develop a role to rival Time Team, and become a paid consultant.' He added, looking enquiringly at Anna, 'After all, I gather from Will that you're paying staff for the Rossington Play this year.'

'Well, only Philly for the admin, and Niri for the research,' she said deprecatingly.

Hugh frowned slightly. 'What about the time you're putting in? You should have a fee too. I'll speak to Will.'

'No, really, Hugh,' Anna expostulated, 'that's not…'

'Nonsense,' Mike snapped, 'you've got to make a living, even if you will fritter away your time on a host of different things.'

'Have you never thought of bringing all you do together?' James asked her. 'Settling on a base, and operating from it?'

'How do you mean?' she asked, puzzled.

'Well,' he leaned his elbows on the table and steepled his fingers together, a gesture that she realised Hugh frequently made too, 'writing, producing and acting are all part of the same kind of creation, putting an imagined scene before a public. You do all three now, and train others to perform as well. You could carry on doing those things from a set base, a place that people will associate with you, even if your own acting takes you further afield.' The strain in James' face eased as he thought about the idea. 'You could also develop your base,' he went on, 'bring people to you for events, and maybe students or local people for dramatic experience. Capitalise on your skills,' he pointed out, stabbing a finger towards her. 'Use them in as many ways as you can.'

Anna was staring at him. 'I've never thought of that,' she said slowly. 'I wonder if I could. The trouble has always been that I like all these aspects of drama, and I particularly like showing local details in greater national events. I've never really thought that they could all fit into a pattern.'

'That's your trouble,' Mike said abruptly. 'You never stop to think, you just follow the latest whim.'

She glanced at him impatiently. 'Well, why not? We can't all follow straight narrow paths like yours, nose to the ground, never looking around.'

Lucy hastily pushed back her chair, startling Ben, who sprang up as well. 'I'd better get started on the washing up. Does everyone want coffee?'

Anna got to her feet too as murmurs of assent answered Lucy. 'I'll come with you. Come on, Mike,' she said pointedly, 'I thought you were going to give us a hand.'

Mike glowered at her. 'What?' he demanded disbelievingly.

Anna's gaze met his and flickered meaningfully to James, then to Hugh, and back to Mike.

'Oh yes, I see,' he said, thrusting his chair back so hard that it fell over. 'I do so enjoy washing up, I must join you,' he said with heavy sarcasm. He was about to stomp up the orchard when Anna caught his arm.

He swung round, brought up short by the tray of bowls and empty pudding dishes that she pushed towards him.

'Be careful,' she advised. 'Mind the gates, and the door. Make sure there are no cars coming down the drive. Don't trip over the dog.'

He scowled darkly and walked with exaggerated care up to the wicket gate that Lucy was holding open.

Anna flashed a brilliant smile at Hugh and James, then she followed Mike with a tray laden with glasses.

James watched them go and turned to find Hugh's amused eyes were on him. 'She's lovely,' James said, 'as well as talented. I hope Mike realises his luck.'

Hugh smiled. 'That incisive mind of yours has slipped up,' he commented. 'Anna and Mike are forever niggling at each other. Mike thinks his luck's in if Anna isn't around.'

'I think,' James said slowly, 'the jury is still out on that subject. Time will tell which of our brilliant legal minds has sorted the evidence best.'

He sighed, the deep lines in his face becoming more pronounced. 'And talking of legal matters, Lucy said you've already endured a visit from Bel and Alex.'

Hugh nodded, his expression hardening. 'Out of the blue. I hadn't,' he admitted ruefully, 'opened my personal post. One of my authors has got an unexpected problem with his work. He's been accused of plagiarism. Brother Ambrose, at Ravenstow Abbey. You remember, I told you about his book on monastic herbalists and their work.'

James nodded. 'Yes, when you were last in London. It sounds very interesting. Can you deal with the problem?'

'We can prove that it's an unfounded accusation,' Hugh said grimly, 'but we've got to go through the whole process of rebuttal. That's been taking up my time over the last few days.'

'Difficult,' James agreed. 'I'm sorry Edward has landed this difficulty on you too.'

'On us both,' Hugh corrected. 'You'll find it just as awkward as I will. And I'm sure Bel and Alex have spent much more time hectoring you.' He studied the older man. 'Did you know Edward was doing it?'

James shook his head. 'I would have advised him against it, he knew that.' He linked his hands together, resting his elbows on the table. 'Let's be frank, Hugh. You know, and I know, that Alex is going to run through any money he gets. I don't know where your father's legacy to Bel went, and I haven't asked. But Edward has paid Alex's debts time and again over the last couple of years, and Alex has always come back with yet another little difficulty, or another amazing opportunity.' He looked penetratingly at Hugh. 'Don't think Edward didn't know that Alex would never stop coming. But he felt an obscure loyalty to your father, a need to help his son.' He frowned. 'I suppose,' he admitted reluctantly, 'that I feel it too. I just differed with Edward about how best to do it. I've never felt that endlessly supplying money would help Alex to sort his life out.'

'I'm not sure anything would ever do that,' Hugh said.

'Maybe not,' James admitted. 'And I know he's relied heavily on you as well to get him out of difficulties. But you've got your own commitments now, your wife, your business, your lovely home, and the family I expect you'll raise here.'

'But there's still Alex,' Hugh finished. 'And Edward has certainly made him our concern for a while.' He paused, making a mental calculation. 'Several years, in fact. At least,' he cocked a questioning eyebrow at his uncle, 'Bel said the money was in trust until he's thirty. I'm sure she'll have that fact right.'

'Of course,' James said. 'Well, Hugh, I don't agree with what Edward has set up, but I wouldn't be happy to overset it.'

'No,' Hugh said, 'neither would I. So that's it, isn't it? We have to abide by his wishes, and cope with Bel's anger and Alex's demands.' He sat back in his chair, absentmindedly watching the chickens.

The birds had settled on a bare patch of earth near the upper hedge. The majority seemed to be fascinated by the few who were vigorously wriggling and squirming in shallow dips, fluttering their wings, ruffling their feathers and sending clouds of dust into the air around them.

'What are the terms of Edward's will?' Hugh asked suddenly.

James sat back too. 'They're very simple. The bulk of his fortune goes to you without any condition.' Hugh's eyes widened in surprise. 'One hundred thousand to Alex, to be invested and held in trust until his thirtieth birthday. He is to receive the interest on it annually. And,' James sounded resigned, 'the trustees, that's you and me, have the power to authorise exceptional payments from the capital amount.' He met Hugh's eyes with a grimace. 'The rest, just over three hundred thousand, is divided between his favourite charities.'

'How much am I looking at?' Hugh asked quietly.

'I can't be sure yet,' James said, 'but I should think at least a million pounds.'

'I can see why I'm not Bel's favourite person,' Hugh commented. 'Not, of course, that I ever was.'

'Edward wasn't in our profession,' James said, 'but he felt very strongly about justice. Particularly where you were concerned. We never said anything to you about your father's will, but that didn't mean either of us felt it was right.'

Hugh felt an unexpected surge of emotion, although his face stayed impassive. These two men, his uncles, had been living busy lives of their own when he had been dumped on them by his father, but they had made sure Hugh could call their homes his. They had, he realised, been his real family, the people who had wanted and cared for him, not just because of the blood tie, but because he was a child in need of affection and encouragement.

'Well,' he said lightly, 'we don't seem to have any alternatives. Are you happy to sort out the investments?'

'Yes,' James said firmly. 'You've got more than enough to deal with. I don't want to add to it.' He glanced back at the house. 'You and Lucy have achieved a huge amount with Withern. I haven't seen much of it, but it looks very nice now.' He smiled suddenly, his tired face relaxing. 'I thought you were making a big mistake when I saw the photos you sent me before you bought it. But apart from anything else, it should be a good investment.'

'In the long term I'm sure it will be,' Hugh agreed. 'But we don't plan to leave here for a long time. You must let me show you around after we've taken your bags up to your room.'

'Oh no,' James said quickly. 'I haven't come to impose myself on you. Especially when you've got friends here.'

'Mike's already decamped to my study,' Hugh said, 'so that you can have his room. Everyone is glad you've come to visit us at last, so you certainly can't expect to get away without staying for a couple of nights at least. Will's around too, and he'd be furious if he misses you. He's technically on study leave,' he explained with an ironic grin, 'with a friend from school. They'll probably get down to some work once they go back to Will's place next week. Niri,' Hugh's expression was amused, 'always makes sure they do. They've been friends for a couple of years now. He spends quite a lot of time with her parents in Corrington when they want a taste of town life.'

He saw that his uncle was looking undecided, and made his final bid. 'Bel and Alex are staying over in Coombhaven, so we should definitely present a united front next time they call. Bel's mode of operation has always been divide and rule.'

'There's an advantage in knowing how the other side thinks,' James said. He relaxed back into his chair. 'Alright, Hugh, you've persuaded me. In fact,' he confessed, 'I do have another call to make while I'm down here.'

'I didn't know you had friends in this area,' Hugh commented.

'I don't,' James said. 'But there's a silver collector in Coombhaven that Edward was in frequent touch with. An American lady, I believe. I thought I'd go and meet her.'

'I see,' Hugh said, obviously puzzled.

James smiled suddenly. 'Silly of me, I told Alex about it in London, but of course you don't know yet. Edward,' he explained, 'left me his silver collection. It doesn't mean as much to me as it did to him, but I'd like to learn more about it.'

'Of course,' Hugh sounded enlightened. 'It was mainly Georgian, I think. It's lots of little things, isn't it? Boxes, spoons and the like.'

James nodded. 'Yes, I had no idea there was such a variety. I've brought them with me, it's so easy to carry them around. I'll get them out for you to see if you like.'

'He always showed me his latest addition whenever I visited,' Hugh remembered. 'Many of them were beautifully decorated. I'd like to see them again.'

'And Edward kept a note of all their histories. So you see why I can't miss a chance to make contact with somebody knowledge-able,' James said. 'She got in touch with me when she heard of Edward's death. I knew her name, of course. Edward frequently mentioned it and I think there was often a friendly rivalry over pieces. In fact, she was keen to buy his collection, but when she heard I'm keeping it she was very willing to advise me about it. So it will be nice not to have to rush my visit. I do hope Mike won't be too uncomfortable if I take over his room.'

Hugh laughed. 'Come on, James, you know perfectly well that Mike can sleep anywhere. Remember the number of times he slept on the floor of your flat.'

'Of course I do, but as you're both older he might find it less comfortable.'

'I'm not always sure that Mike is really older, in attitude and thoughts anyway. He's got his tent in the back of his car now, in case there's chance to join the students camping in the top meadow.'

'What students?' James was puzzled.

'They're working on a minor survey Mike's set up,' Hugh said. 'He's being very mysterious about the old storehouses beyond the farmyard, and insisted on doing some investigation.' Hugh shrugged. 'I'm letting him get on with it, but I've no idea what he's expecting to find.'

'I must go and see what he's up to,' James said, intrigued. 'Maybe I'll be able to weasel some information out of him.'

'Maybe,' Hugh agreed. 'I think Ambrose is curious too. Mike's involved in a big excavation at Ravenstow Abbey, so Ambrose knows him pretty well. Well, Ambrose insisted on coming here tomorrow for our next discussion, so my guess is that he'll be slip-ping up to the storerooms too. Maybe you should go together.' He smiled suddenly. 'Do you know, James, maybe something good will come out of this business with Edward's will. We may persuade you to come down more often. Especially,' he groaned, 'if Alex keeps presenting projects that need capital investment. As I'm sure he will.'

'I can deal with his demands,' James assured him. 'If you're happy to rely on my judgment.'

'You know I am,' Hugh said. 'But it doesn't seem fair to leave it all to you.'

'Just keep backing me up,' James said. 'That will be wearing enough.' He frowned. 'There's already a project Alex wants money for. Some boat idea, part of a holiday tour scheme, I think.'

'I've heard of it,' Hugh said dryly. 'Ask him for detailed plans and figures. You probably won't hear any more about it.'

'Maybe,' James said doubtfully. 'But you're right, Hugh, I would like to come down more often. I only get to see you occasionally when you're in London, and I don't get to see Lucy at all.'

He pushed his chair back and stood up, stretching his back and shoulders. The chickens by the upper hedge stirred, but settled down again when James strolled to the lower fence and gazed down the meadow.

'How far does your land go?' he asked, as his eyes ran over the swathes of bluebells.

'Down to the river.' Hugh came to stand beside him. 'And,' he waved a hand to his left, 'over to the hedge there. Beyond that it's part of Fran's farm. It was her wedding to Anna's father that we were celebrating today.'

'How nice,' James said. 'I presume Anna's happy about it.'

'Very.' Hugh's crooked smile touched his lips. 'She feels a great responsibility has been taken off her shoulders. Anna always sees the bright side of everything, but there wasn't really a dark side for anyone to find in this. Except,' he added slowly, 'perhaps for us, if we lose Fran as a neighbour. She's become a good friend.'

'Is that likely?' James asked, his eyes idly following the line of willows and alders that edged the river at the foot of the meadow.

'I think so,' Hugh said regretfully. 'I can't really see Richard

Evesleigh living there. He's got a gem of a Georgian house between here and Will's place. But I gather from Anna that Fran doesn't want to live in it, so I'm not sure where they'll end up.'

'They'll sort it out,' James said comfortably. 'Do you have a footpath along the riverbank?'

'No.' Hugh followed James' gaze to where a man stood, half hidden under the trees. 'That's a chap called Hector Trone. I've given him permission to moor his boat below the meadow for a while. You can just see it through the trees. We,' he said lightly, 'only run to a much smaller one, which we keep down at the landing stage.'

'It's years since I went boating,' James mused. 'Do you remember, down in Dorset, when you were first interested in bird-watching?'

'Of course I do,' Hugh said. 'It was one of the formative experiences of my life. The first time I saw a kingfisher. And we met that photographer, who let me help him when he was taking pictures of the kingfisher nest in the bank.' He laughed suddenly. 'I'll never forget the shock of finding that young birds turn their bums and squirt at the light.'

He glanced at his uncle's face. 'Let's go out while you're here. We'll pack a picnic and go down towards the sea.'

'What a nice idea,' James exclaimed. 'Yes, I'd like to do that. Will Lucy come?'

'I think it'll just be you and me,' Hugh said. 'She and Anna have some catching up to do. Mike will be dying to get to work once his students arrive. And Will and Niri will, I suspect, be haunting Fran's farm.'

'I didn't realise Will was here until you mentioned him,' James said. 'It must be a couple of years since I saw him. I suppose he's going on to university soon.'

Hugh nodded, commenting, 'You'll see quite a change in him. But he still talks just as much if you get him started on his interests.'

'Are they the same?'

'Not exactly,' Hugh said. 'I'll leave you to find out for yourself. Let's go down to the river now and I'll introduce you to Trone. You'll probably know his work, his pen name is Flim; he writes those exceptionally good satirical political commentaries.'

'Why, yes, I read them,' James said. 'I wouldn't have thought he was a country person. He always seems to be appearing in society photos, you know, the Earl of Blank, Lady Somebody, Flim at the races, the ball, the whatever is happening.'

Hugh shrugged. 'You're probably right. He certainly doesn't seem very handy with his boat. I think he's really only looking for some peace to write a book,' Hugh said, opening the gate into the meadow. 'But I haven't pressed him about it. We've had some good discussions on a whole range of subjects. He's very well informed.'

James passed through the gate, leaving Hugh to fend off the few adventurous chickens that thought they saw an opportunity to enter wider feeding grounds.

'Won't Lucy be bringing the coffee soon?' James asked suddenly.

'We won't be long,' Hugh said cheerfully. 'We'll just say hello.'

James looked doubtful, but fell into step beside his nephew to stroll down the slope towards the river. There was a well-defined path over the rough turf, meandering through the bluebells. The scent of the flowers filled the air around them, and overhead a lark sang his thrilling notes, so that they seemed to fall throbbing from the sky.

As they approached the landing stage Hugh caught James' arm, pointing over the trees. James looked up to see the distinctive shape of a heron, making its stately way above the water with long steady wing beats.

Withern's rowing boat sat quietly beside the landing stage, barely moving on the surface of the fast-flowing water. A little further along was a sleek white cabin cruiser.

'He does himself well,' James commented in a low voice.

'Oh, it's hired from the boatyard in Corrington, the town

upriver from here,' Hugh said. He called out, 'Hector, hello, are you in?'

Silence fell around them as Hugh waited for an answer. James watched the waterweed streaming in the strong current, and the small round bird that bobbed up and down on the rock that edged the far side of the river. He caught Hugh's arm, 'What's that?' he asked softly, pointing towards the bird.

Hugh glanced at it. 'A dipper. He's often here.' His eyes ran over the boat. 'I don't think Hector's in, but I'll just try the door.'

He leaped lightly onto the deck, and a few steps took him to the closed door that led into the cabin. He pulled at the handle, knowing at once that it was locked.

'No luck,' he said, jumping back onto the bank. 'I didn't think he'd be going far when you saw him. He'd only just come back from town with his shopping.'

'Well, maybe it's just as well,' James said. 'Lucy will probably be wondering where we are.'

They had just returned to the landing stage when a voice hailed them from the corner of the field. Hugh looked up sharply, and saw Hector coming towards them.

'Looking for me, Hugh?' he asked. 'I'm afraid I was trespassing in the corner of your field.' He indicated the binoculars, shiny and new, that hung across his chest. 'There's a very good spot for watching the river. But,' he smiled, 'I expect you know that.'

Hugh nodded. 'It's not a good time to tramp over there,' he said. 'We're keen to get up our numbers of nesting larks, and it's best not to disturb them.'

'Oh, I was very careful,' Hector said. 'I wouldn't dream of damaging a nest.' He looked enquiringly at James. 'Have you brought me a visitor?'

'My uncle, James Carey,' Hugh said. 'James, this is Hector Trone, best known to his readers as Flim.'

'You mustn't go around blowing my cover, Hugh,' Hector said in mock reproach. 'I'm here incognito.'

'But I'd have known you from your photographs,' James said

mildly. 'You're in the papers such a lot.'

'Yes,' Hector was gratified. 'That's true. Look, come aboard and have a drink.'

'Well, actually, we only came down for a quick stroll,' James said. 'We're due to join the others now. And here, I think, comes the search party.' He gestured up the field.

Will was loping down towards them, but Hades reached them first, his tongue hanging out of his grinning mouth as he threw himself on Hugh.

'Down,' Hugh said automatically. But Hades had already turned his attention to James, sniffing him curiously, then recognising his scent and licking his hand effusively.

'Keep him away from me,' Hector said, sounding strained. 'I really don't like dogs.'

'Oh, he's alright,' Will said, arriving in time to hear this. 'Hello, James, I heard you were here. What a shame you missed the barbecue. We've eaten everything. It was pretty good.'

James grinned at him. 'But I was in time for some pudding, Will, the best part of any meal. How are you?'

'Hades,' Hugh called.

The big dog looked at him reproachfully, coming slowly to Hugh's side. He looked hopefully over to the river and began to drift towards it.

'No, Hades,' Will said, and the dog turned his head to his master with obvious disbelief.

'Lucy said,' Will repeated his instructions verbatim, 'if you want any coffee you'd better come and get it.'

'We're just on our way,' James assured him. He turned to Hector. 'It was very nice to meet you. I hope you enjoy the rest of your stay.'

'Why don't you join us?' Hugh said impulsively to Hector. 'We're at the coffee stage, I'm afraid. But I'm sure there'll be enough for one more.'

'It's very kind of you,' Hector said, 'but I wouldn't want to intrude.'

'Nonsense,' Hugh said. 'I'd like to introduce you to my wife.'

'Well, in that case, I can't really refuse,' Hector said.

Further up the slope, Hades was once again running ahead of Will as they retraced their steps towards the orchard. Will was frowning, remembering that Lucy had not wanted Hector to join the party. Had Hugh forgotten, Will wondered. Well, it was too late now, the bloke was coming up with the others. What a strange, precise way of talking he had, as if, Will grinned suddenly, he was giving a speech.

'Doesn't that dog disturb your birds?' Hector asked behind him.

Will rolled his eyes. Where had Hugh got this bloke?

'Hades is very well trained,' Hugh remarked. 'All of our dogs have to be if we're going to walk over farmland.'

'You've got more?' Hector was horrified. He slowed and came to a stop. 'Look, Hugh, maybe this isn't such a good idea. Why don't you and James come down to me later on for that drink? More butch than coffee, don't you think?'

Phew, Will thought, overhearing this. That gets us out of an awkward situation.

'We're virtually there,' Hugh said. 'You might as well come in for a few minutes. We can put the dogs in the house.'

Will pushed open the gate into the orchard, letting Hades rush through to greet Ben as if they had been apart for hours. He strolled over to Niri, who was sitting at the table sipping from her cup of jasmine tea. Bending down, he said softly, 'There's going to be trouble. Come indoors with me.'

She looked up at him in surprise. 'Sssh,' he warned as Hugh came into the orchard with James. 'Niri, this is James,' Will said more loudly, waving at the older man. 'Hugh's uncle.'

'Will,' Hugh said, coming to join them as Niri stood up to greet James. 'Take Hades into the house, would you? Hector's really scared of dogs.'

Will looked meaningfully at Niri. 'Come on, Niri, bring your tea with you. We can sit in the back garden and see if Josefina comes home.'

Lucy had been chatting to Mike and Anna at the far end of the table. Her clear laugh rang out as Hugh approached her. She glanced round, her hazel eyes lit with amusement. 'Listen, Hugh, to what Anna heard in Coombhaven.'

'Later,' he replied. 'Lucy, Hector's come up for coffee, but he's seriously scared of dogs. Can you take Ben up to the house? Will and Niri have already gone with Hades.'

Lucy stared at her husband, the laughter dying out of her face. She got to her feet. 'You stay with your friend, Hugh.' She glanced furiously at Anna. 'We'll carry on our conversation up at the house.'

She turned, stalking away. Caught by surprise, Ben scrambled up quickly to follow her.

Hugh stared after her, remembering too late that she had not wanted Hector to join the party. He looked apologetically at the others. 'I forgot,' he said.

Anna pulled a face. 'Never mind. I'll go with her, Hugh.' She got up and moved away.

Mike hesitated, then stood up too. 'I'll join them. Leave you to it, mate.'

Hugh stood in the centre of the orchard, James just behind him, and watched as his friends went out into the lane.

'Just a quick coffee here, Hugh,' James said. 'Then we can join them again.'

Before Hugh could reply, Hector leaned over the gate. 'Is it safe?' he called.

THREE

'My God,' Hugh exclaimed, dropping the newspaper he had been glancing through as he waited for slices of bread to toast. 'I'd better warn Mike.' He belted his dressing gown more tightly round his waist as he walked swiftly to the back door, pulling it open and running down the steps.

'What's that all about?' Will demanded, looking round the kitchen table at the others. He got to his feet and went over to the window.

The farmyard outside had been transformed from the expanse of compacted earth that it had been a year ago. A wide winding path of granite slabs ran between waves of bleached ornamental grass tussocks to the two huge stone barns that stood on the far side. Minor paths branched off left and right to the subsidiary buildings, forming rough squares of evergreen shrubs. Here and there were trees, sometimes in large stone containers. Benches and chairs were dotted around, some against the brick buildings, others in paved areas in the newly formed garden.

Will spent no time admiring his sister's creation. His gaze went straight to the barns, whose sloping tiled roofs and great curved doorways still dominated the scene. Eventually the grasses and shrubs would conceal most of the path, but now in their infancy he could easily see that Hugh had not gone that way to his company office. Will glanced to the left, towards the old dairy and washroom that Hugh had made into his study. There was no sign of Hugh there either, so Will's eyes moved automatically to his favourite buildings on the right, the cart houses and stables.

'Maybe it's something in the paper,' Niri suggested, picking it up to scan the pages Hugh had left open.

Will started. 'Maybe,' he agreed, pressing his face against the windowpanes and trying to peer to the left.

'Wait till you see Hugh's study,' Niri said to James. 'It's in part of the old farm buildings. You know,' she explained, as James looked uncertain, 'the dairy, brewhouse and washroom. The places where the farmer's wife did all her work.'

James nodded. 'Yes, of course. I suppose there must have been a lot to do in a place like this.'

'They'd have been self-sufficient here once,' Niri said. 'The brewhouse has been kept pretty much as it was, still with the cider press as Lucy wants to use it for their own apples. I was sorry Hugh had to change the other buildings, but he's done it very cleverly. The dairy and the washroom have been knocked into one room internally, and it's surprising how big a space there is.'

'Even with all the books lining the walls,' Will said over his shoulder.

'Is that where Hugh works from?' James enquired.

'Sort of, when he's on his own,' Will said. 'But the main publishing office is on the mezzanine in the left barn. That's where he works with his new assistant, and that's where all the files and things are. The books he publishes are stored in the barn below.' He stiffened. 'Who's this?'

'Who?' Niri asked quickly, as she got up to collect the toast.

'I don't know,' Will said impatiently. 'Some woman's just come into the yard and dumped a bike by the stables. I wonder what she wants. Maybe,' he swung round, 'it's Josefina from Fran's farm.'

He opened the kitchen door, holding onto Hades who was keen to go outside. 'Where's she gone?' Will demanded in exasperation, going out onto the top step for a better view. After a few seconds he came back into the room, closing the door behind him, and leaning back against it, grinning.

Niri stood still, the basket of toast in her hand, staring at Will. 'What's so funny?' she asked.

'It must be Hugh's assistant,' he said. 'I didn't know she was coming today. Hugh must have forgotten too. And of course Mike spent the night on the couch in Hugh's study. I guess the assistant goes there when she arrives, and Hugh has gone to warn Mike. Anyway, she's gone straight in. She's, umm, unusual looking.'

'What do you mean?' Niri asked, putting the plate down and resuming her seat at the table.

'Well, alternative, I suppose. Very short scarlet hair, definitely dyed, and long earrings with shells and feathers. Baggy green trousers, baggy purple top. A huge belt, yellow, I think it was, with lots of strands hanging down her bum. I wonder,' Will laughed out loud as he sat down and reached for a piece of toast, 'who's going to get the worse surprise? Her or Mike.'

In the study Hugh had finally succeeded in waking Mike, who stared up from under the duvet, blinking blearily at the overhead light that was shining into his eyes. He was an incongruous sight in the room, a place of neatness and order, designed for calm reflection and reading.

The central archway showed where the two outbuildings had been opened into one space. All the walls were lined with books, generally serious-looking hardbacks in sombre colours. Here and there a stretch of leather bindings showed a discreet gold lettering on their spines.

Broad seats had been built under the windows, and modern armchairs of different styles were grouped in one corner of the room around a low coffee table. This was clearly a place to sit and read, warmed by the crimson carpet on the floor and the brocade curtains screening the windows.

But the huge oak desk that filled the furthest part of the room was a sign that work was done here. It was heaped with tidy piles of papers and obviously new books, edged by a matching oak stack holding a couple of printers and a scanner.

Mike was still half-asleep as he threw the duvet back. He heaved himself round to sit on the edge of the couch that ran at an angle across the inner part of the room, where the door from the farmyard opened into the fourth corner. He was clad only in a pair of shabby boxer shorts, his upper body showing an odd mishmash of healed cuts and dark patches of old sunburn from his years of outdoor work on different excavations. His chin bristled with stubble and his red hair stuck out at odd angles as he scowled at Hugh.

'Okay, so it's morning,' he grunted. 'What's the rush?'

His discarded clothes were scattered on the floor nearby, half hidden by a layer of books that had been left haphazardly over them. Hugh was glancing at them irritably. 'I suppose you were up reading half the night.'

'Of course I was,' Mike growled, rubbing his face. 'What's the problem?' He straightened abruptly. 'Have the students turned up?'

'No,' Hugh said shortly. 'But my assistant will arrive at any moment, and she usually comes here first for the office key. I haven't got around to having another one cut yet.' His eyes ran over Mike. 'I don't want her to burst in on you and get a nasty surprise. I'll head her off, but you'd better get up.'

He had barely finished speaking when the door behind him opened and a woman came in, the strands of her yellow belt swinging jauntily. 'Hello, Hugh, I saw the light was on, but I didn't expect...' she began in a strong Liverpudlian accent. 'Oh, I'm sorry,' she said, stopping abruptly, 'I didn't know you had company.'

Hugh turned to face her. 'I'm sorry, Maggie, I'd only just remembered you were coming in today. We've got an extra guest at the house, so Mike's made use of the couch in here.'

Maggie's face was naturally ruddy, but embarrassed colour was running up her throat as she averted her eyes from Mike, who was glaring belligerently at her. But she replied without a tremor, 'That's alright. I'll go straight to the office if you'll give me the key. I've got plenty to be getting on with until you come.'

'Yes, that would be best,' Hugh said with relief. 'I'll be there as soon as I'm dressed.' He glanced at his watch. 'There are a couple of things I want to run through with you before Brother Ambrose arrives. And you might check those details I mentioned about the plagiarism issue. I want all the facts I'll need when he's here.'

She left without another word, shutting the door behind her with exaggerated care, and Hugh looked back at Mike. The two men met each other's eyes, beginning to grin. 'It could have been worse,' Mike said philosophically. 'Since when have you had an assistant?'

'For a fortnight. She works three days a week for me, but she's flexible about which ones she does. So she's only here today because I wasn't working yesterday,' Hugh said, glancing at his desk. 'Business has been building up, and the admin takes far too much of my time. It was lucky timing, really,' he added. 'Maggie has just moved down to the area into a rented cottage on a farm this side of Coombhaven. She sent out her cv as soon as she got here and I got in touch with her straightaway. She worked for an academic publisher in London, so her background couldn't be better. I can't believe how much of the routine stuff she's already dealing with. I can rely on her totally, she just gets on with what needs doing. I couldn't have found anyone better, I just wish she could do a full week for me. It's nice as well for Lucy to have somebody around if I'm away.'

'I could do with an assistant to do all my forms,' Mike grumbled. 'I hardly ever get my hands dirty on a dig these days.'

'Maybe you should follow James's advice to Anna,' Hugh said lightly. 'Set up on your own.'

Mike snorted. 'That's not so easy for some of us. And you can't really think Anna's going to do something so serious.'

Hugh lifted his shoulders in a casual shrug. 'Who knows? But

I'd better get back to the house and dress. There are some things I need to run over with Maggie, then I want to spend some time with James. Brother Ambrose is calling by later this morning to discuss this wretched accusation.' Hugh began to collect his books from the floor. 'Oh,' he said over his shoulder, 'I think James is keen to have a look at those storerooms you're so interested in.'

Mike scowled as he watched Hugh replacing books on the shelves. 'There's nothing to see,' he growled. 'But bring Ambrose up when he's here. He's bursting to have a look too, and I want a word with him about the work at the abbey. And leave that one,' he leaned forward to remove the book from Hugh's hand, 'I haven't finished with it.'

Hugh glanced at the title of the book, and saw it was Eamon Duffy's *The Stripping of the Altars*. His brows rose in surprise as he passed it over.

'I'll bring James up with Ambrose. I'm sure they'll get on,' Hugh said. 'I'll be interested to hear how your dig at the abbey is going too.'

Mike stood up and stretched his arms high above his head. 'Aaargh, I could do with some coffee.'

'Get your kit on then, and come over to the kitchen,' Hugh said. 'I don't expect anyone's hurrying away from breakfast. Except Anna and Lucy,' he added. 'They went out walking early.'

Mike grimaced as he pulled on his trousers. 'In the dog house, Hugh?' he asked bluntly.

'Just a bit,' Hugh admitted, opening the curtains at the windows. 'I quite forgot about not bringing Hector up to the orchard. He's such an interesting chap I just thought Lucy would like to meet him.'

'I don't know,' Mike said doubtfully, his voice muffled as he yanked his shirt over his head. 'She's not interested in that sort of thing, is she? Political commentary, social stories, and all that,' he said vaguely.

'Oh well,' Hugh said philosophically as he opened the door, 'she'll get over it.'

Mike was following him, pausing at every step to look at the shelves he was passing. He pulled down another book from the shelf. 'I didn't know you had this.'

'Not now, Mike,' Hugh said, waiting in the doorway. 'Come and have a shower. I'll get Will to make some fresh coffee for you. And if you have time, do take James around the farmyard buildings for me.'

'Okay,' Mike agreed, leaving the study with a last longing glance at the bookshelves. 'If I've time, and if,' he added sardonically, 'Will doesn't do it first. And I'll have to see to the students whenever they arrive.'

'Surely they won't be here before lunch?' Hugh asked, shutting the door firmly and locking it.

'Depends when they started,' Mike said as they set off across the yard garden. 'They're both coming separately from Oxford according to Mersett, so if they left yesterday and camped on the way, they could be here any time. Oy,' he shouted suddenly, creating a burst of scent as he brushed past the daphne that partially concealed the dairy. 'Will! Where are you off to?'

Hades spun round and raced towards Mike as Will stopped at the foot of the steps that led down from the back door. Niri was descending them behind him as Will looked across to Mike.

'Morning,' he said, grinning at the sight of the dishevelled archaeologist fending off the excited dog. 'Sleep well?'

Mike ignored this. 'Where are you off to?' he repeated grumpily. 'I need you to get me some coffee.'

'Sorry, Mike,' Will said blithely, 'we're going to see Josefina. At Fran's farm,' he added, seeing Mike's baffled expression. 'In case she needs any help.'

'I'm sure she'll welcome you with open arms,' Mike said morosely. 'Don't mind me.'

'Great, see you later then,' Will said, as Hades came back to him, pausing momentarily to sniff at a clump of grass. 'Come on, Niri, we can't hang about here. She'll probably already be busy. Farmers,' he glanced at Mike, who was stomping up the steps after Hugh, 'have to be out early, unlike some people.'

Mike muttered under his breath, but Will had already gone out of hearing.

The old waterlogged ruts in the farmyard entrance had been levelled, and the earth compacted, so that Will and Niri no longer had to press against the prickly tangle of hawthorn by the pond to get out into the lane. Lack of rain meant the level of water in the pond had shrunk, leaving a rim of dry earth around its edge, which Hades began to sniff.

Will paused to point out the small holes that were visible in the crumbling soil. Before he could speak there was a sudden movement behind the reeds. A large heron rose heavily into the air, wings beating hard as it climbed upwards at a steep angle, clearing the top of the sallows with a narrow margin. Will and Niri stood watching it straighten out and fly sedately down towards the river.

'We must remember to tell Hugh we saw it here,' Will said. 'Anyway, those holes are water voles' emergency exits. Their main entrances are in the overhanging turf bits. Lucy found some of their lawns last year,' he added enthusiastically. 'Cropped turf around their holes,' he explained, as Niri looked enquiringly at him, 'with stacks of grass for food supplies. Just like tiny haystacks really.'

'Why is it so muddy just there?' she asked, pointing to a shiny wet slope that Hades was approaching.

Will whistled and the big dog paused, looking over his shoulder. As he began to amble back towards his master Will explained, 'That's where the stream comes down from the spring. Lucy had the lower part of its bed widened so that water spills out from it more widely down the pond bank.'

'Why?' Niri asked in surprise. 'Is it particularly useful for some plant?'

Will laughed. 'A good try,' he acknowledged. 'But actually it's for mud, to encourage house martins and swallows to nest. They've used the eaves and the stables in the past, and Lucy wants to make sure they still have mud to build with. She's made shallow dips around the yard garden as well, to fill with water when it rains and act as artificial puddles.'

He pointed to the side of the house, whose coat of ivy was now neatly trimmed and cut away from the roof. 'She's made slots into an attic up there, too, for swifts. They should be arriving soon, so we'll see if they use the gaps.'

'She's thought of everything,' Niri said. 'I wonder if she's at a bit of a loose end now so much has been done.'

'Oh, she'll find something else to do,' Will assured her. 'Lucy always does. Come on, Niri, if we hang around here any longer Mike will come out and expect me to cook him a full English breakfast.'

Will grabbed her arm and pulled her into a run until they were out of sight down the lane that continued past Withern towards Fran's farm. High hedges rose above their heads on either side. Hawthorn was in bloom, creating white patches in the mixture of green from spindle, elder, hazel and dogwood. Wild roses already flourished a few flowers, delicately tinged with red.

Will and Niri slowed to a walk, passing under the shade of the trees, oak, beech and wild cherry, that grew here and there out of the hedges. Birdsong was all around them, and there were scurryings and rustlings in the hedges. A blackbird shot out of one of the underlying ditches with a loud alarmed call, darting across low in front of Niri.

She stopped, startled, and Will laughed. 'I forget you grew up in a town,' he said.

'We have blackbirds in town,' she said, unruffled. 'He just surprised me.' Her eyes followed the path the bird had taken, over the stile on the left into the field beyond. She looked slowly up the slope to the summit, crowned with trees that hid an old quarry.

'Has Lucy done anything with the quarry?' she asked suddenly.

Will paused, one hand on the field gate on the other side of the lane. He looked across at Niri, his face unusually sober. 'I don't know. She hasn't said,' he answered. 'And I don't like to ask.'

'No, I don't expect you do,' Niri said quietly. 'It doesn't have pleasant memories for her, after what happened there. Shall we go back that way later and see what it looks like?'

Will looked uncertain. 'I don't know,' he said at last. 'What if she sees us?'

'We're just taking the long way back to Withern,' Niri pointed out.

'Maybe,' he said unenthusiastically.

Loud barking from the farm rang across the field behind them. Will swung round, and pushed the gate open. 'Come on, Niri,' he called, setting off at a great pace. 'Hades has probably already got there. He knew where we were going.'

She followed him, carefully closing the gate. By the time she set off Will was well across the pasture, oblivious to the purple orchid spikes colouring the field. Loud peewit calls followed Will's progress and startled lapwings rose up nearby, black and white against the sky as they spread their wings.

Will left the farmyard gate open for her, and through it she saw the pebble-dashed bungalow that sat among a huddle of lean-to sheds. Fran's old blue Fiesta hatchback was parked near it, and a tabby cat sat on the bonnet, surveying the scene around. Chickens scurried around the edge of the field beyond the bungalow, and in front of the car Will stood talking to a tiny woman in faded blue overalls, her long black hair wound into a knot on the back of her neck, the coils of a hosepipe lying loosely by her feet. Hades was springing around the yard, trying to tempt a collie bitch to play with him.

'Hello, Bess,' Niri said softly as the bitch came up, her whole body moving eagerly with her wagging tail. 'Are you missing Fran?'

'She does,' the woman said, overhearing this. 'Always she looks at the door for Fran. But she is a good dog, she comes with me when I tell her. She was pleased to see your dog. I knew he was a friend.'

'This is Niri,' Will said. 'She's staying with Lucy as well. We're going back to my place soon, to do some studying. But it's not far away. It would be easy to come over if you need a hand.' He turned to Niri. 'Josefina had three lambs born last night. One of them kept her up until this morning.'

'Hello, Niri,' Josefina said, as Niri murmured a greeting. 'It is good that you and Will have offered to help. The lambing, though, it is not difficult. Fran has mostly Jacobs, for their wool and for breeding. These are new to me, but I think they lamb well. Last night was nothing, one of the Closewools, I think Fran called them.' She looked enquiringly at Will.

'Yes, that's right.'

'It was just a little help that was needed, to get the front legs out.' Josefina added, 'Would you like to see? The lambs are all very nice, and the Jacobs are so little and so pretty with their black spots. Fran is telling me these sheep are very hardy, so the lambs are left outside.'

'Yes, I'd like to see them,' Niri said. 'What about Hades, Will?'

'I'll stay here with him,' Will said. 'I want to talk to Josefina.'

'In the field behind the bungalow,' Josefina directed Niri. 'Do not get too close to them.'

She waited until Niri had passed round the bungalow to the gate into the far field. 'I am glad you came, Will. I was wondering whether to talk to your sister.'

'Lucy won't know,' Will said. 'Plants yes, birds possibly, but not farming.'

'This is not farming,' Josefina said. 'When I was out last night, this morning that is, I walked through the fields to look at the stars. And I heard men, two men, talking. Their voices were low, but at night the sound carries. They were down by the river. I wondered, should there be people there at that time?'

Will frowned. 'No, there shouldn't be. And it's the close season, the wrong time of year for night fishing. Unless,' he added thoughtfully, 'it's poachers. I'll tell Lucy or Hugh. It might be rustlers too,' he said, 'after the sheep. They're a growing problem, but I haven't heard of any trouble round here. And this is so far from the road it wouldn't be easy to get the animals away. Not without alerting Lucy and Hugh. It's not as if the rustlers could get the sheep down the river.' He drew in his breath sharply. 'Yeah, I've got it. That Hector bloke must have had visitors. Heck, Lucy'll be mad if he starts holding parties.'

'Who is this Hector bloke?' Josefina asked.

'He's got a boat moored just past the Withern landing stage. Hugh gave him permission. He's writing a book or something, so Hugh was bound to be interested.' He met Josefina's puzzled stare. 'Hugh runs a publishing company, you see. So he likes people who talk about books.'

'I see,' Josefina said. 'Then if it was this man, it is not a problem for me. But I will be careful. If there are rustlers out there I do not want them to take Fran's sheep away. What would she say to me if she came home here and saw they were all gone.' She broke into a hearty laugh, which startled Will.

'I must get on now, and clean the yard,' she said, mopping at the tears that streamed down her cheeks. 'You and Niri, you will come to see me again. We will tell more jokes.' She picked up the hosepipe in one bony hand, and reached for the tap with the other. 'Take your dog now, Will. Bess knows, she will stay away if she does not wish to have a bath.'

Thus firmly dismissed Will called Hades. The big dog left Bess reluctantly, although the bitch had already retired from the game to lie in the porch. Hades followed his master hopefully round the side of the bungalow. 'Heel,' Will instructed, spotting Niri some distance down the pasture. He leaned on the gate watching her and the Jacob sheep that grazed near her still figure, noting the two tiny lambs that were kept firmly on the far side of their mother. Beside him Hades propped his head on one of the gate bars and surveyed the scene too.

'Hi, Niri,' Will called after a while, feeling Hades shifting restlessly, 'we should go.'

She walked up to him without haste. 'They're lovely, and so very small,' she said. 'I wish I'd brought my camera.'

'Well, we'll be coming again. And Josefina said there are calves in the upper fields,' Will offered. 'We may see those if we go back on the top path.'

'Why are you in a hurry to get back?' Niri asked, falling into step beside him as they skirted the rear of the bungalow, passing through the overgrown garden and returning to the lane.

'I'm not really,' Will said. 'But James said at breakfast that he was going to ask Mike to show him over the storerooms that the students are going to be working on. I thought it would be interesting to muscle in if we can. Mike's being so mysterious about it, it would be cool to guess what he's up to.'

'Why is Mike so secretive about these storerooms?' Anna asked Lucy.

'Is he?' Lucy replied without much interest, her attention on Ben as the collie lay in the field, snuffling the air around him.

'Oh yes,' Anna said firmly as she reached for the flower-patterned thermos. 'Very.'

She had been sprawling elegantly on a grassy bank a couple of fields above Fran's farm. Now she sat up, pouring herself more coffee and offering the thermos to Lucy, who shook her head.

Lucy had led them on a circular tour from Withern after an early breakfast, along the river and back through the farm fields. Her route, Anna had noted, had avoided the Withern landing stage, and so had not passed Hector Trone and his boat. Instead, they had gone through the orchard and walked diagonally across the meadow, treading carefully over the grass, listening to the larks singing overhead and the occasional piercing call of lapwings.

A narrow gap in the hedge led to the riverbank beyond the landing stage and the visitor's boat. Here the alders edging the water were already in leaf, and yellow-rimmed pussy willow buds were casting a faint dusting of pollen over the grass. Lucy had pointed out a scattering of pink coral-like flowers in a damp hollow. Butterbur, which would soon be hidden by huge cabbage-like leaves that had once been used to wrap butter in farmhouse kitchens. A couple of male orange-tip butterflies danced erratically near a clump of lady's smock, whose pale fragile flowers fluttered above the water.

It had been a gentle stroll, different to the strenuous walking they usually undertook on the cliffs near their family homes. Lucy had maintained an intermittent commentary on what they saw, but generally they relaxed into a friendly silence. That, Anna thought, was how they saw the kingfisher, darting in a flash of brilliant turquoise from a branch over their heads away downriver ahead of them.

But even now, as they sat over the coffee and biscuits Lucy had brought with them, Lucy was showing no sign of making confidences, of the usual chatting exchange of news. Anna tried again to break through the unseen barrier that Lucy seemed to have erected around herself. 'Why is Hugh so taken with this Fone man?' she demanded.

A faint smile touched Lucy's lips. 'Trone,' she corrected mildly. 'I haven't the faintest idea. He sounds a crashing bore to me.' There was a faint trace of bitterness in her voice that made Anna look at her alertly.

'Look, Lucy,' she said bluntly, 'what's up? And don't,' she added forcefully, 'tell me it's nothing. We've been friends long enough for me to know there's something wrong, and for you to know you can tell me anything you like.'

Lucy had been lying back, watching the occasional cloud drift across the blue sky. Now she sat up, wrapping her arms around her knees. Ben's head lifted, then lowered resignedly again to rest decoratively between two clumps of primroses.

'Is it Hugh?' Anna demanded. 'Things seem a bit frosty between you.'

'No, it isn't Hugh. Not really,' Lucy said slowly. 'Perhaps it's both of us. But mainly it's me.'

'What do you mean?' Anna asked anxiously.

Lucy brushed back a strand of chestnut hair and turned to look at her friend. 'Do you remember, at Berhane's place at New Year, she mentioned a seed bank in Ethiopia?'

'Umm, no,' Anna admitted after a second's thought. 'What is it? Somewhere that sells seeds?'

'The opposite,' Lucy said. 'They identify, catalogue, store and keep safe seeds of all kinds of wild plants, especially those in danger of being lost. There's so much that depends on it. We don't know yet what uses so many plants have, yet human activity destroys their habitats. At least the seed banks give us a chance to restore them in the future, to investigate plant uses that we don't yet know about.'

'It sounds interesting, rather like what you were originally going to do in Peru,' Anna said. 'It must be very important work.'

'It is,' Lucy said emphatically, her eyes glowing with fervour. 'The one in Ethiopia that Berhane mentioned was a traditional one, a safe place where a few farmers stored seeds that could be used if future crops failed. Talking to Berhane about it reminded me of just how important the banks are. And,' she added grimly, 'how much I wanted to help save the world's plants.'

'And so?' Anna prompted. She was beginning to get an inkling of where the conversation was going.

'And so I kept an eye, just a casual eye, on what was happening. And on the jobs.'

'And there's one you want to apply for,' Anna guessed.

Lucy shook her head, her hair swinging from side to side. 'No.' She was silent, obviously debating whether to continue. 'No, I've applied for it,' she said.

'And Hugh isn't happy about it,' Anna said. She frowned. 'That doesn't sound like him.'

'Hugh doesn't know about it,' Lucy said. 'It's a maternity leave post, full-time. An amazing opportunity.' Her face was alight with enthusiasm. 'It's a co-ordinating role, maintaining contact with other botanic gardens and seed banks, identifying potential places for expeditions to identify and collect new plants, cataloguing the duplicates that are sent in.' She saw Anna's blank stare. 'The country of origin keeps seeds in its own bank, but duplicates are sent to other banks for extra security, to make sure that if one of them is destroyed the plants don't all go with it.'

'Wow,' Anna said rather feebly. 'I can see why you want the job.'

'I went to the interview last week. And,' Lucy stared down over the meadow, 'I've been offered the post.'

'Oh gosh, I see,' Anna said. 'It's going to be awkward telling Hugh at this stage.'

Lucy nodded. 'I start at the end of May. And they want me there for an induction course next week, and to arrange times to talk to Sally, who's having the baby,' she said. 'So I've got to get things moving here.'

Anna stared at her. 'You've accepted it,' she said blankly. 'Without telling Hugh?'

Lucy's hands gripped her knees. She turned to look at Anna again. 'It all happened so quickly,' she said. 'I didn't really expect anything to come of it. But everything that I raised as a problem, they've resolved for me. I can do three days in Hampshire, stay on site with Ben, and work from home for the other two days. So we'd be here most of the time.'

Anna was frowning. 'But why on earth haven't you discussed it with Hugh?' she asked.

'Well, he hasn't been here,' Lucy said. 'And things have been a bit difficult.' She looked down at her fingers. 'I haven't told you, or anyone, but I've been seeing a doctor.'

Anna's heart missed a beat as she remembered how long it had taken Lucy to recover her strength after she had been injured the previous year.

Lucy saw how anxious Anna looked and said quickly, 'I'm alright. At least in most working parts. It was about having a baby. And I can't. Ever.' She finished bleakly.

'Because of last year?' Anna asked carefully.

'Yes. The fall injured something inside me, and I won't be able to get pregnant again.'

'Have you told Hugh this?'

'Oh yes,' Lucy said, and now the note of bitterness was more evident. 'And he doesn't mind.'

'Well, that's good, isn't it?' Anna was puzzled by Lucy's attitude. 'It would be awkward if he was desperate to become a father.'

Lucy laughed harshly. 'He doesn't want to become a father. He didn't want the baby I lost. He doesn't want to look at adoption or surrogacy. He thinks we've got a good life, and should count our blessings, or words to that effect.'

Anna was silent, absorbing this, wondering how to respond. After a few minutes she asked cautiously, 'And do you want a baby then?'

'I hadn't thought about it, really,' Lucy said. 'Then when I found I was pregnant it was such a surprise, and I realised I was happy, really happy about it. For a couple of hours, until it was all over.'

'Lord, Lucy, what a mess. I'm so sorry,' Anna said. 'I'm sure Hugh doesn't know how much it means to you.'

'Because everything's okay for him. His business is successful, he's got the house he wanted, I'm there all the time. If,' she added, 'he still wants me.'

'Of course he does,' Anna said forcefully. 'Surely that isn't why you've gone for this job.'

Lucy smiled suddenly. It was a tired smile, not the usual gamine one that lit her pointed face. 'It isn't revenge, Anna. But it's my life, what I wanted to do. What I still want to do. And I can do it. If I'm not going to have a family, why shouldn't I?'

'I see.' And Anna did. 'Well, you're going to have to tell him. It's a shame Bel and Alex have turned up. Everything's going to hit him at once.'

'He's hardly been here at the same time as me,' Lucy said defensively. She pulled a wry face. 'And I've been putting it off when he has. Oh well, I'll get it over with when James leaves. I've already started winding up things here with the Wronham Trust.'

'Of course,' Anna exclaimed. 'I thought you'd just taken on more work with them. Aren't you managing their heathland survey as well as the coastal one?'

'Yes. But that was another piece that fell into place. When I discussed it with Miles Raden, the director, you know, he agreed to second me to the seed bank. We're in frequent contact with them, so it'll be valuable experience for whatever else I may do with the trust in the future.'

'It is meant to happen, I see that,' Anna said. 'When things fall into place so well you can't miss the chance.'

Lucy swung round eagerly. 'That's it. I just can't. You do understand. Thanks for not telling me to sit back and appreciate my lovely home and my charming husband.'

'Of course I understand,' Anna reassured her robustly. 'And Hugh will too. He's always known how much your work means to you.'

'He understands that, I know,' Lucy said sadly. 'But I've made it difficult, I know that too. Oh well, I'll just have to sort it out.' She got to her feet, dusting down her jeans. 'I'm glad I've told you, Anna. I've been going around feeling that everyone could see I had a guilty secret.' She bent to stroke Ben as the collie came up eagerly to lick her hand. 'When you're working in London you must come down and see us. I'll show you round the gardens, the living plant collection is impressive. And you can stay over. There's a sofa bed in my flat.'

'I'm not going to be in London so much, especially with this autumn's play in Stratford. But I'll get down to see you somehow. And I expect you'll be putting Hugh up too,' Anna ventured. 'He's in London quite a lot.'

'He'll probably be too busy,' Lucy said indifferently. 'Even though he's got this assistant now he still seems to be in the office all the time. If he isn't away visiting authors. In fact I seem to see more of Maggie than I do of Hugh. She's always around, talking books and authors with Hugh if he's here, wondering where he is if he's late. Look,' she added more brightly, 'there are Will and Niri coming up from Fran's farm. Let's meet them.'

'They seem to be going up towards the quarry,' Anna said. 'I haven't been there recently. Have you been since,' she paused for a fraction of a second, 'since last year?'

'Oh yes,' Lucy said. 'I'm not letting it become a problem. I still go up to watch the badgers in the copse beside the quarry. You should come some time.'

Mike looked up with a scowl on his face as the two dogs bounded excitedly over to him. 'For God's sake,' he growled, 'this isn't a public entertainment. We're trying to get some work done here.'

The woman on his left looked round with a startled air from the wall they had been examining, flinching as Hades approached her. Little and round, she barely reached Mike's shoulder. Her circular staring eyes under a straight-cut fringe gave her a comical appearance, enhanced by her rosy cheeks. Anna was irresistibly reminded of one of the painted wooden dolls she had inherited from her grandmother.

The man on Mike's right was the opposite to little and round. Stoop-shouldered and gaunt faced, with a straggling ginger beard and long ginger hair streaked with white, he studiously ignored Ben, sniffing round his ankles, and only glanced quickly. Ageing hippy, she assessed him, in his forties, perhaps recently redundant, indulging in a new hobby.

'Well,' Mike snarled, interrupting her thoughts. 'Have you come for something special?' He saw the look of alarm the woman student shot at him, and tried to modify his own expression. 'It's alright, Laura. They're friends of mine, just getting in the way.'

The man was staring intently at the blank dividing wall. 'I see what you mean, Mike,' he said earnestly. 'It's...'

'Yes, yes,' Mike interrupted. 'Just get your tents set up, then you can get to work.' He shepherded them out of the storeroom and turned back in the doorway, blocking most of the light, glowering at the visitors.

'Do come in properly, Mike,' Anna said impatiently. 'We can't see a thing otherwise.'

'There's nothing to see,' he said crossly, edging into the room again, 'and there won't be if we can't get on with our work. First James and Ambrose, now you lot. It's enough to make a saint swear.'

Will was looking round curiously. Mike was quite right, there was nothing out of the ordinary to see. It was a square, stone-built room, one of two in a solitary building a few yards up the slope beyond the barns. Will had only been in it once before, and all he could remember were heaps of old farm tools and fraying sacks, tubs of obsolete fertilisers and pesticides. They had all been cleared out when Lucy and Hugh had first started renovating the farm, but nothing else had been done to this building.

'Do you have plans for the place?' he asked Lucy suddenly.

'What?' His sister started, caught by surprise. 'Oh, no, we haven't discussed it. After all,' she waved a hand towards the farm-yard below, 'we've got plenty of buildings closer to the house, which are more useful.'

She looked at the room more carefully. She knew the low tiled roof was still in good repair, and they certainly would not want birds to settle in its eaves. But perhaps, she thought with a flicker of enthusiasm, if the door is left open it might encourage fly-catchers to nest here.

There was a thick layer of earth over the floor, but it had been swept clean when the room was cleared. The window was wide and deep, the only thing that seemed strange to Will. He said as much to Mike. 'That window is unusually wide and deep, isn't it?'

'Hummph,' Mike grunted uncommunicatively.

'Is the other room the same?' Will persisted. 'Are you interested in that as well?'

'Almost. Yes. Are you going now?' Mike enquired, leaning back against the wall, oblivious to the crumbling distemper as he folded his arms across his chest.

'Really, Mike, you could give us a guided tour,' Anna reproached him mischievously.

'Right, gather round,' he said with exaggerated patience. Attracted by his tone, both dogs came to sit in front of him as he continued to speak. 'One room, square, stone-built, used in recent memory as a storeroom. Next door one more room, nearly identical to this.' He pointed to the windows, one beside the door, one in the opposite wall. 'Wide, deep, glazed windows.' Turning to the door he said, 'One doorway, carved stone rim, thick wooden door with metal hinges.'

'It's very well-built for a storeroom,' Niri commented. 'Perhaps it was used for something before that. But there's no fireplace, so it can't have been lived in. Do you know how old it is, Mike?'

A corner of the archaeologist's mouth twitched in what might have been a smile. 'I'm not telling you until I know for sure,' he said firmly.

'Did you tell James and Ambrose anything?' Will demanded.

Mike shook his head, grinning now. 'Nope. And they're both more skilled at interrogation than you lot.'

'I thought they'd still be here,' Anna said, moving towards the door. 'Did you run them off?'

'No need,' Mike said. 'They,' he emphasised the word, 'have both got things to do too. Ambrose was keen to talk to Hugh about his book. And James was bursting to get into Coombhaven to see this woman about his collection.'

'Oh yes,' Anna said, stepping out into the sunshine, 'he was showing me the pieces last night and telling me all about them.' Her dark blue eyes sparkled. 'He's got life histories for nearly all of them, and I picked up some ideas for community plays.'

Mike snorted, as he shut the door of the storeroom behind Will. He reeled a little as the dogs pushed past him to race away. 'Bloody hell,' the archaeologist snapped, looking over Anna's head down the slope towards the farmyard. 'Now we've got Hugh coming to look round.'

Hugh caught his words as he reached the group. 'Not me,' he said mildly. 'I've already had a good look round and can't see anything there that seems unusual. So I'm waiting to be surprised.'

He looked at his wife. 'Ambrose has just left, he sends you all his love. Maggie can cope with the rest of the paperwork, so I'm just off to Coombhaven. I'm meeting James at this woman's, Meryl something or other, in the centre of town. He's calling by the hotel on his way, to talk to Bel and Alex. If he can persuade them to have a proper discussion he's taking us all to lunch at The Fighting Prawn, down by the estuary.'

Mike groaned. 'Another modern pub name for a decent old building.'

Hugh lifted a shoulder in a slight shrug. 'The food is good. Not,' he added glumly, 'that I'm likely to enjoy it, given the company and the topic.' He met Lucy's gaze. 'I can't imagine you want to come too.'

She shook her head at once, her smooth chestnut hair swinging out and back around her head. 'But I could meet you afterwards and we could walk out by the river for a bit.'

Hugh's eyes flickered with surprise. 'Fine,' he said. 'We could go on to Kingston Sands for tea at the café. James may like to drive round and meet us.'

Reflecting that this should give her at least an hour to break her news to Hugh, Lucy nodded. 'Okay.'

Beside her, Anna thought ruefully that Lucy really could not have picked a worse time to reveal her recent activities. Hugh's meeting with his stepmother and brother could not be expected to go well.

FOUR

Hugh strode along the broad esplanade beside the river Torre in Coombhaven. To his right stretched the lawns and neat flowerbeds of the municipal park that edged the esplanade. An elderly couple sat on a bench, basking in the sunshine, smiling benignly as he passed them. They were vaguely familiar and he murmured a greeting, edging at the same time around a stumbling toddler. The child's mother was approaching, trundling in front of her a pushchair laden with shopping bags. Her head was bent over her task, but she looked up as Hugh reached her, her eyes going beyond him to the toddler. She yelled angrily as she saw the child bend down to try to touch a seagull.

Hugh winced at the sound of her shrill voice, which momentarily pierced his preoccupation. He had left his car at The Fighting Prawn, the inn further down the estuary, hoping to clear his head by walking into town. But he had found he could not appreciate the salt smell of the sea, nor watch the gulls wheeling overhead. The exposed flats around the central channel of the river were hosting a variety of small birds, scurrying about, probing with long beaks, curved or sharply pointed, into the mud. The skirling cries of oystercatchers should have alerted him to their presence, for normally he enjoyed watching the birds, their pink legs and orange beaks conspicuous against their black and white plumage. Today not even the call of the curlew flying downriver caught his attention.

He was sure, had been from the start, that Bel and Alex would not be reconciled to maintaining the trust. There was no argument that he or James could advance that would convince them of the rightness of carrying out Edward's wishes. It just left him and James to stand on the letter of the law.

Hugh frowned. No doubt Alex needed the money. The frown deepened. He probably needed it badly, he usually did. Hugh cast his mind back. He had not seen his brother since his marriage to Lucy, nor for some time before that. It must be about five years since Alex had last touched him for a large loan, and Hugh had sworn then that it would be the final time.

His uncles had occasionally passed on details of Alex's activities. Teaching English in Morocco had been followed by crewing for a Turkish yachting enterprise, tour guiding in the Caucasus and Georgia, taking divers out around Crete. I suppose, Hugh thought grudgingly, the main link is travel and physical activity. Maybe he could make a go of an enterprise that involved both. Hugh laughed out loud in his disbelief, startling the pair of tourists poring over a map nearby.

Catching their alarmed eyes, Hugh smiled charmingly, noticing that he had already reached the harbour at the foot of the town. To his left there was a view along the cobbled street that led to the quay, where boats were stranded in low water, their masts clustering overhead like bare trees in a forest. The neat Georgian houses edging the harbour had once housed sea captains and merchants, and now were generally converted to nursing homes and offices. They underpinned the rows and rows of houses that lined the hill terraces above.

The high street ran steeply uphill towards the converted courtyard of The Old Inn, where Isobel, Lucy's grandmother, had a small mews house. It was a shame he was not going there with Lucy, Hugh thought fleetingly, and taking Isobel out to Garraway's, the coffee house they all liked so much. At the thought of Lucy, Hugh felt a twinge of conscience. He had perhaps not been listening to Lucy enough just lately, he thought a touch guiltily, nor even seeing as much of her as he would like to. Yes, he had been busy, but even so he should make more effort. Hugh realised suddenly how very much he was looking forward to going walking with his wife that afternoon. It was a long time since they had done anything like that, just the two of them.

Well, he thought, stepping off the narrow pavement to avoid a group of chattering women, just this dreadful lunch to get over and then I'll sort things out with Lucy.

The hotel he had suggested to Bel and Alex was right at the top of the high street, one of the old coaching inns, but Hugh did not intend to go that far. They could meet him down at The Fighting Prawn. He would prise James away from his silver collector and go down there in his uncle's car, which must be in one of the nearby car parks.

Halfway up the high street Hugh branched right along a narrow curving road, and began looking at the house names. Beyond the first few early Georgian period cottages the buildings were more modern, dating from the 1950s onwards. Wisteria House was the one he was searching for, the home of James's collector. There it was, a narrow three-storey house at the near end of a recently built terrace, set back behind railings and a small garden.

He opened the gate, wincing away from the bright red geraniums and blue lobelia that had been recently planted out into the pots of varying shapes and sizes that filled the garden. Mounting two shallow steps he rang the bell, frowning as he saw that the front door was fractionally ajar.

Careless, he thought, noticing the security chain that hung loosely beside the edge of the door. He rang the bell again, waiting with growing impatience. Finally he pushed the door open, but it jammed on the litter of letters scattered across the mat. He picked them up and pushed the door further back. 'Hello, may I come in?' he called loudly. 'James, it's Hugh.'

His words fell into silence. As Hugh waited, glancing round

the crowded hallway, he felt uneasy, unable to appreciate the very fine collection of Tunbridge-ware boxes that cluttered every surface.

There was a flicker of sound, so faint Hugh barely caught it. Straining his ears, he waited. It came again. This time it was clearly audible. Someone was groaning, groaning heavily.

Hugh stepped forward, listening hard as he dropped the letters he held onto a half-moon table against the wall. There it was again, the groaning, coming from the room on the right. Its door was ajar too, and Hugh pushed it carefully. It swung smoothly inwards before hitting an obstacle and shuddering to a halt.

Hugh stepped through into the room and stopped aghast at the sight that met him. Chairs were overturned, china cups and plates smashed in a welter of biscuit crumbs and spilt coffee. A delicate Regency dining table lay shattered across the body of a man. It was James, who was trying to crawl out from underneath it, his fingers scrabbling feebly on the faded Persian carpet.

Hugh hurried forward, his heart thumping. He grabbed the table, heaving it off his uncle and falling to his knees beside him. James was unrecognisable, his face badly bruised and bleeding, one eye swollen shut. From the harshness of his breathing Hugh feared he had broken ribs, perhaps a damaged lung. And his left leg protruded at a strange angle, undoubtedly broken.

'Hugh.' It was a faint whisper. Hugh crouched closer, ducking his head close to his uncle's, one hand taking the fingers that still groped towards him. 'The boy,' he heard. 'The boy.'

The fingers that Hugh clasped stilled as he looked quickly around. To his horrified gaze there appeared to be bodies everywhere. He touched James' wrist, desperately searching for a pulse. There it was, but so faint.

Hugh released his hold, and ran his hands gently over his uncle's body. He could feel the broken rib bones under the blood-stained shirt, and bit his lip. It was best not to move the older man at all, he decided quickly, checking that James could breathe safely.

Hugh stood up and looked around. He seized the thick cotton cloth that was tangled in the ruins of the table and laid it carefully over his uncle, hoping it would be enough to keep him warm. After a second's thought he removed his mobile phone from his pocket and pulled off his jacket, laying it on his uncle too.

He turned back towards the entrance and felt a jolt of shock as he saw his brother lying in a crumpled heap behind the door. A long stride, and Hugh was beside him, bending over the prostrate form. Hugh let out his pent-up breath with a sigh of relief. Alex had not been beaten as badly as their uncle. In fact, the only obvious damage was a reddening mark on his jaw. Knocked out cold, Hugh guessed. He considered moving his brother into the recovery position, deciding rapidly that it was better to leave him as he was.

He moved past Alex to the figure that lay on the floor next to the sofa, half screened by the shattered table. Bound and gagged, soft grey curls standing up in wild disarray above terrified eyes, the woman who lay there strained away from him.

'It's alright,' Hugh reassured her hastily, bending over her to pull the gag out of her mouth. He stood up again immediately, pressing the emergency code on his phone as he said, 'I'm James' nephew. I'll ring for an ambulance and the police, then I'll untie you.'

His call was answered at once and he spoke briefly into the phone, emphasising the urgency of James's condition. He did not have much doubt that the police would arrive promptly, nor the ambulance either. Both had stations just at the top of town, so had only to skirt round the one-way system.

He gently rolled the woman onto her side and began to pick at the knot that tied her hands tightly behind her back. Even at this moment he noticed the rope, one of the finer kind sold at the local chandlery. Surely it had not been lying conveniently to hand in the house. The intruder must have brought it.

Where the rope cut into the woman's wrists the skin was torn and bleeding, a sign that she had struggled to free herself. The knot was expertly tied, and Hugh was finding it difficult to loosen it.

'A knife,' the woman said hoarsely. 'Get a knife from the kitchen.'

'Of course.' Hugh went swiftly back into the hall and through a door at the back, beyond the stairs. It was a small kitchen, but there was a prominent block of knives on one of the counters. Hugh seized the smallest one and hurried back to the dining room. He inserted the tip carefully under the rope, between the woman's wrists, and sawed slowly until it fell apart.

'Ah,' she sighed in relief and rolled back, attempting to sit up.

Hugh put an arm round her shoulders, lifting her enough to prop her against the sofa. As he knelt down to work on the rope around her ankles she began to rub her wrists.

'How is he?' she asked after a moment. 'Your uncle?'

'Not so good,' Hugh replied. 'What the hell happened here?'

'He tried to stop them. Two of them,' she said as Hugh sat back onto his heels, the remains of the rope in his left hand. Her voice was rasping and she put up one hand to massage her throat. 'Do you think I could have a glass of water?'

'Of course.' In the kitchen Hugh dropped the knife and the rope onto the counter and began to open cupboards, searching for a glass. Finding a shelf of neatly stacked mugs he grabbed one and filled it quickly from the tap.

He hurried back to find the woman trying to get to her feet. 'Wait a bit and I'll help you up,' he said sharply.

She sank back down to the floor and accepted the mug he held out to her. Gripping it tightly between shaking hands she raised it to her mouth. A little spilt down her chin, but she sipped carefully before taking larger gulps of water.

Hugh crouched beside her, waiting until she finished. He took the mug from her hand and put it down on the floor beside the sofa. 'Alright, let's get you up,' he said briskly, getting to his feet. 'Then you can tell me what happened here.'

He leaned forward to put his hands under her arms, but she

shook her head. 'No,' she said urgently. 'I've got a dodgy hip. Let me roll over onto my hands and knees, then I'm sure I'll manage.'

Hugh stood back, watching anxiously as she manoeuvred herself, until she eventually pulled herself up against the sofa, collapsing onto it with a sigh of relief. 'That's better,' she said, her breath coming in short gasps.

He studied her, noting the pallor of her face. He picked up the mug and offered it to her again. She waved it away. 'How is he?' she asked, a soft American drawl becoming more noticeable as she stared down at James.

He lay very still, his shallow breathing barely stirring his chest. Hugh moved to sit on the floor beside his uncle, putting one hand lightly on James's wrist. 'The ambulance will be here soon,' he said obliquely. 'And the police. What the hell happened?' he demanded again.

She shook her head disbelievingly. 'Two men burst into the room. James had put out his silver, and I had just opened my own showcases when it happened. I was so shocked I didn't know what was going on, but your brother was quick off the mark, tackling them at once. My goodness,' she gasped, turning round in dismay. 'I forgot, how is he?'

'Knocked out,' Hugh said curtly. 'He'll come round soon.'

'One man hit him hard, very hard,' she said quietly, 'and he went straight down. It was lucky he didn't catch his head on the door, he just slithered down the wall. Your uncle was trying to tackle the other man, but,' her eyes filled with tears, 'he was getting the worst of it.' She searched up the sleeve of her jumper, pulling out a flowered handkerchief to mop her eyes. 'The first man just grabbed me before I'd even moved. It was so quick, I was trussed up before I could do anything.'

Hugh frowned as he saw her rub her cheek. 'Did he hit you?' he demanded.

She nodded slowly. 'I think I screamed. It must have been then. More of a slap, than a hit, I suppose. It stunned me, but didn't knock me out.'

'But could you see or hear what was happening?' Hugh asked. 'Did they go straight for the silver?'

'No.' She shut her eyes, then opened them, filled with horror as she stared at him. 'The first man, the one who'd hit your brother, went over to your uncle. James had fallen to the floor by then, and the man attacking him was kicking him while he lay there. The first man,' she said the words with stunned disbelief, ''joined in. James wasn't resisting at all, they could just have taken the silver and gone. But it was as if they really wanted to hurt him.'

Hugh's face was grey and strained as he listened. His mind was filled with a burning anger that he had never experienced before.

The woman was looking at him sorrowfully. 'I'm so sorry,' she said. 'I'd have given them the silver rather than have this happen. It's very dear to me, much of it belonged to my great-grandfather, but it isn't worth this.'

He nodded, unable to answer. After a minute, he asked, 'What brought it to an end?'

She frowned. 'I'm not sure. I think there was a noise at the door. But something startled them. They grabbed the showcases and emptied the contents into a couple of bags and just left without a backward glance.'

She looked embarrassed. 'I was too afraid to do anything, I just lay on the floor, keeping as still as I could, praying they wouldn't come back. Then when I was sure they'd gone I tried to free my hands.' She looked down at her swollen and bloody wrists. 'But the rope was too tight.'

'Did you hear the front door shut?' he asked suddenly. 'It was ajar when I got here.'

'Yes, I did,' she said, 'but it doesn't catch unless you really push the lock, so it would have bounced open. That's why, you see,' she leaned forward, 'I'm sure I shut it when James and your brother arrived. I had to push it as usual. How on earth did these men get in?'

As she spoke they heard voices outside the house and Hugh got swiftly to his feet. As he reached the hall two people in bottle-green uniforms came briskly through the front door.

'Emergency call,' the first paramedic, a man, said shortly. 'Where do we go?'

'In here,' Hugh said, stepping aside to allow them to enter the dining room. 'Two unconscious men. The worst is the older one here. The other is just behind the door. And this lady has been very badly shocked, she needs checking over too.'

She waved a dismissive hand as the male paramedic bent over James. 'There's nothing a good strong cup of tea won't sort out for me.'

'Just stay there,' the paramedic said without looking up. 'We'll take a look at you when we've finished with the men.'

Hugh stood staring down at his uncle's frail and battered body as the paramedic worked on it. The other, a woman, was checking Alex, but came back quickly to her colleague. 'Out cold,' she said. 'Almost certainly concussion.'

'Call through to the hospital in Corrington,' the man said. 'This one will need the intensive care unit. We'd better take the other one there too.'

He turned to the elderly woman, who said firmly, 'No, don't bother about me, I haven't been hurt. I'll ask my doctor to come round.'

His eyes ran over her quickly, noting the colour that was beginning to return to her pale face as she patted her hair, trying to tidy her disordered curls. 'Make sure you do,' he said as his colleague finished her call. 'Shock can catch up with you later on, when you're not expecting it.'

He turned to his colleague. 'Let's get the stretchers.' As he finished speaking, they were leaving the room.

'I heard it was a call from you,' another man's voice said from the hall.

Hugh spun round, recognising it at once. He was plainly glad to see the tall man, impeccably dressed in a grey suit, who the paramedics were acknowledging as they left the house.

'Rob,' Hugh exclaimed in relief. 'Thank God it's you.'

Inspector Robert Elliot looked at him with a hint of surprise in his eyes. The two men had known each other for some time, and had been in various tight corners together in the last few years since they had both come, for different reasons, to the West Country. In all that time he had never seen the imperturbable Hugh so disturbed.

The inspector's eyes went past Hugh, assessing the situation in the dining room. 'Do you know them?' he asked quietly, making way for the paramedics as they returned.

'Yes,' Hugh said. 'My uncle, and my half-brother.'

'Were you here when it happened?' Elliot asked.

Hugh shook his head. 'I was meeting James, my uncle, here to go on to lunch. I didn't know Alex would be with him.'

Elliot moved into the room, keeping back against the wall as the paramedics lifted James onto the first stretcher and moved over to Alex. 'Was this how you found the place?' Elliot asked Hugh.

'Not exactly,' he confessed. 'I moved the table, it was lying over James. And I used the tablecloth to cover him.'

'Unavoidable,' Elliot said. 'There was obviously quite a fight here.'

Hugh's mouth tightened. 'A beating. A very deliberate beating of an elderly man who can't have been a threat.'

'Out of the way,' the male paramedic ordered as the first stretcher was lifted from the ground.

'I'll come with you,' Hugh said as James was carried past him. 'I'm related to him, to them both,' he added, sensing imminent dissent.

'Don't hang around then,' the man said. 'We won't wait for you.'

'Elliot,' Hugh said urgently, 'this lady…' He broke off in some astonishment, looking at the woman, who was now sitting more comfortably on the sofa. 'I'm so sorry, I don't even know your name,' he apologised.

She gave him a faint smile. 'Hardly surprising.' She looked at the inspector. 'I'm Meryl Harper,' she introduced herself, 'and this is my house.'

'This,' Hugh said quickly, 'is Inspector Elliot of the regional crime unit. Can you tell him what you told me?'

'Of course,' she said.

'Catch up with me at the hospital, Rob,' Hugh said over his shoulder, following the paramedics as they took Alex out of the house.

Lucy stood at the reception desk in the hospital emergency ward, wondering where to go. Hugh's message had been so very brief. James was badly hurt and on his way to the hospital, Hugh was with him.

A tea trolley rattled along the corridor to the right of the desk, stopping at every door. The corridor that ran to the left was empty, stretching off into the distance without a sign of movement. An orderly was approaching from the lift behind her, pushing a wheel-chair whose occupant had one bandaged leg stuck stiffly out in front of him. There was nobody to ask for directions, except perhaps the orderly.

Lucy was moving forward to intercept him when a woman's shrill voice caught her ear. The hysterical tone in it jarred her memory. Bel, of course, Hugh's stepmother. What on earth was she doing here? Surely she wasn't that concerned about James?

Lucy looked down the left corridor and saw that two people had appeared at the far end. She began to walk reluctantly towards them, unable to miss the sound of Bel's hectoring. The other person, a man in a white coat, was speaking too as Lucy neared them. His tone was low and soothing, but he was not Hugh.

'He's my son,' Bel was saying over the other man's words, 'and I insist that he's seen by the consultant now. I don't care what else he's doing, I want him here at once.'

'Really, Mrs Carey, there's no need to be so concerned. Your son is already beginning to come round. Mr Perera will be here as soon as he can, but we really don't anticipate any problems with your son.'

'This just isn't good enough,' Bel raged, stopping dead. 'I shall complain to my MP.'

'Bel.' Lucy started at the sound of Hugh's voice close to her shoulder. He put a hand on her arm, but continued to speak to his stepmother. 'Try to control yourself. You won't do Alex any good if he comes round to hear you ranting. Try for a little of the gentle caring mother and sit at his bedside. I'm sure,' Hugh added mendaciously, 'that seeing you there when he regains consciousness will do him a power of good.'

Bel hesitated, unable to deny that she thought so too. 'I'd do it happily,' she compromised, 'if I thought you could be relied upon to look after your brother's interests. But I've learned to know better over the years.' She stared at Hugh with intense dislike. 'You couldn't even be bothered to collect me. All I got was a message to say Alex was in hospital.'

Hugh closed his eyes briefly, struggling to retain his barely regained equanimity. 'I came in the ambulance,' he said. 'I can't be in two places at once.'

'Much good that did Alex,' Bel retorted.

Hugh's patience snapped. 'I came with James, who's in a much worse state than dear Alex. So just get out of my hair, Bel, and look after your son.'

Bel's face crimsoned with fury, which warred with curiosity. 'James?' she said. 'What happened to him? I suppose,' she rallied, 'my boy was hurt in this fight to protect his uncle.'

To her surprise, Hugh said with a bleak smile, 'Something like that may be true. So go and smile at our little hero.'

A nurse had appeared at the doctor's elbow during this exchange, murmuring in his ear. The doctor straightened up and spoke before Bel could say more, 'Your son has recovered full consciousness, Mrs Carey. Perhaps you would like to go and see him?'

Bel caught her breath, coughing, but turned and hurried down the left corridor after the nurse. The doctor glanced apologetically at Hugh. 'It takes some people badly, the shock,' he ventured.

Hugh nodded without saying anything.

'Do you want to see him as well?' the doctor asked. 'Only for a few minutes, I'm afraid. The police have said they'll be here shortly, and they'll want to talk to him. Then your brother must get as much rest as he can, now and for some time.'

'I'll wait,' Hugh said. 'His mother will be quite enough. And I want to see Mr Perera as soon as he's finished with my uncle.'

The doctor nodded. 'Of course. If you want to sit down over there,' he pointed to the chairs lining the wall beside the reception desk, 'he'll be here when he can.'

The doctor went back down the corridor towards Alex's room, and Hugh, his hand still on Lucy's arm, steered her towards the seats. He released his hold and sat down heavily on one of them, burying his head in his hands.

Lucy sat beside him, looking anxiously at him. She put a hand on his shoulder. 'Hugh,' she said tentatively, 'how is James?'

The shoulder under her hand stiffened. 'Bad. Very bad.' The words were muffled, hidden by his hands. He dropped them, saying savagely, 'Bloody Bel. It's always Alex. He'll get better. James may not. He's in a very bad state. If I hadn't walked from the estuary, if I'd only parked closer, I might have got there in time to help him.' Hugh's shoulder sagged suddenly and he turned his head away from Lucy.

She stared at him, not sure if she had heard him correctly. Before she could find a way of asking there was the sound of brisk footsteps from the right corridor and Hugh looked round quickly.

He got to his feet slowly, waiting for the approaching man to reach them.

'Hugh Carey?' the consultant asked. He was a slight figure, his expression impassive as he asked the question.

Hugh nodded.

'James Carey's son?'

'His nephew,' Hugh said. 'And next of kin.' He searched the other man's face. 'How is he?'

'Let's sit down,' Mr Perera indicated the chairs, looking enquiringly at Lucy who had also risen to her feet.

'I'm Lucy Rossington, Hugh's wife,' she said quietly. She resumed her seat as the consultant pulled out a chair, turning it so that he faced her as he sat down.

Hugh, though, stood in front of them for a second longer, before he sat reluctantly next to Lucy.

'I won't beat about the bush,' Mr Perera said. 'James Carey has suffered a number of injuries. One of these has caused a blood clot on his brain.'

'Is it operable?' Hugh asked at once.

'Yes, but your uncle also has a serious heart condition,' the consultant answered. 'That has been badly affected by the attack. We must take it into account when we decide what to do next. My main instinct is to wait a while and see how he progresses.'

Hugh was looking stunned. 'I didn't know,' he said blankly. 'About the heart condition, that is.' He gathered his wits with difficulty. 'Can I sit with him?'

'Of course. But,' Mr Perera added, 'your uncle is on life support. It may be a shock to see him so.' He hesitated, but saw that Hugh was waiting for him to continue. 'It's difficult for you, I understand that, but do you know what your uncle's wishes would be if he has to continue on life support?'

Hugh stared at him, not fully understanding at first. Then the words hit him like stones, thudding hard into his stomach.

'Would he want the machine switched off?' he asked numbly. 'Would he want to die? Is that what you're asking?'

'I'm afraid it is.'

Hugh shook his head dazedly. 'No, we've never discussed it. There never seemed to be a reason to. He isn't that old a man, and I always thought he was in good health.'

'I see,' Mr Perera said. 'Well, we'll deal with it if we come to it. Would you like to come to your uncle now?'

'I'd like a few words with my wife first,' Hugh said.

Mr Perera nodded, and got to his feet. 'I'll let the nurse know you'll be coming. She'll be there with him all the time.' He strode off back down the corridor.

Hugh sat frozen, staring after him. Lucy sat beside him, unable to think of anything to say. At last she asked, 'Is there anything I can do while you sit with James?'

Hugh turned slowly, his eyes unfocused at first, then settling on her face. 'I don't know. I can't seem to think.'

She put her hand on his. 'Do you want to tell me what happened?'

'Yes,' he said after a few minutes, 'yes, I do.' He gathered his thoughts with a visible effort. Before he could open his mouth there was the sound of footsteps again, firm and unhurried. He looked up quickly, and experienced an overwhelming mixture of feelings when he saw Inspector Elliot approaching, another familiar figure at his side.

The Rossington circle knew Detective Sergeant Tom Peters well from their earlier forays into crime and mayhem. He was a man of middle height and girth, really rather square, Lucy always thought. His rubicund face and twinkling blue eyes, together with the heavy tread and thick-fingered hands, gave him a traditionally bucolic look. But they belied the shrewdness of those blue eyes, and the acuity of the brain behind the look. Today he looked unusually sober as he reached them, affected perhaps by the atmosphere of the hospital, perhaps by the knowledge of Hugh's personal connection with the victims.

Hugh's own face was expressionless as he grappled with the emotions that assailed him. Disappointment warred with relief that it was not the consultant, irritation at the inevitable delay in going to his uncle fought with thankfulness that he would only have to repeat his story once. At the moment, he thought wryly.

'Hello, Rob,' Lucy greeted the inspector, cutting into Hugh's confused thoughts. 'I should have guessed you'd be here. It's good to see you, although I'm sorry it's trouble that brings us together again.'

'Strictly speaking, it shouldn't be my case,' Elliot replied, looking down at them with concern, 'but when I saw Hugh's name on the emergency call I thought I'd better go. You all have a habit of getting into situations that develop badly.'

'You'll be involved in this one,' Hugh said bleakly. 'As well to get in at the beginning of a murder case.'

The inspector's expression altered, sharpening. 'I'm sorry. I hadn't heard that your uncle had died.'

'He hasn't. Yet,' Hugh replied. 'But he's going to. And I have to decide when.'

Elliot was frowning. 'I don't understand you.'

'He's on life support. I don't entirely know what that means yet. But from the direction of the consultant's questioning it sounds as though it will be an issue of how long we want to keep him on it before agreeing to let him die.'

The inspector glanced around. 'Tom, could you see if you can get some coffee. I should think we could all use it.' He ignored Hugh's impatient gesture as the sergeant retraced his steps towards the lift, which was opposite the drinks dispenser. Elliot sat down on the chair the consultant had used, carefully hitching up his trouser legs. 'What exactly has the doctor said?' he asked quietly.

His demeanour helped Hugh to retrieve his own normal equilibrium. 'Look,' he said in a firmer voice, 'let me tell you what happened from the beginning. I'll go through the medical situation later; Lucy doesn't need to hear it all again.'

He sat back in the chair. 'Briefly, James is my uncle, one of the two who pretty much brought me up. Alex is my younger half-brother. Bel, his mother, is here. You'll be bound to meet her soon.'

Elliot picked up the tone of Hugh's last words and correctly interpreted them. Hugh couldn't stand his stepmother, the inspector thought. I don't expect I'm going to like her much either.

'They're all down here to discuss the will of my other uncle,'

Hugh continued. 'He left his estate between Alex and me, with Alex's in trust until he reaches thirty. James and I are his trustees.'

'How long have you known this?' Elliot asked, warily conscious that Hugh was presenting the facts as if he were once more practising as a barrister. Which could, the inspector reflected, simply be because he's so closely involved with them.

'Since yesterday evening,' Hugh replied simply, 'when Alex and Bel turned up at Withern. What with one thing and another, I haven't,' his lips twisted in a faint smile, 'been paying enough attention to my post, and they couldn't get me on the phone. James came down shortly after, for the same reason.'

The bland expression on Elliot's face did not alter, but his mind registered several thoughts. Family trouble. Difficult relationships. And money, especially inherited money, usually caused dissension.

Sergeant Peters returned, carefully balancing four plastic cups in his hands. Lucy got up quickly to help him, and with a slow smile he passed two over to her. 'There's sugar in my pocket, if you want some,' he said, jerking his head towards it.

'Thanks, but we don't take it,' Lucy said, sitting back down and passing one cup to Hugh.

He took it absentmindedly, obviously startled when the heat burned his fingers. Putting it down on the chair beside him, he said, 'As James was down here he planned to visit a silver collector in Coombhaven to discuss the collection he inherited from his brother. That was Meryl Harper, of course. An American, I think, although she looks as though she's been in the house for some time.'

Lucy had been watching Tom Peters out of the corner of her eye, fascinated as always at how such a chunky person could fade into the background. He had passed the inspector his cup, and sat silently down next to Lucy. In spite of his unobtrusiveness, she knew he was very much engaged in what was being said.

At Hugh's words, though, Lucy's attention returned to her husband. She glanced at him, wondering how he was deducing so much about Meryl Harper.

Hugh saw her surprise, and added, 'I only got her name as I was leaving her house to come here. I expect James mentioned it, but I didn't remember. And,' Hugh saw Lucy still looked puzzled, 'from what I saw of the house it was stuffed with collections of all kinds. I can't imagine she's only got those in place recently.'

'I noticed too,' Elliot said. 'All those little boxes in the hall. I don't suppose you had chance to notice, but the dining room was crammed with china cabinets, and pretty much every spare inch of the walls was covered with peculiar pictures, made out of materials. I expect they're something special. Anyway,' the inspector collected himself abruptly, 'she's lived there ten years, and was in the area before that.' He anticipated Hugh's question as the other man opened his mouth. 'That loose front door lock interested me. But there've been no unusual callers recently, nobody unusual who might have noticed it. The only people who've come to the house in the last few days are the cleaner and the gardener. Both fairly new, it's true, so we'll check them out.' He smiled a little. 'The gardener is shared with most of the street, it seems. A woman, although that's maybe not so unusual these days, and very generous with spare plants. She's responsible for planting the pots in the front garden, and I got the impression that Ms Harper wasn't too keen on the colour scheme.'

Elliot changed the subject, bringing the conversation back on track. 'Was your brother interested in silver too?'

'Definitely. But not that sort, only the sort that can be spent.' Hugh made the sardonic comment without thought and at once regretted it.

The inspector saw the fleeting expression of irritation that crossed Hugh's face, and registered a further thought. Hugh didn't like his brother much either.

'Did they leave your place together?' Elliot asked.

Hugh stared at him, confused for a second. His face cleared. 'We only had room for James at Withern. Alex and Bel are staying in Coombhaven, at The Coach and Horses at the top of town.

James called in there on his way to Meryl Harper, to arrange a lunchtime discussion with us.'

Hugh glanced at Lucy. 'I've left my car at The Fighting Prawn. I came here with James in the ambulance.'

'I'll sort it out,' she said. 'One of the others can come over and take me down there. I'll drive your car back here for you and collect my own. I'd better go into the inn as well and tell them why you didn't turn up for lunch.'

'The others?' Elliot picked up her comment. 'Who else is staying with you?'

'Anna, Mike, Niri and Will,' Lucy said. 'That's why there wasn't room for Alex and Bel. As it is, Mike moved into Hugh's study to free up a room for James.'

Neatly explained, Hugh thought appreciatively. He must remember never to underestimate Lucy's skills.

'Of course,' Elliot exclaimed. 'It was Anna's father's wedding, wasn't it?'

'Yes,' Hugh agreed, realising afresh how friendly Anna and the detective had become. 'I thought you might have been there.'

'I was on duty,' Elliot said. 'At least,' he added, 'the ceremony seems to have gone without trouble.'

'Fortunately,' Hugh commented, 'the bride and groom had left before my family began to arrive.'

'Did your uncle, or your brother, for that matter, mention anything about their intentions, their activities, their friends, down here?' Elliot asked.

Hugh's brows drew together. 'You think they could have a connection with the robbery?'

The inspector shrugged. 'I can't know yet. It seems unlikely, but,' his eyes narrowed thoughtfully, 'the operation doesn't have the feel of a casual job. And there was no reason for your uncle to be attacked so savagely. Two men could have subdued him very easily without doing so much damage.'

'Yes, I know that,' Hugh said painfully. 'I follow your reasoning, but it doesn't make any sense. Who would want to hurt

James? And why come down here to do it?'

'What's his occupation?' Elliot asked.

'He's a solicitor in Clerkenwell, but there can't be anything controversial there. He deals with family law.'

'We'll have to check his recent cases,' Elliot said. 'Can you let me have the name of his firm?'

'He'll have business cards in his wallet,' Hugh said. 'I'll get you one of those.'

'Anyway, we'll presume your brother decided to go along with your uncle to Ms Harper's until we know otherwise,' Elliot said. 'How did you arrive on the scene?'

'I was meeting James there,' Hugh said. 'I left my car at the inn by the estuary and walked up. I wanted to clear my head.' Again he mentally berated himself for saying too much. 'A full day of partying with Mike and Anna usually has that effect.'

Elliot said nothing, sipping his coffee as he waited for him to continue.

Hugh, appreciating the tactic, went on, 'I didn't know precisely where her house was, but it was easy enough to find. We've come to know the town quite well since Isobel, Lucy's grandmother, moved into her house further up the high street. Anyway,' he feared he was beginning to ramble, so concentrated harder on his story, 'I found the Harper house easily, at about twelve-thirty, I should think. James's appointment was for eleven, and he thought an hour and a half would be more than enough time.'

Hugh paused, picturing his own arrival at Meryl Harper's house. 'There was no answer when I rang the bell, and I saw the door was slightly ajar.' He glanced at Elliot enquiringly. 'Did she tell you the door doesn't latch properly unless the lock is pushed or pulled?'

The inspector nodded.

'And that the intruders were disturbed while they were beating up James?'

Elliot nodded again.

'Well, it may be worth checking the time of the post delivery, and see if the front door was open then,' Hugh said. 'When I pushed the door further open it caught on half a dozen envelopes on the hall floor. I picked them up and put them on the little table there.' He looked rueful. 'It was a purely automatic action.'

'You think the post delivery disturbed the intruders,' Elliot commented. 'If you're right that could narrow down the timing for the attack. I presume you didn't see any sign of the attackers when you arrived? A couple of men with bulky bags legging it down the street?'

'No,' Hugh said. 'I've been racking my brains, but I don't recall seeing anybody. I was standing in the hall, in fact I think I called out, when I heard a noise. Groaning,' he said, his face set. 'It came again, more clearly, so I followed the sound into the dining room.'

Lucy saw his hand clench. Hugh was aware of it too, and consciously relaxed it.

'The room was a shambles,' he said. 'It was a general impression. I can't say I noticed exactly, just that the table was knocked over and broken, because it lay over James, who was sprawled on the ground in the middle of the room.' He grimaced at Elliot. 'It was only after I'd moved it and done what I could for him that I saw Alex, partially hidden by the door. He was out cold. And then I saw the woman tied up on the ground beside the sofa. I hadn't seen her at first because the table screened her. It was lucky,' he added, 'that I didn't throw it over her when I moved it.'

He turned to Lucy. 'Could you go and see how she is?' he asked. 'She wasn't physically hurt much, but although she was badly shaken she refused treatment from the paramedics. It would be worth making sure she has arranged to see her doctor.'

'Of course I'll go, if you give me her address,' Lucy said. 'I can easily do it before I drive your car back here. I've got Ben in my car, so I'll take him with me and walk him up through the town.'

Hugh remembered vaguely their plans for an afternoon walk, plans that seemed to have been made a lifetime ago. He dismissed the memory, concentrating again on what had happened that morning.

'That's it, really,' he said to Elliot. 'I took out Meryl Harper's gag, her own scarf, I think. I went to the kitchen for a knife and cut the ropes, they were tightly tied, professionally I'd say. She was bound at the wrists and ankles. But she coped very well.'

'Yes, a competent woman,' the inspector said. 'She was insisting she was quite alright when Tom and I left her.'

'Well, that's all I can tell you,' Hugh said, getting to his feet. 'I'll get down to James's room now.'

Elliot and Sergeant Peters rose too, the first with lithe ease, the latter planting himself firmly on his feet. 'Thank you for taking the time to talk to us,' the inspector said. 'Let me know how things go.'

'Of course,' Hugh said. As he spoke he was scribbling in a small notebook that he had taken out of his pocket. He ripped out the page and gave it to Lucy. 'Meryl Harper's address. I'll see you at home when I can.'

'I'll come back here when I've got your car sorted out. We'll see what to do then,' she said. 'And I'd better find James' car too, if you can get hold of his keys.'

He nodded and strode off down the corridor without another word, leaving his coffee untouched on the chair.

'It's hit him hard,' Elliot said, watching him go.

'He was very close to his uncles,' Lucy said, standing up too, 'but I think James was always his favourite. They often met up when Hugh was in London, and he stayed with James whenever he was in town for any length of time.' She watched Hugh until he disappeared from sight. 'And now,' she said heavily, 'it looks as though he'll have to decide whether or not to end James's life support. Are you,' she turned to the inspector, 'going out to Withern? Only they don't know what's happened yet, so I should tell them.'

Elliot was about to make a light-hearted comment about the appearance of policemen on the doorstep, when he remembered how often members of the Rossington circle had got into difficulties. His unannounced arrival could easily cause alarm. He felt a twinge of annoyance when he thought how unlikely it was to be seen as a purely social call, even by Anna.

'Ring them up then,' he advised Lucy. 'I won't be going immediately. In fact,' he looked startled, 'I had almost forgotten about Hugh's brother. What sort of state is he in?'

'I imagine he's not too bad,' Lucy said. 'At least, he's conscious again and I didn't hear that he was badly hurt in any way. He's in a room down there,' she gestured to the left. 'And,' she added, 'his mother's with him.'

'Ah yes, his mother,' Elliot commented. 'I'd better meet the lady.'

A slight smile touched Lucy's lips. 'You won't be able to avoid her.'

'Ah well, let's get it over with, Tom.' Lifting a hand in farewell, the inspector walked off along the corridor. As he followed, Sergeant Peters winked companionably at Lucy.

FIVE

Anna pulled James's dark Jaguar into the farmyard at Withern with a sigh of relief, swinging the car round into the wide parking area. It was already packed with cars, including Mike's battered red Passat and the old Landrover that Anna used when she was staying with her father. As she edged the Jaguar into a space, stopping it with its nose towards the old stables, she was vaguely puzzled by the other cars there. There was a bright yellow Mini, and a nondescript Escort. The students, she thought suddenly. The cars must belong to them. She leaned her head against the steering wheel of the Jaguar for a moment before getting out, just as Lucy's Suzuki drew up beside her.

She waited until Lucy had got out of her car and released Ben, who sprang out with relief, rushing over to Anna, then racing into the yard garden. 'Let's make some tea,' Anna suggested as she fell into step beside her friend, noting how tired Lucy looked.

'That's just what I need,' Lucy said. She was staring at the bicycle leaning against the stable wall. 'That woman is still here,' she said with exasperation. 'Maggie,' she explained as Anna looked puzzled. 'She'll be over as soon as we get into the house, anxious to know why Hugh isn't in the office.'

Lucy's expression lightened as Ben slid to a halt in front of her, his pink tongue lolling out of his mouth. 'Poor Ben. You've been really short-changed recently.' She glanced at Anna as they moved towards the house. 'He hasn't been out much for the last couple of days, and we didn't go far with him this morning. Of course,' she sighed, 'Hugh and I were going for a long walk along the cliffs this afternoon.' She grimaced. 'My confession time. I don't know how I'm going to tell him now.'

'What's this?' Mike demanded, emerging from the gateway as they reached the back steps.

Ben gave a bark of delight and fell on him, prancing about his legs. Lucy started, looking nervously over her shoulder.

Anna swung round to face him. 'Really, Mike,' she said crossly, 'don't creep up like that.'

'Rubbish, woman,' he said, 'if you weren't talking so much you'd have heard me coming. Anyway,' he waved a hand at the Jaguar, 'what's this? A present from an admirer?'

Anna's eyes narrowed, but Lucy intervened quickly, 'It's James's car. Anna came out to Corrington with Will and Niri to drive it back.' She brushed a strand of hair out of her eyes. 'They've stayed to have something to eat in Coombhaven, but they've been very good. They drove me down to The Fighting Prawn to pick up Hugh's car, then they took Anna round all the car parks until they found James's Jaguar.'

Lucy glanced at Anna. 'Hugh didn't want me to wait at the hospital, but I don't have any idea how long he'll be there.'

'What's this?' Mike demanded again, more forcefully. 'What's happened?'

Anna and Lucy stared blankly at him. Ben gave up trying to interest any of them in playing a game and wandered over to the stables.

'Of course,' Anna said, with sudden understanding. 'You weren't here when Lucy rang.'

She saw Mike's face darkening and added quickly, 'Hugh's fine. It's James who isn't. He was attacked in a robbery at the silver collector's.'

'What?' Mike exploded. 'What silver collector? Can't you tell a decent story?'

'Listen carefully,' Anna said sharply. 'I won't be repeating it. James told you about the silver collector, I know he did. And you mentioned her yourself.'

Mike made rumbling sounds, but Anna carried on, 'Well, James went to her house in Coombhaven and two men burst in, knocked Alex out, tied up the woman, beat up James and stole the silver.'

Mike stared disbelievingly at her. 'James? Why would they hurt him? And Alex? What was he doing there? And...'

'Shut up, Mike,' Anna snapped. 'We don't know the answers either. And I don't expect Rob will yet.'

'Elliot?' Mike groaned, clutching his hair. 'Bloody hell, I suppose he's on his way.'

Before Anna could reply he asked gruffly, 'How bad is James?'

'Very bad, I think,' Lucy said. 'The doctor was asking about whether to take him off life support.'

'When he doesn't need it?' Mike asked awkwardly.

'I think,' Lucy said carefully, 'he meant if it wasn't helping.'

'God!' Mike blurted out. 'This will hit Hugh hard.'

Lucy closed her eyes for a second. They flew open when a woman spoke from behind them.

'I'm so sorry, I couldn't help hearing. If there's something wrong, is there anything I can do to help?'

They were all taken by surprise, turning to look at the woman who had come along the path that led across the yard garden from the barns. She was standing in the shade of the witch hazel that stood in a large terracotta pot, ignoring Ben, who sniffed around her feet before wandering off again.

Mike stared at her. Her very short scarlet hair was definitely familiar, and so was the Liverpudlian accent. With an effort of concentration, he remembered who she was. Hugh's new assistant. Mike's eyes rested on the long earrings with shells and feathers that dangled almost to the shoulders of her baggy purple top.

'Maggie, thank you,' Lucy said politely. 'I'm sure Hugh will tell you about it when he can. Briefly, his uncle has been badly injured and Hugh's at the hospital with him now.'

'Oh, I'm so sorry,' Maggie said, biting her lip. 'But he needn't worry about work, I know what to do. At least,' she hesitated, 'I will need to talk to him about Brother Ambrose's book. I'm not quite sure what to do about it next. I haven't dealt with plagiarism issues before.'

'I'll let Hugh know,' Lucy said. 'I'm sure he'll be back sometime this evening, he'll have lots to sort out if he's going to be at the hospital for any length of time.'

'Well,' Maggie said, 'I was just going home. But if you don't mind, I'll go for a stroll and come back to the office later and do some tidying up. Then when Hugh comes back he can tell me what needs to be done.'

'Yes, fine,' Lucy agreed rather absentmindedly. 'I'm sure he'll be grateful.'

'Let's get you that tea,' Anna said, taking her arm. 'You barely had a chance to touch your lunch.'

'Okay,' Lucy said, allowing herself to be drawn up the steps to the back door, with Anna at her side, and Mike clumping heavily behind her. She was aware that Maggie still stood where they had left her, staring after them. Perhaps, Lucy thought, they should ask her in for tea.

Anna shook her arm. 'No,' she said.

'No what?' Lucy asked in surprise as she entered the kitchen.

Mike pushed the door hard behind them, so that Ben accelerated to get through the closing gap, casting him a reproachful look. 'No, don't ask the woman in,' Mike said. 'That's what you were thinking, isn't it? She's always getting in where she isn't wanted,' he added unfairly. 'She came bursting into Hugh's study this morning before I had chance to get any clothes on.'

'That must have got her morning off to a fine start,' Anna commented.

'Of course it did,' Mike said complacently. 'Women always like something to talk about.'

'And laugh over,' Anna agreed. 'Lucy,' she said quickly,

avoiding Mike's eyes as she filled the kettle, 'sit down. I'll make tea. There's still plenty of wedding cake, isn't there?'

Lucy nodded. 'The cake tin's in the larder,' she said, as she sat down. Ben sniffed at her hand, licking it twice, before he lay quietly down beside her. She looked at the table, still littered with lunch bowls and plates. Everything had just been left after Hugh had rung through with his terrible news. She knew she ought to be thinking of what to do, but she felt quite numb with shock now that she had got back home.

'I expect Will finished off all the cake before he left,' Mike said pessimistically, gathering all the crockery together and carrying it over to the worktop. He clattered it rapidly into the dishwasher, before striding to the larder and taking out the tin. 'Amazing,' he exclaimed, 'Will's barely touched it.'

'No,' Lucy said absently, 'he and Niri were eager to get off to see Josefina again. They'd eaten and gone by the time we heard from Hugh.'

Anna was slicing bread. 'Cut some slices of cake then, Mike, and we can have toast with some of the paté. There must still be plenty of that. Will doesn't like it and Niri won't eat it.'

'Good idea,' Mike said. 'I tell you what, I'll make the tea. Then we can get our heads together over this.'

Anna turned from the toaster she had just put on and stared at him in surprise. 'We can't do anything, Mike. Just wait to hear from Hugh. And hope James gets better.'

'Well,' Mike said roughly, spooning tea into a pot, 'we've sorted out worse. And James is a decent bloke. I like him. Let's find out who did it.'

He lifted the kettle and poured boiling water into the pot, spilling enough to create a pool on the worktop. He glared at Anna as he banged the kettle back down. 'I can manage,' he snarled, snatching several pieces of paper from a reel of kitchen towel and dabbing at the puddle.

'Right,' he said, putting three mugs down on the table. He carried over the teapot and fetched a bottle of milk from the fridge.

'Now let's get things sorted out.'

Anna brought the toast, thickly spread with paté. 'Help yourselves,' she said, putting the plate down and taking a seat between Mike and Lucy. 'Why don't you give us a summary of what we've told you, Mike,' she suggested. 'Then we can see if you've understood, at least,' she amended her sentence hastily, 'if it all makes sense.'

He swallowed a mouthful of toast, glowering suspiciously at her. 'Right,' he said thickly. 'James went to see this silver collector, robbers got in, dealt with Alex, beat up James, pinched the goods. James is in hospital on life support. What I don't understand is why Alex was at this woman's house too.'

'Hugh doesn't know,' Lucy said. She sipped her tea, flinching as it burned her lips. 'James went to the hotel to arrange a lunch meeting with Alex and Bel, so Hugh thinks Alex may just have tagged along with him after that.'

Mike grunted as Lucy cautiously sipped her tea again. 'Probably wanted to get away from his mother,' he commented.

'Perhaps,' Lucy conceded. She glanced at Anna. 'But they're going to be a problem. I suggested to Hugh that they would have to come here now, but he won't hear of it.'

'Keep them away,' Mike advised. 'Hugh's got enough to deal with without them on his back.'

'But Mike,' Lucy said, 'they'll have to stay in the area while James is so ill.'

Mike snorted. 'Don't you believe it. They don't care a toss whether he dies or not.' His eyes narrowed. 'Unless,' he said slowly, 'James has left dear Alex something in his will. Alex is always after money. He'll want to know if he's going to get it or not.'

'He can't be that bad,' Anna expostulated.

'Don't you believe it,' Mike said darkly.

'But how can we leave them in a hotel?' Lucy persisted.

'Easily,' Mike replied bluntly. 'Just make sure they don't expect you to pick up the bill.'

'And there's bound to be a police investigation,' Anna said suddenly, 'so Alex at least will have to be around for a bit.'

A knocking on the back door startled them, and sent Ben racing over to it, barking furiously.

'And here he is, the conquering hero right on cue,' Mike said gloomily. 'Inspector Elliot, riding to the rescue again.'

But when Lucy opened the door she found she did not recognise the woman standing outside. Ben though stopped barking and went up eagerly to greet the tiny woman in faded dungarees.

'I am sorry to bother you,' she said. 'I am Josefina. Are you Lucy, Will's sister?'

'Yes.' Lucy hesitated, then said, 'Look, do come in, but I'm afraid it isn't a good time.'

'I know this,' Josefina said, stepping briskly into the kitchen. 'Anna, hello. I am hoping that all is well with Fran and Richard.'

'I haven't heard anything,' Anna said, noting how Josefina's eyes had moved on to Mike, running openly over him. 'I guess no news is good news.'

'This is Mike Shannon,' Lucy said. 'A friend of ours. Mike,' she glanced at him, 'you know Josefina is looking after Fran's farm.'

Mike nodded at Josefina, one hand firmly clutching his mug as he muttered a greeting.

'The archaeologist.' She pronounced the word carefully, enjoying his surprise. 'Will told me of you. That you are making a big discovery.'

Mike scowled. 'Bloody Will. Always exaggerating.'

'But this is not what I came for,' Josefina exclaimed. 'You must excuse me. Will and Niri came to help me this afternoon with the lambing.' Lucy's heart sank. She really did not see how they could help with another emergency.

Josefina took her eyes away from Mike, glancing sideways at Anna. 'It is busy, you understand, and they like to help. It is a nice time, lambing. Especially,' she added, with a quick grin, 'if you only do it for a few hours. But Will and Niri had to leave suddenly just as they arrived. An emergency, Will said.' She was looking at Lucy now. 'I know nothing more. He has not come back. But I have come to say that if I can help, you must tell me. I should like to assist Fran's friends.'

Lucy's twinge of guilt was overwhelmed with a surge of relief. 'Thank you,' she said. 'I'll let you know if there's anything, but at the moment we're just waiting to hear from Hugh, my husband.'

'It is Hugh who is hurt?' Josefina demanded.

'No, his uncle, who was staying with us,' Lucy replied. 'But Hugh wants to be with him.'

'Of course,' Josefina agreed. 'Will tells me that publishing is what Hugh does. This I do not know, so I cannot do anything about it. But if you need to be driven, or to have shopping brought, that I can do.'

'Thank you,' Lucy said again, wondering what else she could say.

'I will go now,' Josefina said, turning to the door as she spoke. She paused to stroke Ben, who was still sniffing her trousers. As she crossed the threshold she looked back at them. 'You will remember I am there if you want me.'

Mike moved to the window as Josefina shut the door. He leaned close against the glass, peering out. 'She's gone,' he announced. 'What the hell did she come for?'

'You heard her, Mike,' Anna said. 'This is the country. People help their neighbours.'

'People like to be the first with the gossip,' he retorted. 'All those questions, she wanted to know what was going on.' He frowned. 'That's suspicious. What,' he demanded suddenly, glaring at Anna, 'do you know of the woman?'

'I didn't interview her,' Anna said stiffly. 'Fran was satisfied with her references. And Fran wouldn't leave her animals with anyone she didn't trust.'

'Huh!' Mike said. 'You must know something about her.'

'Well, I think she's Bulgarian, and she answered an advert Fran put in a farming paper. Although,' Anna remembered, 'I think she came through an agency who'd picked up on the advert.'

'We should keep an eye on her,' Mike declared.

'You could do it,' Anna said sweetly. 'She obviously liked the look of you.'

Mike glowered. 'I've got work to do.' His expression lightened. 'We can get Will to do it. He'll be there anyway, and if he thinks he's helping our investigation he'll keep out of our way while we get on with the serious stuff.'

Anna stared at him. 'Mike, I can't believe you're saying this. Why the sudden urge to play the detective?' Her eyes sparkled. 'We didn't do much at New Year, did we? You felt left out of the action.'

Before he could expostulate the back door burst open and Will came in, followed more sedately by Niri. Hades pushed past them, rushing over to Ben.

'Lucy, we've just seen Josefina,' Will said. 'She still needs help with the lambing. Is there anything else we can do here? Have you heard how James is?'

'No, I haven't, Hugh hasn't rung yet. But thanks for everything, Will, and you too, Niri, you've both been a great help,' Lucy said. 'Go down to the farm. I can always call you if I need you again.'

'Okay. We'll be back for dinner. I guess Hugh will be home by then.' He glanced at Mike, suddenly suspicious. 'What are you doing here? Has something else happened?'

'No,' Mike said. 'But we've just been deciding to keep an eye on what happens in the area. And you could tell us what goes on down on the farm.'

Will looked puzzled. 'There won't be many people visiting,' he said. His expression cleared. 'You're thinking about Josefina, aren't you? She's alright, you know. But,' his eyes brightened, 'there were those men she overheard on the riverbank.' He glanced at his sister. 'I told you, remember.'

Lucy nodded. 'Yes, but I'm pretty sure it was Hector Trone with some friend of his. There've been no poaching or rustling problems reported around here.'

'What…?' Mike began, absentmindedly stroking Hades as the big dog rested his head on the archaeologist's knees, his eyes fixed on the half-eaten slice of toast that Mike had put down on his plate.

Will interrupted. 'Lucy can tell you about it. We'll get off.' He glanced at the table. 'We ate in Coombhaven, at Garraway's.'

'I was sure you wouldn't starve,' Anna said.

As Will turned to the door Niri caught his arm, saying something quietly. 'Oh yeah,' Will said. 'Niri thinks we ought to go back to the manor. Can we collect our things later?'

'You will need our rooms, won't you?' Niri asked Lucy. 'Hugh will want to bring his brother back here, and perhaps his step-mother too.'

'I think,' Lucy said slowly, 'we'd rather you didn't go. Hugh doesn't want to have Alex and Bel here. And,' she ended heavily, 'there's no question at the moment of James coming back.'

'I'm sorry,' Niri said. 'We weren't sure how seriously he was hurt. Is he really so bad?'

Lucy nodded.

'Lucy, I didn't realise,' Will said apologetically. 'That's a real shame. He's a cool old guy. Well, okay, we'll hang around for a few days and give Hugh an alibi.'

'Does he need one?' Inspector Elliot asked from the doorway, stepping aside for Will and Niri to pass him. Hades paused to sniff his legs, before following his master down the steps.

But Ben barked and ran towards Elliot, his tail waving wildly as Anna exclaimed, 'Rob, you startled us.'

'Conspirators are always edgy,' he commented, stroking the excited collie. He came further into the room and she expected that he would greet her as usual, with a kiss on the cheek, but he simply smiled round generally at them all. Behind him Sergeant Peters carefully closed the door and moved to stand near the window.

Mike snorted as he swallowed the last piece of his toast.

'Conspiracy be damned!' he half-snarled, half-coughed as the crumbs caught in his throat. 'We're just making sure that Hugh doesn't have Bel and Alex invading Withern.'

'Ah yes,' Elliot said blandly. 'I have met them both.' He allowed his semi-official manner to drop. 'I can see your point.' He glanced at Lucy, who pushed out the chair beside her. 'How is James Carey?'

He sat down, carefully hitching up his trousers. Anna pushed the remaining piece of paté and toast invitingly towards him, but he shook his head. 'Not for me, thanks.'

Mike leaned across and picked the toast up, taking a big bite and chewing loudly.

'There hasn't been any change,' Lucy said. She looked at her watch. 'Hugh said he'd ring at five. He's a little late.'

'What about the woman in the office, whatshername?' Mike said suddenly. 'That woman who dresses like a clown, always butting in where she's not wanted. Is she still hanging around waiting for him?'

'Maggie,' Lucy supplied automatically, as Ben sat down beside her, his golden eyes bright and alert. She glanced towards the yard garden and the barn that Hugh used as an office. 'I'll go over and see when I've heard from him. She's a workaholic, but she mustn't stay forever waiting for Hugh to get back.'

'Would you like tea, Rob?' Anna asked, getting to her feet. 'I can make some more.'

'Please,' he said gratefully.

Anna looked enquiringly at Sergeant Peters as she filled the kettle again. He nodded, returning his attention to the others.

The inspector pushed his chair back from the table, turning it sideways so that he could rest one arm on its surface and stretch his legs out in front of him. 'This is just going through the motions, really, but I have to ask you if you can remember anything that James Carey may have said that might have a bearing on the case.'

'Like what?' Mike demanded.

'Well, did he mention the visit he planned to make?'

'Yes,' Anna said from behind him. 'You must remember, Mike, he talked about it yesterday evening. I was interested in the silver things he'd inherited from his brother. They're mainly little things, patch boxes, vinaigrettes, nutmeg graters, apple corers. He has fascinating histories for most of them. You know,' she added as Elliot looked puzzled, 'who made them, who owned them, how they were used. I thought I might be able to make a community play out of one or two of the stories.' She looked enquiringly at the inspector. 'Was the collection he went to see the same kind of thing? I suppose I assumed it was.'

Elliot nodded. 'Yes, Ms Harper has given me a detailed list, and it's very similar to what you've described. Apparently,' he looked a mild query at Mike, 'they were very popular items in the eighteenth and early nineteenth centuries.'

'I wouldn't know,' Mike said. 'I'm not interested in those kinds of things.'

'But do you remember James Carey talking about them?'

'He was full of it,' Mike said gruffly. 'I stopped listening after a while.'

The inspector sighed. 'It sounds as though he'd have mentioned it at any opportunity. And he could have done that several times before he even came down here. That blows the possibilities wide open.'

'Were Ms Harper's things particularly valuable?' Anna asked as the kettle came to the boil. 'I assume her stuff was stolen too.'

'It was,' Elliot replied. 'We don't know the value of James Carey's collection. Hers was estimated at nearly £10,000, and I gather he had a number of exceptionally rare pieces that may have had a high individual value.'

'The price of silver has risen,' Mike commented unexpectedly. 'We're having to take extra care of silver items in museums. The silver itself can be worth more than an object's historical value.'

'Even so,' Anna said, 'would Ms Harper's things be worth the effort? After all, the thieves can't really have known James would have his there too.' She looked thoughtful. 'Could they?'

'People have been killed for much less than one silver collection, let alone two,' Elliot said.

Lucy's mobile rang and she picked it up quickly from the table. Her expression of anticipation faded. 'It's Will,' she said, seeing the alertness of the others. 'Hello, Will.'

She listened to Will's voice, faintly audible to the rest of the people in the room. 'No, there's no further news. Yes, that's fine, if Josefina's sure.'

She closed the connection and put the phone back on the table. 'Will and Niri are staying to dinner with Josefina.'

'There you are,' Mike exclaimed emphatically. 'She wants to pump Will for information.'

'She's had plenty of time to do that already,' Anna pointed out, bringing the teapot to the table and pouring some tea into a mug, liberally splashing it with milk before passing it to the sergeant.

'Who is Josefina? And why should she want to pump Will?' Elliot asked, pouring tea out for himself.

'She's the woman looking after Fran's farm,' Anna explained. 'And Mike thinks she's a suspicious character.'

'Why?' Elliot asked the archaeologist as he added milk to his mug.

'She was here this afternoon,' Mike said, 'much too interested in what's going on. Besides,' he added belligerently, 'she's a fake, I just know it.'

'Did she meet James Carey?' Elliot asked.

'No,' Lucy said, 'I'm sure she didn't.' She dismissed the subject. 'It sounds as though they'll be eating soon, so I must think about what we can have. I can't seem to get my mind to work.' She brushed a strand of hair off her cheek, tucking it wearily behind one ear.

'Nonsense,' Mike said forcefully, as she pushed her chair back. 'We'll send out for pizzas. Are you staying, Elliot?'

'No, much as the thought appeals to me, I'll have to get back to the station,' the inspector said.

'Did James Carey say anything else at all that might be relevant?' Elliot caught Mike's eye, and elaborated, 'Did he have any odd encounters, was he worried about something?'

'Of course he was, poor bloody bloke,' Mike grunted. 'He faced having dear Alex on his doorstep for the next ten years or so.'

'Why is that?' Elliot asked, suddenly interested.

'This bloody trust, that's why,' Mike said.

Beside him, Lucy sat back, resigning herself. Mike was going to let it all out. And after all, there was no reason why Elliot should not know. But she knew that Hugh would be furious to have his family problems exposed.

'Hugh and James have to administer it on Alex's behalf until he's thirty. That's why dear Alex and Bel are here, to harass Hugh into refusing to act or into breaking the trust, whatever,' Mike finished vaguely.

'I see,' Elliot said noncommittally. 'Interesting, but it doesn't seem to have an immediate bearing on the robbery and the attack on James Carey. After all Alex Carey was injured in that too.'

'Hmmph,' Mike snorted. 'He was probably trying to get out of the place.'

Anna suppressed a giggle. Mike could just be right.

Elliot ignored the byplay. 'Did James Carey speak to anybody else down here? What about this woman you mentioned from Hugh's office?'

'Her.' Mike gave a short laugh. 'Efficiency incarnate, to hear Hugh talk. One of those women who can do things better than men, I reckon.'

'I don't think James met her,' Lucy intervened. 'She did come in this morning, but she only saw Hugh. Oh, and Mike.'

'In nearly every sense of the word,' Anna said, not quite under her voice. She added quickly, more clearly, 'What about your students, Mike? Did James talk to them when you were showing him over the storerooms?'

Elliot looked faintly puzzled for a second, then he asked the archaeologist, 'Are you running a dig here?'

Mike shook his head vigorously. 'Nothing so definite. I've just got a couple of students doing some preliminary research on the storerooms beyond the farmyard.' He frowned in memory. 'They'd arrived by the time I was showing James and Ambrose around, but they were busy putting their tents up. I was showing them over the storerooms later on when this lot,' he glowered round the kitchen, 'turned up for a guided tour. Then the students went over to Ravenstow Abbey, where I'm running the main dig, to see what the place is like. I'm giving a talk there tomorrow, but it doesn't hurt them to have a good look in advance and think up questions. I went over myself to check on a few points, and I'd only just got back from there myself and had another quick look at the storerooms when Lucy and Anna came home.'

'Mike, why didn't you say you were giving a talk?' Anna asked. 'We can all come for the laugh, that is, the experience.'

He glowered, but Elliot asked, 'Was there any sign that James Carey had met either of these students before?'

'He didn't rush over and fall into their arms,' Mike said sarcastically. 'I'm not even sure he noticed them. He was more interested in finding out what I'm doing at the storerooms.' He glared round at Anna. 'Like everybody else. Some people just don't seem to have enough to do.'

Anna's eyes had widened. 'What about the man on the boat?' she asked eagerly. 'Didn't James speak to him?'

'Of course,' Lucy breathed. 'But Hugh was with him, so he'll know what was said.'

'Who is the man on the boat?' Elliot demanded.

'Some bloke who asked Hugh for permission to moor near our landing stage,' Lucy said. 'A political satirist, or something like that, who's looking for peace and quiet to write a book. Hugh goes down to chat to him most evenings, so he'll know more about him than I do. I haven't met him, but James spent some time with him and Hugh yesterday evening.'

'What's this man's name?' Elliot asked, as Tom Peters held his pencil poised above his notebook.

'Umm,' Lucy hesitated, 'something odd.' She looked appealingly at Anna, who shrugged.

'Hector Trone,' Mike said unexpectedly. 'Writes as Flim for one of the national dailies.' His tone was disparaging.

Anna looked at him admiringly. 'That was clever of you, Mike.'

'Hugh mentioned him enough,' Mike grunted. 'I suppose you weren't paying attention.'

'I'll go down and have a chat with him,' Elliot said, getting to his feet.

'I'll show you the way through the orchard.' Anna stood too. She froze, one hand on the back of her chair as she listened to the sound of a car driving into the yard.

'That must be Hugh,' Lucy said, as the collie sprang up. 'It sounds like his car.' She got up and ran to the door, pulling it open as the silver Audi came to a stop beyond James's Jaguar. Ben was already racing down the steps, and Lucy was not far behind him. The others followed more slowly and had only reached the yard when Hugh got out of his car.

Lucy stopped a short distance from him, but Ben was wriggling round him in delight. Hugh stroked him absentmindedly, but his eyes met Lucy's.

She was horrified to see how dull they were, how rigid his grey face was. Afraid to ask anything, she hesitated, wondering how to find the right words.

'He's dead,' Hugh said flatly. 'James died. It was his heart.'

At least, Lucy thought thankfully, Hugh didn't have to make any decisions. Aloud, she said, 'Hugh, I'm so sorry. Look, come in and sit down. Rob is here too.'

Hugh's gaze went beyond her to the group at the foot of the steps. 'Good.' The dullness left his eyes, to be replaced by a hard coldness that Lucy had never seen before. 'I want to know how this investigation is going.'

There was a patter of footsteps coming across the garden from the barns. Lucy's heart sank as she glimpsed the tall figure that was hurrying towards them through the shrubbery. The bright colours of her clothes flashed conspicuously in gaps in the greenery. Efficient Maggie undoubtedly was, Hugh was forever singing her praises, but she was also becoming ever present.

'Hugh,' Maggie said as she reached them, her face set in worried lines, her hands tightly clasped on the wide belt that held in her billowing shirt. 'I waited to see what I could do. I was so sorry to hear your uncle was ill.'

'Not ill,' Hugh said abruptly. 'Dead.'

Lucy drew in a sharp breath at his curtness, aware that Maggie's body had stiffened with shock.

'But yes,' Hugh continued, his voice level and toneless, 'if you can wait I'll come across to the office shortly. I'm going to be tied up for the next few days, so you'll need to keep things ticking over. There's nothing you can't handle without me, but I want to keep an eye on the plagiarism case.'

'I've got all the papers ready for you to read,' she said briskly. 'It won't take long. And you can be sure I'll manage everything else. I'll be glad to do anything I can to help.'

Hugh nodded, and turned away, walking towards the house. Lucy was aware that Maggie stood still, watching him go. She ventured a small smile at the other woman, who did not see her at all. Maggie's eyes were fixed on Hugh, watching him walk up the steps to the back door with Inspector Elliot close behind him. Lips tightening, Lucy followed her husband.

It was with a sense of relief that Hugh pushed open the wicket gate into the orchard opposite Withern. Although the first stars were showing the evening was still light. It was warm after the unusual heat of the day, and Hugh was glad he had not bothered to put a jumper on over the short-sleeved shirt he wore.

There was a faint clucking from the hen house as he passed it on his way to the bottom gate. A gentle breeze feathered against his face as he entered the meadow. His feet brushed silently through the grass, the delicate scent of the bluebells rising around him.

Below, the river glimmered green as it flowed under the alders and sallows. A late moorhen scooted through the reeds, its red blaze dulled into greyness by the dusk. Hugh paused as he reached the trees at the bottom of the meadow, glancing at his watch. It should be time. And here they came, the first rooks flying in, followed by more and more, until they swirled around in a dense cloud. Suddenly a few peeled off, trailed by a growing stream of their brethren, diving down into the copse edging the meadow, choosing their roosting sites for the night.

The air was filled now with their loud cawing, harsh and unmusical, but oddly communicative. Birds were fending off neighbours who were too close, perhaps commenting on their habits, maybe comparing amicable notes about feeding grounds.

How James would have liked to see this, Hugh thought. Although he was naturally a townsman, he had loved to see country things.

Hugh's feeling of relaxed wellbeing began to dissipate. James would never see this. And Hugh planned to make sure that somebody paid for that.

He deliberately lifted his stiff shoulders, moving them until they were more comfortable. A brief chat with Hector, he thought, then I'll get back to the house. I haven't really had a chance to talk to Lucy yet.

For a brief second he hesitated. Hector could wait. But no, Elliot had been down to see him, so Hector must be wondering what was happening. And perhaps a glass of whisky beside the river, some chat about politics might clear his head, Hugh reasoned.

It was silent on the riverbank under the trees. The water flowed past noiselessly, the green weed streaming out in the current. The sound of the rooks had died away as they settled down, and the odd outburst was muffled in the opaque gloom under the tree branches that grew over the bank.

At first Hugh thought Hector was out. The large white boat ahead of him was quiet, barely stirring on the moving water. There was usually the sound of jazz coming from Hector's iPod, but there was no hint of that now.

Hugh was about to walk on past the boat when he saw the dim light glimmering in the cabin. Again he hesitated. But yes, he would see if Hector was there. He could do with his company.

Hugh leaped lightly onto the deck, landing with a soft thud. But Hector did not throw open the door of the cabin. Hugh had to walk over to it and knock. A faint response encouraged him to open it and lower himself down the steps into the space below. It was a composite room, with a neat galley, and fixed table and chairs in the centre, a couch running around the front, and a sleeping area at the back.

Hugh's eyes were drawn at once to the couch, where Flim lay in obvious discomfort. He wore only his boxer shorts, and his shoulders were hunched. But even in the poor light from a lamp Hugh could see the bruises that marked his bare chest and his face.

'My God,' he exclaimed. 'What happened to you?'

'Had a fall,' Hector muttered. 'Need another whisky. Pass me the glass, there's a good chap.'

Hugh turned to the table, where a heap of papers had been pushed to one side, leaving space for a couple of glasses and a nearly empty bottle of whisky. He had just picked up the bottle when a groan from Hector distracted him.

Hugh spun round to see Hector doubled over on the couch, whimpering loudly. 'Here, let me give you a hand,' he said, putting the bottle down again and taking two steps to the other man's side. 'Are you sure you haven't broken any bones?'

'No, no,' Hector muttered impatiently, struggling to sit up straighter. 'Give me a hand, will you?'

Hugh reached an arm around his shoulders to support him and Hector struggled to get up.

'Aargh,' he exclaimed, his weight falling back onto Hugh's arm.

Hugh bent over him, lowering him back onto the couch. 'Lie still for a minute. I'll just check your ribs.' He ran an impersonal hand carefully over the other man's rib cage. Hector flinched dramatically, uttering another cry.

Hugh straightened up. 'There's nothing broken,' he said. 'But you're pretty badly bruised. You'd better lie back and get some rest. I'm not sure the whisky is a good idea.'

'Don't lecture, there's a good fellow,' Hector said, leaning heavily against the cushions. 'Just a drop won't do any harm.'

From the smell of Hector's breath Hugh knew he had already had more than a drop. So a bit more would probably not make much difference.

Hugh picked up the blanket at the foot of the couch and laid it gently over the other man. Hector had an arm raised, almost covering his face, and flinched again at the touch of the blanket.

What a poor creature, Hugh thought, depressed at the sight of Hector. I'm sure he's acting up, just like a temperamental prima donna.

He poured a finger of whisky into one of the glasses, wondering who had used the other. Hector clearly had not been drinking alone. A shadow of doubt clouded Hugh's thoughts. Perhaps that story of falling had not been true.

None of my business, Hugh told himself, as he gave Hector the glass.

'I've had enough of this,' Hector muttered, his shaking hands grasping the glass tightly. 'I'll take the boat back tomorrow. Give me town any day. I'm not cut out for the country.'

'Well, I'll say goodbye then,' Hugh said without feeling any regret at losing Hector's society, 'and leave you to rest. Take care of yourself, and good luck with your book. I'll look out for it.'

He turned to the door as Hector said, 'I'll send you a copy. The least I can do.'

'I'll look forward to it,' Hugh said over his shoulder as he went up the steps to the deck. He felt a huge sense of relief when he stepped outside and felt the fresh evening air on his face. Closing the door behind him he crossed to the side of the boat and jumped over to the bank.

Lucy will be pleased he's going, Hugh thought as he began to walk further along the riverside. And actually, he realised, so am I. I'll walk up to Fran's fields and back along the lane. That should clear my head.

Night had fallen quite suddenly while Hugh was on the boat, but the sky was clear of clouds and the stars were bright in the darkness. He knew the path along the bank well, and had no hesitation in taking it, even though it was deeply shadowed under the trees, whose branches wove blacker patterns against black sky. Starlight filtered through them to sparkle on the river's surface. A tawny owl screeched from the far bank, answered almost immediately by one close to Hugh, the sound almost deafening him.

Hugh's pace slowed. He began to enjoy the sight of the rippling water with the dancing sparks in its darkness, the rustle of small creatures darting into cover in the bushes, the gentle whisper of the leaves moving in the breeze.

He paused when he reached the gap in the trees that led through into Fran's lower field. There was more visibility here, the background was a shadowy mosaic of open fields with darker shapes of hedges and trees running across it. Although he knew the landscape well, still it looked strange in this light, the shapes larger and darker, oddly different in outline.

As he stood staring he saw a lithe figure run out from the cover of the upper hedge and pause to look back. A fox, his golden coat dulled under the starlight, making him a deeper moving shadow among the others.

I hope Lucy's chickens are well locked up, Hugh thought uneasily. He watched the fox lope up the field towards the orchard. I'd better go up and check, he decided.

He was turning to cross the field at a sharp angle towards the Withern boundary, when another movement beyond the upper field edge caught his eye. He paused, trying to see what was there. The upper shape of the hedge altered, the outline of a person momentarily clear on the far side, before it was hidden again. The person appeared to be moving up the far side of the hedge. Hugh was sure it was a man, but corrected his assumption quickly. It's probably Josefina, he thought, remembering that Will had said the ewes lambed outside. She's probably doing a round to check on them before going to bed.

Hugh frowned. But the figure, its head appearing and disappearing at irregular intervals, seemed to be making a direct, if slow, line for the lane and keeping well under cover. Why should Josefina do that? He suddenly recalled Will mentioning poachers or rustlers. Hugh had not paid much attention, thinking Will was exaggerating, but now he wondered.

He altered his direction, beginning to move up the field. It was only a faint stirring of air behind that startled him, but his senses were acutely stretched, aware of potential danger. He swung sharply round, straight into the fist that drove into his face.

Hugh reeled back, and was struck again. He rallied, unsteady on his feet, but able to land a couple of blows on his assailant. There was a satisfying crunch as his clenched fist struck the other person's jaw. Before he could follow up, Hugh felt the wind whistle round his ear. There was a second assailant, one who managed to land a hard blow on the back of his head.

Hugh staggered, vaguely conscious of urgent muttering between his assailants. Unexpectedly he heard the thud of feet as he fell hard on the ground. They were running away.

He lay still, rolling over a moment later and trying to stand. Somebody was running towards him now. They were coming back. He struggled to his feet, but his head was spinning, his legs giving under him as he turned to face them.

SIX

Lucy looked up anxiously as the back door burst open, setting Ben barking. 'Mike,' she said reproachfully, 'you startled me.'

'Sorry,' he muttered, fending off the excited dog. 'But you ought to keep your doors locked.'

'I suppose I should,' she said. 'But, well, we've never had to.'

'If Hugh being beaten black and blue doesn't tell you otherwise, I don't know what will,' he said crossly. He flung himself into a chair, pushing it back with a loud screech of its legs across the tiled floor.

'I know.' Lucy shivered. 'I still can't get over it. The sight of him, so bruised and battered. Thank God,' she said, as Ben pressed against her legs, pushing his head against her hand, 'that Josefina heard what was going on. If she hadn't frightened them off I hate to imagine what would have happened. I keep remembering that James died.' Her fingers stilled on the collie's soft fur, and he nudged her, urging her to stroke him again.

Anna came into the kitchen from the corridor on a cloud of scented air. She was as elegant as ever in cropped black trousers and an Indian cotton shirt patterned in terracotta and red, but her face was paler than usual, with faint lines of strain around her blue eyes.

'How is Hugh this morning?' she asked at once, going across to the kettle. She raised a questioning eyebrow at Mike as she picked it up. 'More coffee?'

Mike nodded, waiting for Lucy's answer, stretching an arm across the table to reach one of the boxes of cereal that were clustered in the centre.

'He was still asleep when I came down. He's going to be very stiff this morning, but it's all bruising, no bones were broken. There wasn't any serious harm done, thanks to Josefina,' Lucy said, nursing her mug between her hands as if she was very cold.

'Not like James then,' Mike said, tipping muesli into a bowl with a grimace of distaste. 'I hate this stuff,' he muttered. 'The attacks must be connected though,' he added dogmatically. 'It has to be Alex behind all this, wanting to get his money.'

'How would beating up Hugh get him his money?' Anna asked, putting a couple of mugs down on the table.

'Inheritance,' he said bluntly, pouring milk generously over his cereal. 'I expect he'll get something from James too, but with Hugh out of the way there'd be all of Edward's money to play with.'

Lucy stared at him. 'No,' she said slowly, 'that can't be right,' she said. 'Even if Alex had it in him to kill, and his own brother at that, surely I'd inherit from Hugh whatever he's inherited from his uncles. We both made wills as soon as we were married, leaving everything to each other.'

Mike paused, his spoon halfway to his mouth. 'I wonder how much Hugh's inherited?' He stared intently at Lucy, as Ben settled down by her chair. 'You could be a rich woman, you know, if they'd finished him off last night.'

'I hadn't thought of that,' Lucy said. She hunched her shoulders. 'I wonder if Rob Elliot has?'

Anna laughed as she put the cafetière down on the table. As she passed Mike she frowned warningly at him. 'You know Rob,' Anna said lightly, ignoring Mike's startled enquiring look as she sat down beside him. 'I'm sure he suspects us all of the darkest deeds until he's got the real culprit.'

Mike snorted, and muttered under his breath.

Anna glanced at him. 'Shouldn't you be wondering why Josefina scared off the thugs? After all, you think she's a suspicious character, don't you?'

Mike glowered at her as she poured coffee into a mug. 'Well, it's easy to criticise my theories. You tell us what's going on, you'll find that's not so simple,' he growled.

'I can't yet,' she said, watching him scrape his spoon noisily around his bowl. 'Didn't you eat earlier, Mike?'

He nodded, swallowing his mouthful of cereal. 'Hours ago. Unlike some of us,' he said emphatically, 'I've been working. So I'm hungry again.' He scowled. 'I should be there, watching the students working on those storerooms. I've only come back to make sure I hear what's going on.'

Lucy had been gazing absentmindedly at her hands, clasped in front of her on the table. At Mike's words she looked up. 'I want to persuade Hugh to see a doctor this morning. He refused last night, so it was lucky Josefina knew enough to check him over.'

'Hmmmph,' Mike grunted. 'How did she know?'

'For heaven's sake, Mike,' Anna snapped. 'Lots of people know first aid. Many farmers must. And I do myself.'

To her surprise Mike's face grew alarmingly red. As she stared at him he bent over the table, dropping his head into his hands. She pushed back her chair, ready to get to her feet, just as a bellow of laughter burst out from behind his fingers.

Anna relaxed, her own lips twitching. Mike raised his head, wiping his streaming eyes on his shirt sleeve. 'That gives you quite a choice. A Florence Nightingale with kung-fu skills. So you can kill or cure.' His face crumpled again and he buried it in his hands.

She said sharply, 'Why don't you go back to your students, Mike? I'll let you know if anything important happens.'

He groaned, lifting his head. 'I should be there. I don't know how capable they are. Adam talks as if he's swallowed a textbook,' he said irritably, 'but I don't know if he understands what he's spouting. And Laura barely says a word, so I don't know if she's even hearing what I say.' He ran his hands through his hair, leaving it standing up in untidy tufts. 'I'd get back, if I could be sure I can trust you to keep me in the picture.'

'Mike,' Anna was reproachful, 'you know you can trust me.' She turned her head, just as Ben sprang to his feet, barking furiously. 'Isn't that your front door bell, Lucy?' she asked.

Lucy was already getting up. 'I can't imagine who it could be. Rob would come round to the back, and we're not expecting anyone else. I hope they haven't disturbed Hugh. Oh,' she glanced at her watch, 'it's probably the postman.'

Mike was staring after her. When she had left the room he turned his eyes to Anna. 'What was that elaborate warning about earlier?'

Anna leaned forward. 'Mike,' she said gently, 'it was thoughtful of you to point out that Lucy could have been a rich widow. The next stage seemed to be you asking her where she was last night.'

She sat back, watching his square face with interest. Astonishment crossed it, followed swiftly by a faint hint of embarrassment, and both emotions were quickly succeeded by annoyance. 'I didn't mean anything of the kind,' he said gruffly. 'And you know it.'

'But you need to be careful,' Anna said. 'Lucy's rather stressed right now, so don't make it worse.'

She stood up. 'If you're still hungry I could scramble some eggs. I don't think Lucy's eaten at all, and we should see if Hugh wants something to eat.' Anna glanced across at Mike as she walked over to the larder. 'Do you really think Alex is behind this?' she asked, one delicately pencilled eyebrow raised.

'Who else could it be?' Mike demanded. 'First James is killed, then Hugh's attacked. What links them? Dear Alex.'

A slight line marred Anna's forehead as she put the box of eggs she had found down on the table. 'But Alex was attacked too. So surely somebody has targeted all three of them? Who would benefit from that?'

'Lucy from the sounds of it,' Mike grunted. 'And you can't be suggesting she's behind it.'

'Of course I'm not,' Anna snapped, bringing a mixing bowl out of a cupboard. 'I can't even believe Alex would be involved in attacks on his uncle and brother. I'm surprised you don't accuse him of killing the first uncle.'

Mike paused, a look of great surprise on his face. 'My God,' he said, 'I wonder if you're right.'

'Honestly, Mike,' Anna groaned, taking an egg out of the box and cracking it into the bowl. 'You're…' She broke off at the sound of voices in the corridor. She stood frozen, the eggshells still in her hands as she stared at him in horror.

'I don't believe this,' he muttered, recognising the shrill hectoring voice almost as soon as Anna had.

'Really, Lucy, I don't blame you, Hugh's never been much interested in his brother. But I would have thought he could at least have come to see how he is today.' Bel had reached the door into the kitchen and followed Lucy in.

Lucy seemed stunned, thought Anna, but the older woman was definitely looking rather the worse for wear. The ultra-fashionable short skirt really didn't quite suit her. Nor did the tight-fitting cowl top under her jacket.

Behind Bel came Alex. In spite of the large bruise on his chin he looked happier than his mother. His linen trousers were barely crumpled, his shirt looked as though it had just been unwrapped. He ambled into the kitchen, pausing to lean against the doorframe and look around the room. An amiable grin appeared on his face as he saw Anna and Mike, and he raised a languid hand in greeting.

'Not much need to ask how he is,' Mike said bluntly. 'He looks fine.' Better than Hugh, I'll bet, he thought.

Anna stared at Bel, fascinated, as the older woman bridled. Really, Anna thought, letting the eggshells drop from her hand into Mike's empty cereal bowl, I've never actually seen that happen so clearly. She watched closely, trying to imprint the movement so she could copy it at some future time.

'Tough as old boots, that's me,' Alex said cheerfully.

At the same moment, his mother said, glaring indignantly at Mike, 'He's always been a brave boy. He insisted on leaving the hospital, although he's got a very bad headache.'

'Don't fuss, Mums,' Alex said without much conviction. 'I had to come and see Hugh once I heard about James.'

'Of course you had, but I don't expect Hugh will thank you for it. But you've just as much right to know what's going on as he has.'

She looked around the kitchen as if she expected Hugh to pop out of one of the cupboards. 'Don't tell me he's gone out already. Without getting in touch with us.'

'No, he'll be here shortly,' Lucy said, sure that Hugh must have heard the racket in the hall when Bel and Alex arrived. 'Won't you sit down and have some coffee?' Beside her Ben stood stiffly, his eyes fixed on Bel.

'I'll make it,' Anna offered swiftly.

Bel glanced at her indifferently, and took a seat at the table, pushing aside the nearest plates to put her bag down. 'Alex,' she said in a minatory tone, 'come here and sit down.' She patted the chair beside her. 'You must look after yourself.'

Mike snorted, half burying the sound in his mug as he raised it to his mouth. At the worktop Anna's lips twitched as she picked up the kettle and went to fill it at the sink.

Alex had moved towards her with an eager offer to help, but he turned reluctantly and obeyed his mother. He met Mike's sardonic stare as he sat down. 'Mothers always fuss, don't they?' he said with an attempt at a matey smile.

'Mine would have me out of bed with a programme of jobs to do, unless I was unconscious,' Mike returned. 'She doesn't believe in coddling.'

'So much depends on the type of family,' Bel said sharply, her eyes running dismissively up and down Mike's stalwart frame. 'I've left instructions with the police that we can be contacted here,

Lucy.' She accepted a couple of mugs from Anna without any thanks, banging them down hard on the table in front of her. 'And I don't want any more solicitors' letters getting delayed.'

'Oh,' Lucy replied, rather taken aback at the implications, especially in view of the suitcases she knew had been dumped in the hall. 'I'm sure we'll be checking the post.'

'And, of course, when we're allowed to go back to London you can just send any callers or letters on to our flat,' Bel pursued. 'I don't know how long we'll have to stay here.'

'The police won't keep you,' Hugh spoke from the doorway, his voice a little slurred, 'as long as they have an address where they can contact you. Although Alex will have to come back for the inquest.'

Ben was the only one not taken by surprise at his quiet entrance. The collie was beside him immediately, his tail lashing furiously. But Anna bit her lip to stop the gasp that almost burst out. Hugh's face was swollen, purplish black in patches.

'God,' Alex exclaimed. 'You look as though it was you in the fight, not me.'

'Good heavens, Hugh, what have you been doing?' Bel demanded.

He came into the room, dropping a handful of unopened post onto the nearest worktop and bending to pet the collie. He straightened up with an effort and took the chair Mike pushed out for him, lowering himself stiffly onto it. 'I had a fight of my own last night, down in one of the fields. If you can call it a fight.' He glanced at Alex. 'Any more than yours was.'

Bel's eyes flashed with anger. 'The poor boy at least tried to defend his uncle. I don't imagine you had such a laudable aim.'

Hugh ignored this. 'I was expecting you, but not perhaps quite so soon.' He looked across the table at Alex. 'Did you discharge yourself?'

'Of course he didn't,' Bel said sharply, leaning across to take the cafetière Anna had just brought over. 'Do you think I'd let him do that?'

'I'm right as rain,' Alex assured his brother. 'Except for a blinding headache, but I've got plenty of pills for that.' He gave a jolly laugh, but no one responded, except for Mike, who stared at him in disbelief.

'He's got to take care not to get stressed, or do too much,' Bel said pointedly, pouring coffee into the mugs. 'Here, darling, sit down and take this.' She pushed one mug towards her son, adding, 'But now that James is dead he wants to take his share of the responsibility.'

'I see,' Hugh said coldly.

As she sat down Lucy looked at him quickly, aware of the effort it took for him to sound so calm. Out of the corner of her eye she saw Mike wrest the cafetière from Bel's grasp.

'Have you spoken to the police?' Hugh asked his brother.

'Yesterday, for what seemed like hours,' Alex said. 'But I couldn't tell them much. I was knocked out cold within seconds.' His expression changed as he added awkwardly, 'I'm sorry, Hugh. I wouldn't have had old James hurt for anything.'

Hugh began to nod, but stopped, wincing slightly. 'You did what you could,' he said with a touch of warmth in his voice. 'At least James knew that. His last words were to ask after you.'

Alex looked down at the table, his face clouding.

'James was fond of you,' Bel said to him. 'We know that.'

Hugh took the mug of coffee Mike had poured out. 'Thanks.' He looked round as Anna tapped his shoulder.

'I'm just scrambling some eggs,' she said cheerfully. 'Mike's hungry again. Do you want some too?'

'Please,' he said gratefully. He began to smile, but stopped quickly as he felt the aching of the bruised muscles in his face.

'I didn't think you'd want much,' she said, pulling the bowl and egg box towards her again.

'Too right,' he agreed with considerable feeling, as she cracked another egg.

'But you must eat something,' Lucy said, pushing the milk towards Hugh as Bel reached for the jug. 'Even if it's just a little.'

'It's alright. I'm not going to fade away,' he said grimly. 'There's too much to do.'

'That's why I'm here,' Alex said quickly, forestalling his mother. 'You can rely on me to help with the arrangements.'

Hugh finished pouring milk into his coffee before he looked up at his brother. 'That's good of you, Alex,' he said mildly. 'But if you're talking about James' funeral arrangements, there's very little to do. He sorted it all out and paid for it some years ago.'

Alex's mouth hung open in surprise, giving Bel the chance to ask sharply, 'Well, what's going to happen?'

Hugh raised an eyebrow as he lifted his mug to his lips. 'James will be buried in the family vault at Highgate, as soon as the undertakers can fix a date.'

Mike was leaning back in his chair, the front legs off the floor, watching Bel and Alex. This brought him down with a jerk that made Anna wince. 'I didn't know you had a family vault until I came to Edward's funeral,' he exclaimed. 'That cemetery is an amazing place, all those elaborate tombs in the greenery.'

'Sad cypresses,' Anna murmured, momentarily distracted from the cooker.

'It's not the sort of topic that generally comes up in conversation,' Hugh pointed out.

'It sounds rather grand,' Anna said curiously.

'Not really. It's just an ornate pile in an old Victorian cemetery. James,' he glanced at Alex, 'will be occupying the last slot in it.'

Alex shuddered. 'Don't worry about that, Hugh. I don't plan to need a space in the ground just yet.'

'What about James' will?' Bel demanded, ignoring this digression.

Now we're getting down to it, Lucy thought, watching the other woman's fingers curl about her mug, but I can't believe she can be so gross.

Hugh put his mug down and sat back, his arms on the table, his hands loosely clasped. 'Alex won't have to worry about that either,' he said. 'Now that James is dead I'm the sole executor of both wills.'

Bel banged one hand on the table in frustration. 'Just what I expected,' she snapped.

Beside Lucy Ben stiffened, and she was aware of his hackles rising. She put a restraining hand on his neck and the collie subsided, a low growl escaping his lips.

'Mums, it doesn't make any difference. I'll be glad not to have to do anything,' Alex said quickly. 'Although,' he added, glancing at Hugh, 'you know I'll help if there's anything you want me to do.'

Hugh said quietly, 'Thanks. I'll let you know.'

'Er,' Alex went on awkwardly, 'er, I suppose you know what's in the will?'

'I know what was in the last one,' Hugh conceded, accepting a plate of scrambled eggs from Anna with a grateful glance. 'But I don't know if James made any changes.'

'Well,' Bel said impatiently, leaning forward, almost bumping into the plate Anna was passing to Mike, 'you can tell us what you know.'

'No,' Hugh said with unimpaired calm, forking the egg up. 'I won't be saying anything until I've read the will.'

'Mums,' Alex put a hand on his mother's arm, 'Hugh's right.'

She sat back, her face suffused with angry colour. 'But, darling, it may mean you can have your boat after all.'

'Yes, yes,' he said quickly, 'but that can wait. Hugh must do things properly.' He looked a little abashed as he glanced at his brother. 'It doesn't mean I'm not sorry about James,' he said carefully. 'I am, very sorry. But if,' he swallowed hard, and continued, 'if he has left me anything you can see it could make a big difference.'

'If he hasn't tied it up too,' Bel said bitterly.

Hugh ignored her as he scooped up another mouthful of egg. When he had swallowed it he looked at Alex. 'Yes, I see that. I won't take any longer than I have to. I'll probably go up to London sometime next week, so I'll pick it up then. I'll let you know the time, if you like.'

'Fine,' he said, visibly relieved.

'We'll go up with you,' Bel said. 'Although I don't fancy hanging around here any longer than necessary.' She cast a disparaging look towards the window. 'All this country, it's very depressing.'

'Never mind, Bel,' Hugh said, remembering the cases he had seen in the hall. 'There's more to do in Coombhaven.'

'Oh yes,' Anna added brightly, suddenly suspecting what was going on. 'The shops are good, you know. There are some unusual independents, crafts, jewellery, that kind of thing. And Corrington has most of the big chain stores.'

'That's something,' Bel said grudgingly. 'I wouldn't want to get in Lucy's way.'

Lucy had been eating small mouthfuls of scrambled eggs from the plate Anna had put down in front of her. Now she shut her eyes briefly. She had known this was coming, but had not seen how to avoid it.

'You won't do that,' Hugh said, noting how Alex was shifting uncomfortably in his chair.

'Then if you can show us to our rooms,' Bel said, 'I'll freshen up before lunch.'

'Your rooms?' Hugh repeated. 'Bel, have you been invited to stay here?' He glanced quickly at Lucy, suddenly aghast. Surely she hadn't!

Lucy shook her head fractionally, a slight smile on her pale lips at the expression on his face. Hugh relaxed, a rueful apology flickering through his eyes.

'Hugh, naturally I expected you would put us up. In the circumstances.' Bel sounded ferocious. 'You can hardly think we would want to be in a hotel with Alex in this kind of condition.'

'I'm sure Alex has felt worse, in much worse places,' Hugh said. 'We're still fully occupied here, and I'm not turning our invited guests out.'

'Well, really,' Bel expostulated.

'Mums, you know you'll be much happier in town,' Alex

urged. 'You liked that coffee shop we found. And there's a well-reviewed restaurant near the harbour. We can go there and see what it's like.'

'Of course I'd be happier anywhere but here, but that's not the point,' she said, her voice rising.

She was distracted as Ben sprang away from Lucy, reaching the back door almost before brisk knocking was heard in the kitchen.

Lucy pushed back her chair and went quickly over to open it. She was half expecting to see Inspector Elliot at the top of the steps, and was taken aback to find Josefina there again.

'Hello, Lucy,' she said. 'I think that you have guests, I do not wish to detain you. But, first, I would like to know how Hugh is today. Second, I wondered if Will and Niri are coming to help with the lambing.'

Hugh joined them at the door. 'I'm multi-coloured, but still in one piece,' he said, 'thanks to you. Won't you join us for coffee? My stepmother is just leaving, so you won't be interrupting anything.'

Oooff, Anna thought. Hugh doesn't pull his punches. I've never seen this side of him before.

Josefina was shaking her head vigorously. 'Thank you. But I am going to be busy today. There was a set of triplets born yesterday and I think that the smallest is not feeding well. I must see to that, but later I have to go out. I hoped Will and Niri would come before that.'

'They're out walking at the moment,' Lucy said. 'But,' she glanced at her watch, 'they'll probably be back before long, and I know they planned to come down to you then.'

'That is good.' Josefina smiled broadly, showing perfect white teeth. 'I have plenty still for Will to eat. But later I must shop.'

Mike snorted, but Alex had evaded his mother's clutching hand to wander over to the door. 'Tell you what,' he said, 'I'll come and give you a hand until Will gets back.'

Josefina looked at him doubtfully. Hugh introduced him

briefly, 'My half-brother, Alex. Josefina,' he explained to Alex, 'is caretaking the neighbouring farm.' He added to Josefina in a resigned voice, 'I expect he's had lambing experience somewhere.'

'Too right,' Alex said cheerfully. 'I spent six months on an Australian sheep farm. There's nothing I don't know about sheep now.'

'I see,' Josefina said. 'Well, if you wish to help…'

'I certainly do,' he said. 'Let's go.'

'And,' Bel said bitingly, 'what do you expect me to do while you play around? I'm obviously not welcome here.'

'You take the car, Mums,' Alex said over his shoulder. 'Cut along to Coombhaven and see if you can get our rooms back. I'll see you later.'

'And how will you get there if I have the car?' she demanded to his retreating back as he hurried down the steps leaving the door wide open behind him. 'And you won't know where I'll be. I may not get the rooms.'

'I'm going into Coombhaven,' Mike said, forbearing to mention that he would be glad to make the trip if it meant removing Alex. 'I'll drop him off.' His eyes glittered as a sudden thought struck him. He would subtly question Alex's story on the way, and, he thought with satisfaction, he could sniff around at the hotel to see what Alex had been up to.

'And I'm sure you've both got mobile phones,' Anna added helpfully to Bel, startling Mike into paying attention again. 'He can ring you to find out if you've got your old rooms again. It isn't very busy with tourists yet, so you should be okay. But there are plenty of other nice places in and around the town centre.' Luckily for Lucy and Hugh, she added in her thoughts.

Bel picked up her bag. 'Well, I can see you've got it all sorted for us.' Without another word she pushed her chair back and stalked out of the room, followed by Lucy.

'Good heavens,' Anna breathed, slumping down in her chair with relief, 'I never thought I'd be grateful for my own mother.'

Mike snorted with laughter. 'I thank God for mine every time

I meet somebody else's.'

'Hmm,' Hugh murmured, strolling over to pick up the letters he had brought in with him. He began sorting through them as he came back to the table. Sitting down again carefully, he said, 'I must try to remember that Alex is what Bel and my father made him. I occasionally see glimmers of what he might have been.'

'Huh!' Mike growled. 'They only emphasised what was there. You or I wouldn't have turned out like that in similar circumstances.'

'You can't know that, Mike,' Anna said, intrigued by the idea. 'You might have been worse.'

'That would be difficult,' he pointed out. He saw her lips twitch with amusement and his brows contracted into a scowl.

A vehement exclamation brought their attention back to Hugh. He had dropped a letter on the table and was leafing through a stack of photographs with an expression of stunned disbelief.

Anna started, spilling her coffee. Mike had picked up his fork to finish a stray crumb or two of scrambled egg, but dropped it onto the plate again with a clang.

'What is it?' Lucy asked. She had come back quietly into the kitchen. Startled at the expression on Hugh's face she walked swiftly to his side. Ben pattered beside her, and came to rest his head on Hugh's knees.

Hugh looked up at his wife, his eyes unguarded and wide with shock. He handed her the photographs without a word, one hand absentmindedly stroking the collie's soft hair.

Lucy flicked through them, her mouth opening slightly in surprise. Leaning forward, she picked up the letter and skimmed through it. 'How did it happen?' she asked. 'Was he involved in it? Or do you think he's received his own demand this morning?'

Hugh was rubbing his ear thoughtfully. 'I don't know,' he admitted. 'That's the answer to all your questions.'

'Excuse me,' Mike butted in sarcastically, 'if it's a private matter Anna and I will make ourselves scarce. Otherwise,' he said explosively, 'just tell us what you're on about.'

Hugh looked across at him. 'Here,' he said, taking the photographs and letter from Lucy and passing them across the table. 'It's pretty obvious.'

Mike skimmed through the pictures and dropped them onto the table to read the letter he held. 'Blackmail,' he snarled disbelievingly. His eyes narrowed, and his voice lowered, 'And it's been set up deliberately. That man, Flom, Flam, whatever he calls himself, that's what he came here to do.'

Anna had got up and draped herself elegantly over Mike's shoulder to see what he was looking at. He spread the photographs across the table to examine them more closely, and she saw them clearly, although they had obviously been taken in dim light.

Two men seemed to embrace on a couch, one caressing the other's battered and bruised body, the whisky glasses on the table witnessing the drinking session they appeared to have just had. The men's features were not identifiable in every picture, but there were two showing the recumbent Hector Trone looking up anxiously at the man who leaned over him. Two more of the photographs portrayed Hugh turning away from Hector towards the table, with the whisky bottle in his hand.

Anna leaned forward to pick up the letter and skim through the brief words. 'What are you going to do?' she demanded, dropping the letter and unconsciously wiping her hands down her jeans.

'Go down to Hector and see what he knows,' Hugh replied, dislodging Ben and wincing as he got awkwardly to his feet. 'God knows, I could do without this right now.'

'I'll come with you,' Mike said, pushing back his chair.

'Hold on,' Lucy said, sitting down at last. 'We need to think about this.'

Hugh glanced at her unsmilingly. 'What had you in mind?'

'Why have you been set up?' she asked, as Ben lay down nearby with a heavy sigh. 'You, particularly, that is. How did somebody know you've got that amount of money to pay out?

Until you got your inheritance from Edward you'd have had difficulty finding £200,000.' A strained smile touched her mouth. 'We'd probably have had to sell the house to get it, and that could take ages. Surely no blackmailer would wait for that.'

'My God, you're right,' Mike declared, banging his fist on the table. 'It's bloody Alex behind this. Anything to get some money.'

Hugh was leaning back against a worktop, making a valiant attempt to regain his usual nonchalant demeanour. 'It's a good point,' Hugh conceded. 'But how could Alex have set this scene up?' Hugh waved a hand at the photographs. 'He would have to be in league with Hector, and I just don't see that pairing. Not unless they're cleverer at dissembling than I give them credit for.'

'Couldn't Alex have set it up to catch both of you?' Anna asked. 'Hector could have been attacked just like you. Surely,' she added, feeling her way through the puzzle, 'Alex could have set the cameras up on the boat when Hector was out.'

'Having brought the specialised equipment with him on the off-chance of using it?' Hugh asked. 'Which would mean that he'd already laid his plans some time ago. That's not like him.'

'And you're all forgetting,' Lucy pointed out, 'that Alex was in hospital last night and yesterday afternoon. When could he have done it?'

Mike's expression of baffled fury made Anna bite her lip to keep back a gurgle of laughter. 'Then Alex has a confederate,' he growled. 'A person with brains. Alex is probably just the cat's paw.'

'Who do you suggest?' Hugh enquired mildly. 'Bel?' His lips twitched. 'It would almost be worth it, just to picture her creeping around the boat fitting the cameras.'

Mike snorted, refusing to be distracted. 'It's bloody Flam himself, I'll bet.'

'I don't know,' Hugh said, 'but I'll find out.' He glanced at his wife. 'You're right, of course. We need to work out the motive behind this. But I'll see what Hector has to say first.'

Lucy had an arrested expression on her face. 'Hugh, I think

his boat has gone.'

He stared at her in disbelief.

'What!' Mike shouted. 'He's done a runner. Guilt, that's why.'

'How do you know, Lucy?' Anna asked quickly.

'After I let the chickens out this morning,' Lucy said, 'I wandered down the meadow. There was no sign of his boat where it's been moored. Of course,' she said fairly, 'he could just have moved it further down the river, out of sight.'

'No.' Hugh sounded furious. 'I remember now. He said last night he was sick of boating and was going back to London. Given the state he was in,' he added deliberately, 'it seemed a fair comment. After all, he told me the bruises had come from a fall.'

'Do you think he was lying?' Lucy asked.

Hugh shrugged. 'Who knows? I had no reason to think so then.'

'What will happen when you don't pay the money?' she asked.

'I don't know,' he said soberly. 'They may just give up.'

'Or try something else,' Mike pointed out grimly. 'This took some planning. Somebody's gunning for you.'

Hugh shrugged again. 'Blackmail never ends until the victim is bankrupt. I'd never start to pay, even if I had something to hide.'

'Murder's a better bet,' Mike growled. 'I'll bet there's many a blackmailer pushed off a cliff or poisoned. All we have to do is find him and deal with him.'

Ben's growl startled him. As the dog sprang up Mike swung round to see what he had heard. So did the others, looking in surprise at the couple who stood just inside the door. A little round woman and a stooping, gaunt-faced man. The woman peered around the man, her circular eyes popping with fright as the dog approached. The man's expression was hidden by his straggling ginger beard and long white-streaked ginger hair. Anna recognised them at once as the students working on the Withern storerooms

Lucy had clearly forgotten who they were. She was looking at them as blankly as Hugh. Before Anna could explain the man spoke.

'Sorry,' he muttered, abashed at being the focus of so many eyes. 'I knocked, but you didn't hear. The door was open, I heard Mike...' He pulled himself up, knowing he was beginning to ramble excuses.

Lucy called Ben, who turned away from the intruders reluctantly, and slowly came back to her side.

'What is it?' Mike demanded, obviously searching his memory for the man's name. He retrieved it with an air of obvious triumph. 'Adam. What's happened?'

'Well,' Adam said, 'you know we've reached the floor level in the western storeroom.' He stopped, looking enquiringly at Mike.

'Of course I do,' Mike said impatiently. 'Handmade encaustic tiles, fifteenth century. You were supposed to be working out from the cleared patch in the centre.' He frowned. 'What's gone wrong?'

'Nothing,' the woman said in a voice barely above a whisper. 'We've been sifting like you said to, and we've found a few things.' Her voice strengthened in her excitement. 'A couple of glass bottles, and a pottery jar. That's only chipped, it's very nice.'

'Well,' Mike demanded. 'Er, um, Laura, surely you haven't stopped because of that.'

'Oh no,' she said, stepping out from behind the man. 'We've found a coin too, but it's too tarnished to see what it is. We looked for a date but we didn't want to rub too hard. And,' she hurried on, 'there's a strange patch on the floor. That's why we've stopped. Adam said we should ask you about it before we go any further.'

She looked at her companion, who had been nodding in agreement all the time she spoke.

'What kind of patch?' Mike asked. Seeing their worried expressions he said, 'Never mind. I'll come and see. You were quite right to stop. Get back now and I'll be right over.'

Nodding shyly at the room in general, Laura backed out. Adam's eyes flickered around the others in the room, not quite looking directly at any of them, before he followed her.

'Do you think they heard?' Anna asked quietly.

'What? Heard what?' Mike asked vaguely.

'Oh Mike,' she said impatiently, 'remember what we were talking about when they came in. Blackmail and murder. It must have sounded strange.'

'Nonsense,' Mike said. 'It was a perfectly ordinary conversation to have.' He waved his hands wildly. 'We were talking about one of Hugh's books, I'll mention it if I get a chance. When I get up there.' He glanced out of the door longingly. A frown crossed his face. 'Damnation, there they are, gossiping with that woman of yours. They'll never get on at this rate.'

'What woman?' Anna enquired curiously.

'Hugh's secretary, whatshername. She's probably checking on what they're doing. She's the kind to run everyone's lives.' He snorted. 'Maybe she's the one running this.'

'Oh, is she superseding Josefina as prime suspect?' Anna asked. 'What have you got against her?'

Mike scowled at her. 'I don't suffer from bias, not like some people,' he said grandly. 'I just keep my options open. Mind you,' his manner degenerated, 'you'd better watch your step, Hugh. You soon won't be able to move without permission.'

'Hmm,' Hugh said, not really listening to this exchange. 'Better not say anything to the students, Mike,' he continued, thinking how obviously false Mike would sound. 'Excuses always cause more trouble than they're worth. Remember Disraeli's mantra, "Never explain. Never complain."'

'That's nonsense,' Mike said forcefully, distracted for a moment. 'How would anyone ever…'

Anna interrupted, 'What are you going to do now, Hugh?'

'I'm not sure,' he replied. 'Funny,' he added. 'I've dealt with all these situations before, bereavement, murder, blackmail. But it was always a professional involvement.' He pushed himself away from the counter and sat down at the kitchen table again, gathering together the photographs and letter. 'Until I knew you lot and got dragged in at the sharp end I hadn't realised how different it would feel to be the victim. Even then,' he ended wryly, 'I didn't expect to be blackmailed. That always seems such a concentrated form of malice.'

'Here's the envelope,' Lucy said practically, although the expression in her eyes showed she was remembering past events too. 'Shouldn't we ring the police about this?'

'Yes, I suppose we must,' Hugh agreed wearily.

'Then I'll just get over to the storeroom now and see what that pair have found,' Mike said. 'I'll only be ten minutes, then I'll be right back.' He glowered at Hugh. 'Don't go wandering off without me.'

'He'll have us to protect him,' Anna pointed out sweetly. 'Don't worry, Mike. You go and play.'

'Thanks, Anna,' Mike said with false gratitude. 'If I hear men yelling in agony I'll know you're in action again.'

Goodness, Lucy thought in surprise, I do think Mike's learning not to rise to Anna's needling. Thinking briefly back to past encounters between the two, she felt a twinge of relief. Their mutual antagonism had often strained the atmosphere.

The archaeologist thundered down the steps outside, then they heard his voice, raised in greeting, followed by a loud monologue. Ben, at Lucy's feet, lifted his head and began to wag his tail.

'Will must be back,' Lucy said, glancing at the door which Mike had left wide open. 'Do you want him to know about this?'

Before Hugh had time to answer a man appeared in the doorway, and Ben leaped up to greet him.

'Good morning,' Inspector Elliot said politely. 'Mike said you were all here. He seemed in a hurry to get away. But then,' he said, smiling, 'people often are when I come visiting.'

'Come in, Rob,' Hugh said, 'and shut the door. I was just about to ring you.'

'Oh,' Elliot said, taking the chair beside Anna as Ben lingered by his side. 'Have you remembered something?' He saw Hugh clearly for the first time. 'My God, what happened to you?'

'That's part of the story,' Hugh said, pulling out his chair and sitting down again. He pushed the photographs and the letter across the table.

The inspector picked them up, his eyes widening as he looked at them. 'Well, well,' he commented slowly, 'we are seeing life down here, aren't we? Robbery, murder, assualt, blackmail. What will we get next?'

'Strange that they're all happening at once,' Lucy commented, watching Ben as he strayed hopefully towards the back door.

Elliot glanced quickly at her. 'Just so,' he agreed smoothly. He glanced at Hugh. 'Any idea what's behind this? Or who?'

'They've only just come and we've been discussing it, of course. But no,' Hugh said reluctantly, 'I can't think what's going on. The first step must be to speak to Hector Trone.'

He saw the quick frown on the inspector's face, and explained, 'He's the other man in the photograph. He had his boat moored just past our landing stage.'

'Had?' Elliot picked up the tense quickly.

Hugh gestured at the photographs. 'These were taken last night. I found him on the couch in the cabin, battered and bruised. He said he'd had a bad fall, and had gone off boating in a big way. He wanted to get back to London as soon as he could. And Lucy noticed that the boat has gone this morning.' He frowned. 'He was obviously in pain when he moved.' Hugh pointed to one of the photographs. 'That was when I was checking his ribs. I'm sure his injuries were genuine.'

Elliot was scanning the photographs with more care. 'Did you have a drink with him?' he asked.

Hugh began to shake his head, stopping as pain stabbed him. 'No, at least not last night. The glasses were already as you see them. And the bottle was nearly empty.'

'So he'd had an earlier visitor,' Elliot commented. 'Could the damage have been caused by a beating?'

'It could have been, I suppose,' Hugh said slowly. 'I had no reason to think of it at the time. But,' he grimaced, 'it could have been done by the two men who set on me after I left him.'

'Ah, so you didn't fall over or bump into a tree,' Elliot said dryly. 'Did you recognise them?'

'No,' Hugh replied. 'It wasn't a totally black night, but too dark to see details, and they came on me quite suddenly when I was coming back from the river through one of Fran's fields. I didn't,' he said with a twist of his lips, 'have time to look closely at them.'

'Did you mark them?' The inspector sounded mildly hopeful.

'I bloody well hope so,' Hugh ejaculated. 'But not very much, I'm afraid.' He looked resigned. 'If it hadn't been for Josefina, I'd probably have come out of it even more badly.'

'Josefina?'

'You remember, Rob,' Anna said, 'she's looking after Fran's farm.'

'Ah yes, you did mention her,' Elliot agreed. 'What was she doing out at that time?' He glanced at Hugh. 'You said it was night. Do you have a clearer idea of the time?'

Hugh considered. 'Sometime after nine, probably before ten. I went down to the boat after supper, a bit later than usual. I didn't stay that long with Hector, he clearly didn't want company, so I walked back along the riverbank, planning to come back through Fran's field.' He pulled at one ear thoughtfully. 'Josefina might be able to narrow it down. Although I don't expect she was clock-watching either.'

'So what was she doing out there at that time of night?'

'Rob, it's lambing time, she'll be out at all hours, checking the sheep,' Anna pointed out. 'In fact, it always seems to me that most lambs are born at night. That's particularly why Fran wanted somebody living in, not just coming over to feed the animals.'

'Any chance that she saw your attackers?' the inspector asked Hugh.

'I shouldn't think so, but I haven't asked her. She came round a while back, but my stepmother and half-brother were here, so I didn't want to talk to her in front of them. Last night,' he smiled ruefully, 'I was just glad she turned up. I was expecting to get badly done over when she came racing up, shouting loudly enough to be a platoon of rescuers.' He glanced at Anna. 'Woman to the rescue again.'

'I spoke to Josefina last night,' Lucy said unexpectedly, 'after we were sure Hugh was alright and tucked him into bed. She saw figures running away, but they were just dark shapes in the night, there was nothing she could identify.' Lucy's eyes rested on the inspector as she commented, 'Beating up seems to have become a common factor.'

Elliot shot an appreciative glance at her. 'I had noticed,' he said.

'Does it mean anything?' she asked.

'Perhaps,' he replied evasively. 'I'd better get down to the river to see if Hector Trone really has moved on.' He gathered the photographs carefully together. 'I'll need to take these,' he said to Hugh. 'And the letter.'

Hugh nodded. 'The envelope's there too. I'll get you a clean plastic bag. I don't expect you carry evidence bags with you.'

'No, I wasn't expecting to need them. I was just calling by to keep you in the picture about the investigation into James Carey's death,' the inspector admitted. 'And there aren't likely to be any prints. These days everybody knows to wear gloves when they're committing a crime.' He took the bag from Hugh and tucked into it all the things Hugh had received. 'If the photographs are published, will they have an effect on your business?'

Hugh shrugged. 'I doubt it. I shouldn't think they'll come out in the national press, if that's what you're thinking. I'm not important enough to be interesting.'

'How are they threatening to expose you then?' Lucy demanded.

He glanced at her, smiling suddenly. 'By sending the pictures to you, I expect.'

'Oh.' Lucy was startled. 'I see,' she said. 'They thought I'd believe them.'

'I wonder how many women would have done,' Anna mused.

'And they'd probably be sent to some of my more prestigious authors,' Hugh said.

'How will you deal with it if that happens?' Elliot persisted.

Hugh shrugged again. 'Like one of our greatest generals. He said "Publish and be damned." I can't say better than that.'

'Who said it?' Anna asked curiously.

'The Duke of Wellington,' Hugh said. 'When one of the most notorious of the Regency courtesans wrote a story of her life, which naturally involved her clients. She offered to leave them out of it for a financial consideration, but Wellington wasn't having any of it. So she damned him to his contemporaries and to posterity as a dull lover, always boring on about military matters.'

'I bet most of them paid up,' Elliot remarked. 'People usually give in to blackmailers.'

He got to his feet, holding the bag carefully. Ben looked round hopefully from his post by the back door. 'I'll put this in my car, then get down to the river. Then I'll come back and tell you about the main investigation. Though there isn't much to say yet.'

'I'll come with you,' Hugh said, standing up. 'If Hector's there I want to hear what he has to say.'

'Okay,' Elliot said reluctantly as Hugh moved towards the corridor. 'But stay out of it. I'll ask the questions.'

Anna pushed her chair back. 'I'd better go and tell Mike,' she said. She saw the look of alarm that flashed across the inspector's face as he looked over his shoulder.

She laughed, tossing back her long curls with one hand. 'Don't worry, I'll keep him occupied. Questions about his work will have him talking for ages. But,' she walked to the back door, 'he's concerned about Hugh, so it's only fair to keep him in the loop. Otherwise,' she added to Lucy, 'he'll never go off and leave us alone until this is sorted out. Do you want to come too?'

Lucy hesitated as Ben watched her eagerly, then decided. 'Yes, I will.' She ran lightly down the steps to the yard, the collie leaping and bounding in front of her, and walked beside Anna out through the gate to the drive.

They took the narrow path that led through the bushes beside the pond, and behind the stables to the meadow at the back of the farmyard. A short distance away from the drive a man was standing under a silver birch beside the path, staring out over the water. At the sound of their approach he turned to face them, ignoring the dog who was sniffing at his ankles.

'Adam,' Anna exclaimed in surprise. 'I thought you'd be at the storerooms.'

His eyes flickered to meet hers, then slid away. 'I'm going to Corrington. Mike wants me to do some work in the record office.' He jerked his head towards the pond. 'There was a heron.'

'He's often here in the mornings,' Lucy said, glad to be distracted from her thoughts. 'He prefers the river in the afternoons.' She smiled at Adam. 'Are you a bird watcher?'

'I don't know much about birds,' he said gruffly. 'But I like watching them.'

'Have you been down to the coast?' she asked. 'It's a good time to see the birds on the estuary at Coombhaven too, if you go when the tide is out.'

He nodded, looking more interested. 'I've been there. I came down here a day early to look around. It's a nice place.'

'Yes,' Lucy said. She saw Ben fidgeting beyond Adam. 'Well, we'd better get on. The dog is desperate for his walk.'

He nodded and turned away, looking back at the pond.

'Let's hope Mike doesn't spot him wasting time mooning around,' Anna commented.

Lucy did not reply and the two women walked on without speaking over the rough turf of the meadow towards the storerooms.

These were a little way up the slope above the barns at the northern end of the yard, close to a few of the remaining trees from the orchard that had once grown here. Beyond the storerooms two canvas tents were perched incongruously on the only level piece of ground on the slope.

Lucy wondered vaguely if she should tell the students how exposed they were to the wind in that spot. There was only a light breeze feathering her skin at the moment, but the weather this

April had been unseasonably hot. It might not last and then things here wouldn't be so pleasant. As Ben paused to sniff an interesting tuft of grass Lucy glanced at the sky. The weather didn't seem too bad, so she'd keep quiet. Her pace slowed as her eyes fell on a thrush running across the meadow, his spots vivid in the bright light. Watching him, her thoughts returned to the treadmill of what she should do and when.

She and Anna did not speak as they walked up the rough turf towards the storerooms. They passed a pile of wooden stakes and rolls of wire. As she skirted large holes in the ground Anna remembered that Lucy was having more apple trees planted here too, so this was presumably where they were going, and nothing to do with Mike's work.

Her attention moved on to the storerooms. The western one at the far end of the low stone building was now fringed with heaps of earth. There had not been any obvious digging outside, Anna noticed in surprise, so it must have all come from the inside.

She stopped just below the storerooms, turning to look down on the lichened tiles of the uneven barn roofs below. She spoke at last, finally breaking into Lucy's reverie. 'Have you told Hugh about your job yet?'

'No.' It came out on a sigh. 'I was going to yesterday afternoon. How can I now?' she demanded.

'Won't you have to leave soon?' Anna asked.

'On Sunday at least,' Lucy agreed, 'to be there in good time for the induction course.'

'He's going to notice you're not here,' Anna pointed out.

'Will he?' Lucy asked, almost below hearing. 'I wonder.'

'Of course he will,' Anna said sternly. 'And you aren't doing either of you a favour if you don't tell him until he sees you packing your bags.'

'I know. But things have suddenly got so awful for him I don't see how I can say now.'

Anna was silent, not knowing how to answer. 'You'll just have to come out with it as soon as you're alone,' she said at last. 'There isn't likely to be a good time in the next few days, however long you wait for it.'

Mike appeared suddenly in the doorway of the western store-room, his tousled head ducked under the low lintel. 'Is this a social call?' he asked suspiciously. 'Or has something else happened?'

'We've just come to update you,' Anna said, as she turned to face him, noticing that the door into the other storeroom was firmly closed. 'Rob's gone down to the river with Hugh to see if that man on the boat really has moved on.' She saw the involuntary step forward that Mike took, and added quickly, 'They're coming straight back so that Rob can update us on the investigation into James's death. But,' she said gloomily as she strolled up to the building with Lucy walking close beside her, 'it doesn't look as though much has happened with it.'

'Huh,' Mike commented, watching Ben as the collie came up to sniff at the piles of earth around the building. 'It sounds like an excuse to come hanging around here.' He looked meaningfully at Anna.

She ignored this. 'I thought,' she said sweetly, 'you'd like to hear what he says.' She glanced at her watch. 'I don't expect they'll be long, but it depends on how busy you are here.'

Mike scowled. 'I can do without all these interruptions. I really want to get over to Ravenstow,' he muttered. 'But,' he struggled with himself, 'as you've bothered to saunter up here to tell me I'll come back with you.'

Anna smiled and stepped forward, peering into the storeroom. 'What was it they found that was so exciting?' she asked, noting how the floor level had been lowered.

Mike caught her arm before she could go in. 'Don't step on them,' he grunted.

'What?' she demanded.

Mike pointed down to the floor. 'They've reached the original layer, with tiles. Decorated, too, although you can't see that clearly yet because of the dirt.'

'Yes, I heard that student say,' Anna said patiently. 'But he found something else, didn't he?'

Mike glowered. 'Yes.'

'Well?' she demanded. As he shifted irritably from foot to foot, she said crossly, 'I'm not going to rush off and gossip about it, if you've made a big find, Mike.'

'I haven't,' he said gruffly. 'It's just interesting, that's all.'

'Can I see?' Lucy asked from behind them.

Mike grunted. 'Oh come in, both of you, why don't you? We can have a party.' He edged aside, letting Lucy stand next to Anna in the doorway. 'If you look at the floor to the left, near the centre of the room between the two windows, there's a patch on the tiles. That's all it is. Nothing exciting.'

He was right. The women peered towards the spot he had described, but neither could make out anything unusual about the small darkened area.

'Adam did well to spot it,' Mike conceded, as they turned towards him, looking disappointed.

'What does it mean?' Anna asked. 'Mike,' a thought struck her, 'you're not looking for something major, are you? Something that the men who beat up Hugh would be interested in?'

Mike stared at her blankly. 'That imagination of yours,' he said at last in a strangled voice. 'I'll never get used to it.'

'Well, Mike,' Lucy pointed out, 'we have had some strange experiences because of hidden treasure.'

'There's nothing like that here,' he said in exasperation. 'Although,' he groaned, 'laymen always think there's treasure if we start digging.'

He stepped back, waving an imperative hand to bring them further into the room with him. 'Alright,' he said, 'I'll tell you what I think. But I don't know,' he emphasised the last word, 'and I don't want my theories broadcast to all and sundry. And especially not to the students. I don't want it cast in my face for years and years if I've got it wrong.'

'Alright,' Anna said quickly. 'We cross our hearts, and promise not to tell.'

'Except Hugh,' Lucy said quickly.

'Not Will,' Mike said urgently. 'He'll talk about it.'

'Okay,' she agreed.

'Look at the shape of it,' Mike said. 'Stone built, carved stone frames around wide glazed windows and the doorway, a thick wooden door with iron hinges, all at least fifteenth century, I think. And now the floor tiles.'

'It wasn't originally a storeroom,' Anna guessed.

Mike nodded. 'I've sent Adam over to the local record office. I want to see if there's any mention of it in the parish records, and I gather from Mersett's tutor's notes that he's pretty good at digging up information. He'd done some research on the place before he came down, too.'

Lucy's eyes widened. 'You think it was a church?'

'A chapel,' he corrected her. 'Niri's research last year about this place didn't go beyond the early eighteenth century, so I need to look further back. I think Withern may have been an abbey barton, perhaps belonging to Ravenstow itself. That's what I want to talk to Ambrose about. Privately,' Mike added crossly. 'There's always somebody else around when I see him, and I don't want everybody knowing about this. But I'm sure Ambrose can dig something up in the abbey records.'

'What's an abbey barton?' Anna demanded.

'A farmhouse from which a few monks ran abbey lands out in the sticks.'

'Would they have had a chapel in such a small place?' Lucy asked in surprise.

Mike nodded. 'That's a good question. But the bartons were also resting places for travellers. This place is on the route from Coombhaven to Corrington and the main spinal route through the South West. They'd have had plenty of visitors going past here on the way to and from the coast. And,' he said, 'the monks would have catered for their spiritual needs as well as providing bed and board.'

'I see,' Lucy said, viewing the stone building in a new light. A quick glance sideways showed her that Anna was staring at it too, obviously already creating a picture around the building from Mike's words.

'Was it always two rooms?' Lucy asked suddenly.

'No, that's the next thing I want to sort out. Laura's next door, working on the wall. It's thick with dust and centuries of muck.'

Anna grinned, thinking of Laura at work in the little room on the other side of the wall. Mike sure knows how to weed out his students, she thought. Laura must be suffocating in there with the door shut, but perhaps if it's open, Anna realised, the breeze stirs up the dust and makes it worse.

Mike's next words caught Anna's attention again. 'I reckon that there was a doorway in the wall, perhaps arches. Monks at the front, you see, and plebs at the back.'

'So,' Anna said, 'what about this mysterious patch.'

'That's later, I think,' Mike said slowly. 'I hadn't expected that. It'll have to be tested, but I think it's mercury.'

She stared at him, puzzled. 'What does that mean?'

'Well,' now that he was started, Mike's original reticence had vanished, 'it reflects a later use of the building, or this part of it after it was fully divided. With the bottles and jar Laura and Adam have just found, if they're all contemporary, and they appear to be as they were found in the same layer of soil...' Mike stopped, having lost the thread of his comment. 'Yes, if they're contemporary with each other it may mean this room at least was used as some kind of workshop.'

'Will you ever find out?' Lucy asked.

'Maybe. If we're lucky. Probably from a tiny reference in some document that doesn't particularly relate to this place. In fact,' he said, almost to himself, 'I've a feeling I may have seen a useful detail in some totally unconnected family papers. I just,' he said crossly, 'have to remember which.'

'That could take years,' Anna said in disappointment.

'Research often does, especially with my dearth of funding,' Mike said morosely. 'Still, that's what makes discovery so exciting, when you eventually find the clue you need. It wouldn't be the same if it all came handed out on a plate.'

'Perhaps,' she conceded, 'but I'm bursting to know now. Still,' she sounded gloomier, 'you're right.'

Mike stared at her in astonishment, wondering if he had heard correctly.

She laughed at him, pushing her long hair over her shoulders. 'Nobody would be interested enough in this to come creeping around at night.'

'But,' he pointed out grimly, 'they don't know the facts.' More mildly, he added, 'Though there've been no signs of illicit work, and I lock both doors at night. Still, you never know. Hugh might have got in the way of their initial foray. They could come again, and if they do I'll be ready for them.'

Hugh and Inspector Elliot were walking down the meadow towards the river, each deep in their own thoughts. A sudden movement startled them. A hare had sprung out of the longer grass below the trees on their right and was racing across the slope below them, curving and jinking despite its speed. As it disappeared from sight Elliot's attention was caught by the sparkling motes the sunlight struck from the water he could glimpse through the willows and alders on the riverbank.

He slowed, aware for the first time of the subtle bluebell fragrance in the air and the sound of larks singing high overhead. Elliot stopped altogether, turning to look back up the meadow towards the house. Only the top of its roof and a single chimney were visible above the fruit trees in the orchard, where the faint hint of pink blossom was more distinct than it had been a couple of days ago.

The view was idyllic, Hugh thought, pausing to wait, wondering what Rob Elliot made of it. He had always thought of the inspector as a city man, but then Hugh thought suddenly, perhaps that's what people thought of me before I came down here.

'And only man is vile,' Elliot said quietly, the words almost inaudible.

Hugh was startled. 'That's hard to argue against right now,' he said.

The inspector sighed. 'In my job, it's hard to argue against it most of the time. You're lucky to have found this place. I used to think I'd miss the city when I came down from London, but now I find I wouldn't mind something like this. Smaller, of course.' He threw off the unusually introspective mood. 'Well, let's get this over with. Incidentally,' he said as they approached the riverbank, 'do you happen to know the details of James Carey's will?'

Hugh paused, his eyes on the inspector. 'As it happens,' he said reluctantly, 'I do. I'm not going to broadcast them just yet, in case James changed anything.'

Elliot was watching Hugh, noting the uncertainty in his voice. 'I won't repeat anything you say,' he commented mildly. 'But you know it would help me to have some idea at this stage. Who benefits, and all the usual ideas.'

Hugh gave a short, unamused laugh. 'You won't have far to look. I'm the sole beneficiary, barring a few charitable donations and a token legacy to Alex.'

'I wondered,' Elliot said. 'Do you have any idea of the figure?'

Hugh shrugged. 'Alex is down for ten thousand pounds, outright, thank God. The rest,' he shrugged again, 'is probably in the region of eight or nine hundred thousand pounds.' He frowned. 'With my inheritance from Edward,' he said bluntly, 'it makes me very wealthy.'

Elliot whistled. 'I'll say,' he commented. 'You certainly won't need to earn a pension.'

'But it does focus your attention, doesn't it?' Hugh retorted wryly.

'Every detail always has my full attention,' Elliot said blandly. 'What will you do about your other uncle's trust for your brother? It makes it more difficult, doesn't it?'

Hugh's smile was twisted. 'Just a bit,' he agreed. 'I end up rolling in money, and keeping Alex's under my control too. How fortunate I've never worried much about being popular.'

'So you won't disband the trust now that James Carey is dead?'

Hugh's face darkened. 'Believe me,' he said forcefully, 'I'd love to. But my position hasn't changed. I have to honour Edward's wishes, however much I would rather he'd done things differently. The fact that James felt the same simply reinforces my view. I'm pretty sure that Alex knows that, whatever he might like to try to believe.'

'What about his mother?' Elliot asked.

Hugh's face tightened. 'You've met her. You can't need to ask.' He straightened up and turned round, walking onto the bank.

A short distance away on the left was the small Withern landing. Hugh frowned when he saw the figure seated on the far bollard, back hunched, gazing down the river. 'We may be in luck after all,' he murmured to the inspector, shielding his eyes from the sun with one hand. He looked down the bank, glad to look away from the dazzling light, but there was no sign of Hector's boat.

Frowning, Hugh lowered his hand as he stepped out of the sunbeams piercing the tree canopy and walked onto the landing stage. His footsteps thudded dully over the wood, and the figure started, turning round quickly.

'Maggie,' Hugh exclaimed in surprise as he recognised the short scarlet hair. 'What on earth are you doing here?'

Maggie's colours were as vivid as ever, he thought irrelevantly, blinking as he took in the tight orange and yellow trousers and the sky-blue tunic that hung to her knees. Huge iridescent green beads dangled to her waist, swinging with the violence of her sudden movement.

Her hand pressed against her breast, stilling the beads, her eyes wide with shock, his assistant got up. 'Hugh, I didn't hear you coming.'

'I didn't mean to startle you,' he said formally, thinking he had never seen the imperturbable Maggie so shaken. 'I didn't know you were here.'

'No, of course you didn't.' She was rapidly recovering her usual aplomb. 'I shouldn't be here really, but it's so beautiful and quiet. I couldn't resist just sitting for a while. I hope you don't mind.'

'Of course I don't,' Hugh said. 'You can come down here whenever you like.'

'I'm not really wasting time,' she said earnestly. 'I was looking for Hector.' A glum note entered her voice. 'But he's gone. I didn't know he was leaving so soon.'

A faint suspicion tingled through Hugh. He remembered Maggie's keenness to come to work, no matter when. He had put it down to her interest in the job, but then it had never occurred to him that there could be another reason. Now, though, it did.

Hector had lacked his usual amusements down here, so had he, Hugh wondered, preyed on Maggie? She was, he realised now, always keen to be praised, to make sure she was noticed, involved in everything. Needing perhaps to be needed. That would make her vulnerable to types like Hector, Hugh thought, to the kind of attention the man could turn on and off like a tap. Damn, Hugh thought sourly, he hoped he wasn't going to lose her. Her efficiency had made his life much easier.

Aloud, he said, 'It was a sudden decision. He told me about it last night.'

'Oh, he didn't mention it in his message,' she said, turning away.

Hugh caught her arm. 'What message?' he demanded.

She looked at him in alarm, and he dropped his hand quickly. 'That's why I'm here,' she said, apologetically. 'I should have said. There was a message from him on the answer machine when I got in, asking for you to come down as soon as you could.' She fidgeted uncomfortably. 'I was coming over to the house to find you when I saw the inspector arrive. I thought,' she said anxiously, 'you wouldn't want to bother with it just then, so I came down to tell Hector you couldn't come straightaway.'

Hector, Hugh noted, first names. Was that a bad sign?

'I'm sorry if I should have said,' Maggie continued.

'No, that's fine,' Hugh said vaguely. He saw that she was staring at him now, obviously noticing the bruising on his face. 'It was good of you to take so much trouble,' he said quickly. He added dismissively, 'I'll come over to the office later, as soon as I can.'

'Yes, yes, I'll be there,' she said, pulling her gaze away. She turned awkwardly, her head bent as she slanted a nervous smile up at the inspector.

Elliot stepped aside to let her pass and watched her set off up the meadow. 'Is she usually like that?' he asked quietly.

'No,' Hugh said with a groan. 'I'm beginning to suspect Hector had a fling with her. I should have noticed, but I've been so busy.' He looked alertly at the inspector. 'But you see what the message means. If he wanted to see me, there's a good chance he's had a similar package in the post.'

Elliot frowned. 'Does the postman deliver to him?'

Hugh was visibly taken aback. 'No, that's stupid of me, of course he doesn't. I think Hector used to pick up his mail in Coombhaven.'

'So how would he have got his package?' Elliot demanded. 'Would he have gone into town this morning looking the way you described him? I have the distinct impression that image mattered a great deal to him. And,' the inspector continued, 'could he have gone there, got his post, returned, left a message for you and sailed off?'

'Hmm, it does seem unlikely,' Hugh said, discouraged. 'I should have asked Maggie what time the message was left.' He scowled. 'We won't even have the chance to hear it ourselves. She always deletes them immediately.'

'These efficient people,' Elliot commiserated. 'Sometimes they make my life harder.'

'Look,' Hugh said. 'As we're here, why don't I show you the route I took last night. Who knows, there may be a clue waiting to jump out on us. At the very least, we'll have time to talk through the situation.'

He moved off along the bank, oblivious this morning to the flash of blue as the kingfisher left his perch on the overhanging willow branch.

Elliot followed Hugh, picking his way more carefully, keen not to snag his suit on the brambles that sent sneaky tendrils out to ensnare the unwary. His eyes were on the ground as they rounded a bend, so he bumped into Hugh when the other man stopped suddenly.

Hugh staggered, and Elliot put out a quick hand to grab him. Regaining his footing, Hugh said urgently, 'Look.'

Elliot released his arm and raised his eyes to look past Hugh. Ahead of them a large white cruiser was entangled in a thicket of sallow that curved out into the water. 'Is it Trone's boat?' he asked quickly.

'Yes.' Hugh had already set off again, his pace so fast he was almost running as he negotiated the rutted path and the creeping bramble tendrils. 'He wasn't an experienced boatman, but I can't imagine how the hell he got it stuck there.'

He got to the nearest point on the bank, the inspector close on his heels. They paused, wondering how to reach the boat. Hugh's eyes ran over the thicket, wondering if it was strong enough to hold his weight. He really did not fancy going into the water.

He drew a harsh breath. Elliot turned swiftly, his gaze searching along the thicket too. He soon saw what Hugh was staring at. There was a bundle caught up in the lower branches, its bulk mainly underwater. The inspector's mouth tightened. That bulk appeared ominously like a human body. Yes, as he stared, trying to make out details, he was sure he saw a pale hand floating placidly on the current that eddied round the thicket.

Hugh was cursing softly. 'How the hell do we get him out?' he demanded.

Elliot glanced up and down the quiet riverbank. 'I don't know about you,' he said grimly, looking at Hugh. 'But I'm at least going to have dry clothes to get back into.' He was shrugging off his jacket as he spoke.

'Should we disturb him?' Hugh asked, ripping off his shirt. 'We'll have to mind the current too. It's surprisingly strong.'

'There's just a faint chance he's still alive,' Elliot said, peeling off his trousers. 'I doubt he can be, but I must see. There's no need for us both to get soaked. Wait here until I know whether I can get him out.'

He lowered himself into the water, flinching at its coldness. Wading carefully out, he held onto various branches until he was close enough to touch the body. He moved it awkwardly, trying to shift it higher into the branches.

'Damn this,' his voice reached Hugh. 'I can't lift him enough.'

'I'll come over.' Hugh was already out of his trousers. He slid into the water, stifling a yell as the piercingly cold water touched his skin, but keeping his eyes on the scene in front of him.

A frenzied barking startled him so much that he nearly lost his footing. Something heavy fell into the water around him, sending up sprays of drops that blinded him for a moment. Hades was swimming around him, sending the water eddying about his waist.

'Hey, Hugh,' Will shouted. 'I know the weather's hot, but isn't it a bit early for swimming?'

Hugh shook his wet hair, wiping his arm across his eyes. 'Will, for God's sake, get Hades out.'

'What...' Will began, startled by his brother-in-law's peremptory tone.

'Will, quickly.' It was Niri who spoke, and she who called out imperatively, 'Hades, come here.'

The dog left Hugh and swam strongly back to the bank. He scrambled eagerly out and raced towards Niri, who was murmuring extravagant praises. She fended him off quickly, but she was already soaked by his wet coat.

The muddied water settled slowly around Hugh, who was looking back to make sure the dog was under control. He winced when he saw Hades shaking himself vigorously over the clothes

Hugh and Elliot had left on the bank.

'Do you want me to come out too?' Will called, his eyes on the inspector, who was struggling to hold the sodden body out of the water.

'No,' Elliot grunted. 'You're more use there.'

'I'll go back to Fran's,' Niri said. 'It's closer than Withern. Alex is there, he can come and help you. I'll get blankets too. And I'll call the ambulance.' She ran off, the dog leaping beside her.

Will said, 'Hugh, I'll get your boat from the landing stage and come down in it. It might be easier to get him into that than take him to the bank.'

'Good idea,' Hugh panted, as he reached Elliot. He gasped as he tried to edge past to the far side of the body, feeling the current tugging at his legs. 'Be quick.'

SEVEN

The early afternoon sunlight was visible through the kitchen windows of Withern, glinting off the greenery in the yard garden. It was a silent group of people who sat around the room. Bowls littered the table, many still half full of soup. Slices of chunky bread lay crumbled on plates. Even the dogs lay quietly on the floor, subdued by the atmosphere, but hopefully flanking Mike out of habit.

For only Mike was still eating. He swallowed his last mouthful and looked round. 'Well,' he said belligerently, glaring across at Hugh, 'I told you not to go off without me.'

'It would still have happened, Mike,' Anna said. 'It wasn't as if somebody attacked Hugh again. Hector was already dead when they found him.'

'At least we didn't like him,' Will commented. He amended hastily, 'I know you did a bit, Hugh, but you didn't really know him well, did you?'

'No, not really. I enjoyed talking to him,' Hugh said. 'Though I don't know that I would have liked him personally very much if I'd known him better.'

'What's taking Rob so long?' Anna asked restlessly. She got up and walked across to the nearest window, peering out across the yard garden towards the barns. 'He's been in your office for ages, Hugh. Surely that woman can't have much to say.'

Hugh hesitated for a second, then said carefully, 'I think there may have been a bit more to Maggie's relationship with Hector than just a visit to the riverside this morning.'

Mike sat up alertly. 'Do you think she did it?' he demanded.

'No.' A smile twitched at Hugh's lips. 'But I do think she may have been amusing Hector during his stay here.'

'Sleeping with him, you mean?' Anna asked bluntly.

'Possibly,' Hugh said. 'He did have quite a reputation with women.'

Anna stared at him for a moment, then glanced at Lucy, one delicately painted eyebrow raised. Lucy made a face and Anna giggled. 'Well, at least we have taste,' Anna said.

'You didn't really meet him,' Hugh pointed out, 'so you can't judge properly.'

'A distant view was quite enough,' Anna said, 'with all the hearsay as well. His social column was a byword for maliciousness.' She shrugged gracefully. 'I can't imagine he'll be missed by many.'

'He was odd,' Will said. 'And why did he want to stay here? I didn't think of that until Josefina asked me.'

'Ah yes, Josefina,' Mike said with a growl. 'I wasn't forgetting her.' The dogs looked up at him, alerted by the tone of his voice.

'We don't know when Trone was killed, do we? But Josefina wasn't anywhere near the river this morning,' Will pointed out. 'She was at the farm with Alex when we came past. That's why we didn't stop. They seemed to be getting on like a house on fire, and we didn't want to get in the way.'

'Lord,' Hugh groaned. 'Bel will really enjoy that news.'

'Oh, I shan't tell her,' Will assured him.

'You won't need to,' Hugh said glumly. 'Alex will make it perfectly obvious. He never learns. And Will,' he went on, 'don't go around saying Hector was killed. We don't know yet if he was, and we certainly don't know the time of his death. There's an outside chance he knocked himself out and fell overboard. He wasn't a very good boatman.'

'Huh!' Will said. 'I know it's murder. I can tell. But, alright,' he added quickly, 'I'll only talk about it with you lot.'

Mike flinched as the dogs sprang up, barking furiously as they raced to the back door.

'Rob!' Anna said in relief, as it opened. 'We wondered what was keeping you.'

'No, we didn't,' Mike contradicted her.

The inspector took no notice of them as he walkedon¢ into the kitchen, with the dogs prancing happily about his legs until he sat down on a chair at the table. He had exchanged his ruined suit for a pair of Hugh's jeans and a faded blue shirt. The casual attire made him look younger, Lucy thought. Until you saw his face as he looked round at them. It was set and cold. Behind him came Sergeant Peters, his bulk still smart in his brown suit. He smiled faintly in a general greeting to the room, fending off the dogs with an expert hand as he stationed himself near the garden window.

Elliot nodded at Hugh. 'You were right. She was spending the nights with him, which may also explain the voices Josefina heard on the riverbank. But Trone rang her last night to tell her not to come. He didn't say much, just that he had another visitor.' He sighed. 'She's in a fair state, but insisting on staying at work.'

'Damn,' Hugh said with feeling. 'She would. I'd better go over to the office and see her.'

'Would it be easier if I did?' Lucy offered reluctantly, one hand on Ben's head as the collie came to sit beside her.

'No,' Anna said quickly, coming back to her seat. 'She's keener on men, she won't like it if it's just you. Both of you go.'

'What makes you say that?' Hugh demanded crossly.

Anna's eyes flickered to Lucy and then to Hugh. 'Instinct,' she said carelessly. 'Lots of tiny things, just the way she is, I can't explain it.'

'Which means you don't know,' Mike grunted.

Anna lifted a shoulder in an elegant shrug. 'As you like,' she said.

The dogs leaped up, barking excitedly as they raced to the back door again. Alex nearly fell over them as he flung the door open and burst into the room. 'We've been hanging around on the farm waiting for you to get back to us,' he said abruptly to Elliot. 'I've got to return to Coombhaven to find my mother, and Josefina needs to be out checking the field animals. If you do want to talk to us, can't you get on with the third degree?'

Josefina was behind him, a tiny figure in her blue dungarees, silent and watchful, with the dogs butting her hands for attention. She bent her head over them, murmuring quietly.

'I hadn't expected to be so long here,' Elliot said. 'I'm sure we can run through things quickly now. Do you have a room we can use?' Elliot asked Lucy.

She glanced at Hugh. 'The sitting room?'

'Your office would be better,' he said, getting to his feet. 'Just across the corridor from here, Elliot. I'll show you. Then I must go out to my study to have a quick look at some notes I was making. And if Maggie insists on working I'd better go over to the barn and make sure she's got something to do.'

'We don't need to go anywhere,' Josefina said quickly, as the inspector stood up to follow Hugh. 'We can answer questions here.' She looked round appealingly. 'I would like to do it here.'

Alex looked annoyed, but leaned back against one of the worktops, saying, 'Why not? We've got nothing to hide.'

Hugh glanced at the inspector, who sat down again, stretching his long legs out in front of him. 'I've no objection,' Elliot said mildly. 'At the moment I don't even know what kind of case I'm dealing with. The man may have fallen overboard.'

Mike snorted as Hugh offered a chair to Josefina. 'People who don't know boats shouldn't take them out. They're just status symbols for some of them.'

Alex stared at him as Josefina sat down, clasping her hands tightly together on the table. 'Of course they are,' he said.

'Were you interested in this one?' Elliot asked him. Behind him Tom Peters perched awkwardly on a high stool, his shrewd eyes watching the people around the table. The dogs settled too. Hades waited at the door for more visitors, but Ben came back to sit by Lucy, his golden eyes bright and alert.

Alex looked warily at the inspector. 'No, I'd never seen the boat until today,' he said cautiously. 'I hadn't been down to the river at all until Niri sent me to the rescue.'

Mike snorted, but Elliot ignored him, focusing his attention on Alex. 'Did you know Hector Trone, as himself or as Flim the political commentator?'

'No, I'd never heard of him,' Alex said immediately.

'Can you answer the same questions please, Miss Kirilova,' Elliot said.

Mike looked round, surprised, before he realised the inspector was speaking to Josefina.

She was at the far end of the table, sitting in front of Alex, and looking both nervous and subdued. She glanced at Hugh, sitting beside her. He smiled encouragingly and she began to speak. 'I know nothing of the boat, or this man, but I have seen them both.' She spread her hands. 'It is partly that I like to walk by the river when there is time.'

'When have you been there?' Elliot asked sharply.

Her hands came together, clasping each other tightly. 'It is mainly in the evening,' she said softly. 'That is when things are sometimes quieter on the farm. The animals are fed and watered. I have checked them too, so it is just a time for waiting, to see if more lambs will be born.'

'And,' Will interrupted, sounding excited, 'that's when you saw the men, isn't it? You remember,' he said impatiently as she turned her head to look at him, 'you saw two men one evening last week, down by the river.'

'Ah yes,' Josefina agreed, her eyes brightening. 'I know what you mean. But I did not see them, I only heard them.'

'When was it?' Elliot demanded.

Josefina looked anxious, but Will said quickly, 'It was two nights ago, after the wedding, because you mentioned it when we met you on Fran's farm yesterday.'

'Ah yes, that is right,' Josefina said gratefully.

'Did you know the men?' Elliot asked.

'No, how should I?' she replied. 'It was dark and they were behind trees. I only heard the sound of their voices, not even the words.'

'Are you sure they were definitely men?'

Josefina looked surprised, then thoughtful. 'I don't know,' she said slowly. 'The voices were quiet, so I assumed it was men talking. I was afraid they should not have been there, that they were up to no good on Fran's farm.'

'They could have been rustlers or poachers,' Will said. 'But we haven't had any in this area. I thought it was probably the Trone man with a mate.'

'I did too, when Will mentioned it to me,' Hugh said. 'But Trone couldn't have been one of the two men who attacked me last night.'

'What's this?' Alex demanded, looking alarmed. 'I thought you were joking about the fight. I didn't,' he confessed, 'want to ask too much about your face while Mums was around.'

'Two men went for me in a field above the river after I'd been visiting Trone. And somebody had obviously beaten him up too.'

'The same people?' Lucy asked.

Hugh shrugged. 'I should think it's likely, but we can't know yet.'

'My God!' Alex said. 'I thought I'd been in some dangerous spots, but this seems a real hotbed of trouble.'

'And guess when it started,' Mike growled. 'Just when you arrived.'

Alex stared at him. 'What's that got to do with it?'

'That's what I'd like to know,' Mike said. 'Especially as we don't know who's going to be the next victim.'

'Why should there be one?' Alex demanded. He looked around the table rather wildly, but nobody answered. Mike snorted, and gave an exaggerated start as Anna poked him in the ribs.

'Stop it,' she said as he turned to glare at her.

Elliot had been listening to this exchange with interest. Now he got to his feet. The dogs stirred, watching him. 'I must get back to the station,' he said. 'But I'll be here again soon.'

'Let us know when you get the post-mortem results,' Hugh said.

The inspector nodded. 'I've asked for them to take priority. But,' he said resignedly, 'I don't know how long it'll be until we hear.'

'You're on good terms with the police,' Alex commented resentfully as Inspector Elliot left, with Sergeant Peters at his heels closing the door firmly behind him. 'I suppose you always were.'

'Elliot and I have known each other a long time,' Hugh said coldly. 'Since we were both based in London.'

'I too must get back to work,' Josefina said, filling a sudden silence. As she stood up she looked across at Alex, who avoided her questioning eyes. She turned away from him. 'Will, do you and Niri want to come with me?'

'Yeah, that'll be cool,' Will said, getting up too.

'But we can't stay long, Will,' Niri cautioned as Josefina left. 'We've got to get back to the manor soon or we'll never get any revision done. I've still got a lot to get through.'

He pulled a face at her. 'Whatever,' he grumbled. 'I suppose so. We'll pick up our things later, Lucy. Will you be here?'

'Probably, but I'll take Ben out for a walk for an hour or so now,' she said, pushing back her chair. 'He could do with a good outing and I need some fresh air.' She glanced at her husband, as Hades pounded happily down the back steps with Will and Niri. 'Why don't you come too, Hugh?'

'I'd like that.' He smiled at her, even though the bruising pulled at his face muscles. 'Where shall we go?'

'Let's go up the hill. I don't really fancy a river walk.'

'Okay.' Hugh hesitated as he stood up. 'Look, you set off and I'll catch you up.' He was already on his way to the back door, skirting the collie, as he said, 'I want to look up a couple of outstanding points on Ambrose's plagiarism issue. We're keen to get it sorted out by next week. And I ought to see Maggie.'

Lucy's heart sank. 'Alright,' she said unenthusiastically, although he had already left the house. Ben was waiting by the door, his whole body alert and eager, and she felt she could not disappoint the dog again. 'Anna, do you want to walk with me?' Lucy asked as she pulled on her walking boots. 'I don't expect Hugh will catch up. Once he starts on work the time gets lost.'

'Actually,' Anna said lightly, 'I'm going up with Mike to look at his storerooms.'

'What?' Mike sat up straight. 'Since when?'

'Since now,' she said firmly. 'Come on. You've been here for at least a couple of hours. Surely you want to see what your students have been doing?'

He glowered at her as he joined her by the door, where Lucy was tying the laces of her boots. 'This sudden interest is unnerving,' he complained.

Anna raised an eyebrow at him, and a faint tinge of colour crept into his face. 'In archaeology,' he snapped. 'A new fad, isn't it?'

'Of course,' she replied. 'I've only just realised its potential.'

'I'll walk up there with you,' Lucy said. She saw Mike's expression and added quickly, 'Then I'll go on up the hill to the ridge. The grass is quite short up there as Fran grazed her sheep on it for a few weeks, and I want to see if there are any flowers coming through. Last year's survey found a few cowslips, I'd like to see if they're showing yet.'

She hesitated, glancing back at Alex, who was standing uncertainly by the table. 'Do you want to come too?' she asked, looking up at the clock on the far wall. 'There isn't a bus into Coombhaven for another hour, or I expect Hugh will drive you in when he's free.'

'I said I'll take him,' Mike said abruptly, glowering at Alex. 'Give me half an hour or so.'

'Okay,' Alex said. 'I'll be ready. Alright if I make myself some coffee, Lucy?'

'Of course,' she said. 'Have you rung Bel?'

'I guess I'd better,' he said, 'before she gets herself into a state.' He stared disbelievingly at his watch. 'It's only just after three o'clock but it feels as if I've been here for hours.' He sighed. 'She's probably been waiting for me since lunchtime.'

'I was thinking about the police being here, and Hector's death,' Lucy said patiently. 'She may hear a garbled story from somebody else.'

'Hell!' he exclaimed in alarm. 'I hadn't thought of that.' He pulled out his mobile phone. 'I don't want her turning up here haranguing the police. It gives the wrong impression, apart from anything else.'

Anna pulled Mike down the steps, wondering if Alex could hear his loud muttering. 'Mummy's darling, that's the impression we've all got. Spoilt rotten. Not grown up.'

'Sssh,' Anna said. 'He'll hear you.'

'Good,' Mike said, and began deliberately to repeat his words more loudly.

Alex overheard Mike quite well. He stood in the back doorway, his mobile clutched in his hand. There was no reply from Bel's phone. He felt a sense of dread. That probably meant she was on her way back to Withern right now. Mike's current comments made no impact on Alex, but his earlier ones rang repeatedly through his head. Mike suspected him of being involved in all this. James's death, this man Trone's death. What else did Mike suspect?

Alex gritted his teeth. He must find Hugh. That was the only answer. Where the hell had he gone? Alex stared round the yard garden, trying to spot any movement through the shrubbery. His eyes lifted, scanning the buildings that edged the garden. There were so many of them; which on earth was Hugh's study? And where were the publishing offices? And Hugh had mentioned some woman who worked for him. Alex frowned. No doubt she'd be staring out of the window if he did find Hugh.

At that moment a door in the building on his left opened, and Hugh came out, a laptop case in one hand, and began to walk alongside the buildings towards the barns. Alex hurried down the steps to intercept his brother. 'Hugh, wait!' he called urgently as he took the winding central path, stumbling against the grass tussocks in his haste.

Hugh looked over his shoulder and hesitated. Reluctantly he branched off on the path that led to the centre of the garden, intercepting Alex by the heavily scented witch hazel that stood in the large terracotta pot at the point where the paths from all sides of the garden converged.

Alex was limping as he reached his brother. 'I've got to talk to you, Hugh,' he said. 'What Mike said, about it all being connected with me. I didn't know, but I think he may be right. And,' he looked hopefully at his brother, 'you're in with the police. You can make it clear I didn't know.'

'Didn't know what?' Hugh demanded impatiently.

Alex sank down on the wooden bench beside the tree and buried his head in his hands. 'Oh God,' he muttered, almost inaudibly.

'Forget the drama,' Hugh advised. 'If you've got something to say, get on with it.'

'Yes.' Alex straightened up, meeting Hugh's eyes with an air of bravado. 'Well, it's to do with money, I suppose.'

'Of course it is,' Hugh said.

'I don't even enjoy it, but everybody does it,' Alex said. 'And there's always a chance that it'll come right. It did a lot at first.' He sounded disgruntled as he added, 'And I didn't see why it wouldn't again.'

'What?' Hugh asked, although he had an inkling now.

'It was just clubs at first, then I had a run of bad luck so I went online. But my luck only changed when I was introduced to a little place in London. A private place,' he said with some pride. 'You wouldn't believe who else went there. Really grand people, actresses, politicians. There were even a couple of writers sometimes,' he said, with the air of a man offering a sop of interest. 'It wasn't just betting, there was dancing and dinner too, a real social evening.'

'Gambling,' Hugh said grimly. 'How much do you owe?'

Alex lowered his head, staring at his hands clenched on the edge of the seat. 'A lot,' he said.

'How much?' Hugh repeated.

'Two hundred thousand, plus the interest,' Alex muttered. 'But that's not the problem.'

'Oh, can you pay it then?' Hugh demanded sarcastically.

'Not the way they want me too,' Alex said. 'You don't have to pay their debts in money, but I hadn't got any information to sell. So I've got to find the cash. I've been holding them off, but there've been warnings.' His voice faltered.

Hugh's eyes had narrowed. 'Were you holding them off with the promise of your inheritance from Edward?'

Alex nodded miserably, his blond hair flopping loosely up and down.

'I see,' Hugh said coldly, his mind racing. 'Is that why James was attacked? Was it a warning to you, or to him? Or did they just want the silver as part of your repayment?' He shook his head. 'No, how could they know in time to set it up?' His eyes hardened as he stared at Alex. 'Unless you told them.'

Alex buried his face in his hands. His voice was muffled when he spoke. 'When I saw him in London James told me about this collector near you. I thought if they had the silver, maybe they'd leave me alone. I never thought they'd hurt him. I did try to stop it.' He dropped his hands and looked up at his brother. 'I had to do something to stave them off,' he blurted. 'They knew I wasn't going to get enough from Edward, even if you and James agreed to give me what he did leave, and they weren't going to wait forever.' He shivered. 'You don't know what they're like, Hugh. If I can't pay, they'll make an example of me.'

'Just a minute,' Hugh said slowly. 'You said they knew your inheritance from Edward wouldn't be enough to pay your debts. Did you tell them that?'

'Do you take me for a fool?' Alex demanded. He flushed as Hugh raised an eyebrow. 'Of course I didn't,' he ended sulkily.

'Then how the hell did they know?' Hugh said. 'And who are they?'

Alex's face wore a look of terror. 'They always seem to know what's going on. They've got spies everywhere.' He saw Hugh's expression and added, 'I know it sounds like paranoia, but it's true. They know so much it's unbelievable.'

'They must have a contact in James' office,' Hugh said. 'I'll get Elliot to look into that.'

'You will explain to him, won't you?' Alex said. 'I didn't know what they were going to do.'

'How does Trone come into the picture?' Hugh asked. 'And the attempt to blackmail me?'

'Blackmail?' Alex said, his voice cracking. 'I didn't know about that.'

'We've established that you didn't know anything,' Hugh said dryly. He was silent for a moment, gathering his thoughts. 'If they know about the terms of Edward's will, they probably know of James's too. And they know that I'm not likely to hand any money over to you. They'd have to be sure of that before attempting the blackmail. You're an easy touch, but they've got nothing on me. So they tried to manufacture something. Trone must have been in on it, God knows why. I don't know why he was killed, if he was. But I have a good idea where to look for the eavesdropper.'

'Josefina?' Alex said. 'I thought it was suspicious that she should arrive at the same time as me. That's why I went to the farm with her this morning. I wanted to see what I could find out.'

Hugh was obviously not impressed with this effort. 'She could have got the information out of Will about the trust,' he said, 'although I can't remember if he knew about it. But he couldn't have overhead me discussing James's will with Elliot. Only one person might have done that.'

'Very clever,' a new voice said. It was strangely familiar, but subtly different. The men both turned quickly and froze at the sight of the revolver pointed at them.

Mike led the way up the meadow above the farmyard, his pace quickening as he approached the storerooms. The sound of a voice made him frown, pushing open the door into the western store-room. 'I hope you're not spending all your time on the phone,' he snarled as he went into the room.

'I hope his students appreciate him,' Anna commented, pausing outside to wait for him.

'I'm sure they do,' Lucy said, her eyes on the collie as Ben sniffed eagerly along the bottom of the hedgerow that led up to the field gate at the top of the slope. 'Hugh once told me that Mike's lectures are always packed, and his digs oversubscribed.'

'Hmm,' Anna said. 'I expect students are guaranteed a good laugh, if they don't get the rough side of his tongue. But he can,' she admitted, 'make archaeology sound interesting.' She came to a halt and looked back to where Lucy stood, looking down on the barns that hid the rest of the farmyard from sight.

'Sometimes,' Lucy said, half to herself, 'I wish we'd never come here.'

'But it's such a lovely place,' Anna said in surprise, returning to her side. 'You've already done such a lot here, and you can do so much more with it. You've got lots of ideas, haven't you?'

'Yes,' Lucy said unenthusiastically.

Anna glanced at her, wondering what to say. 'I almost envy you,' she said at last. 'I've never had a real place of my own to live in and work from, with somebody to share it.'

'What's the point, though?' Lucy asked quietly, almost speaking to herself. 'We never get to do things together any more, Hugh and I. He won't come walking now, you'll see, he'll get caught up in the office. It's been like that ever since we came here. I thought everything would be better once he got an assistant, but nothing's changed at all.'

'When are you going to tell him about your job?' Anna asked, trying to deal with the immediate issue.

Lucy shrugged. 'I was going to do it on this walk, but you can see why it's difficult to find the opportunity. I'll just have to tell him point blank as soon as we're on our own.'

The sound of raised voices caught their attention. 'I'd better see what Mike's up to,' Anna said, glancing at the storerooms. 'Then I'll come on after you. It's such a nice day it'll be good to be outside.' She looked down at her ankle boots. 'I can manage in these, if you're going along the top of the fields.'

She lifted her hand gaily and went up to the western storeroom, following the sound of Mike's loud voice. Lucy looked down for a second longer, then set her teeth and turned away. Ahead of her, Ben caught her movement and hesitated, waiting to see if she was coming. When he saw her walking towards him he lifted his plumed tail, letting it drift behind him as he led the way uphill.

In the storeroom there were only two people, Mike and the student with the straggly beard. Both men were examining the carved stone arch that had been partially revealed on the wall between the two rooms. Anna wondered where Laura was. She did not seem to have been much in evidence today.

'This kind of chamfering is definitely early fourteenth century,' Mike said dogmatically.

Anna was sure from his tone that he was repeating something he had just said.

'Professor Mersett showed us something similar,' Adam said, 'and that was later, fifteenth century. He said it was very easy to mistake the dating on this sort of thing.'

Mike's eyes popped. 'He should know,' he said shortly.

Anna thought it was time to intervene. She was sure Mike's professional reticence about criticising his colleagues would be easily strained. And she knew that he and the pompous Professor Mersett were frequently at daggers drawn.

'Wow,' she said lightly. 'Is it a doorway?'

'No,' Mike snapped, 'it's a bloody bathtub. What the hell does it look like?'

Adam ignored him. 'Yes, Laura and I have been working on it this morning. She's got a headache now, probably from breathing in too much dust while she was working. She wasn't wearing her mask properly. Still, she's gone over to her tent to lie down for a while. See here,' he pointed to the arch, 'and here. There are leaves and flowers carved down the side. They're in very poor repair, but the plaster may have saved them from total destruction. We'll have to get the conservators in straightaway.'

'Good of you to say so,' Mike said, his voice level. 'Anything else we must do?'

'Oh yes.' Adam turned towards him, and Anna saw a distinct shadow of Professor Mersett in his stance. 'Naturally we must...'

Anna tuned out his voice until it was a drone. She came further into the room, looking around. Mike would explode soon, she knew that, so she'd better hang around to shield the unsuspecting Adam. Even if he did deserve the blast he was sure to get. She wondered idly if Laura's headache had developed so the woman could make a strategic retreat.

Niri was deep in thought as she and Will walked along the lane from Withern towards Fran's farm. Will was running over the events of the last few days, developing his theory about Hector Trone. 'You wait, it'll be all to do with him,' Will said. Hades was trying to push under the upper hedge, his nose wuffling frantically, so Will turned to grab his collar and pull him back.

'Perhaps,' Niri agreed. 'Will, why did Josefina want to go back to Withern? She'd only just asked us to come down to the farm.'

'Well,' he said in surprise, 'I don't know. Something she'd forgotten, that's all she said. You heard her.'

'Yes,' Niri agreed slowly. 'I don't like this, Will. I want to go back to the house too.'

'Come off it,' he said, startled, coming to an abrupt stop. 'You can't really think she's got something to do with it. That's what Mike reckons, but you know he always gets bees in his bonnet.'

'Maybe. But she did turn up just as all the trouble started,' Niri said, turning as she spoke. 'I don't want to go to the farm anyway. I'd rather get on with revision at your place, otherwise the time will be gone before we've done anything.'

'Oh alright,' Will agreed reluctantly. 'If Josefina's not at the farm, I suppose there's not much point in going anyway.'

He walked beside her in frowning silence. Hades had gambolled ahead, eager to meet Bess, the farm collie. He suddenly realised there had been a change of plan, and came galloping after his master, overtaking him in a small cloud of dust. The big dog slowed down, sedately leading the way towards the drive into the Withern farmyard.

Will suddenly paused. 'Look,' he said, 'there's a badger slide down this bank and through the hedge. We can get up it to the top and see if we can spot what the police are doing down by the river.' He called Hades, who stopped and turned slowly to see what was happening now. At the prospect of a jaunt into the fields he brightened and came racing back.

Will was already on top of the hedge bank, staring across the pasture towards the river. 'They're still down there,' he said. 'There are a couple of uniforms coming back up to the lane gate where they've left their cars. Gosh, Lucy must be wild. They're bound to be disturbing the nesting larks. I bet she's mad at Hugh. It wouldn't have happened if he hadn't let that bloke moor here.'

Will stiffened, falling silent, letting Hades wriggle past him to the top of the bank.

'What?' Niri demanded from the lane below. 'What is it?'

'I can see Josefina,' he said slowly. 'She's talking to a man.' His eyes narrowed. 'It's Inspector Elliot.'

Niri stared at him, watching his expression. 'Are you sure it's her?' she asked. 'They're a long way off.'

'Yeah, I'm sure. I'm going to see what's going on,' he said, slithering back into the lane. In his haste he caught his trousers on a stray bramble, and slipped the rest of the way down on his backside.

'Will, are you alright?' Niri asked hastily.

'Yeah, yeah, don't fuss,' he said. 'Let's get along to the orchard and cut through. I don't want to miss them if they're coming back.'

He set off at a rapid pace. Hades struggled indignantly back through the hedge and raced after him.

Niri had to run to catch up too. 'Will, is it a good idea?' she asked. 'There must be a reason she's there.'

'You bet. Mike'll gloat if he's right about her.'

'Will,' Niri caught his arm. 'Who's that?' she demanded urgently.

He stopped beside her at the bend in the lane. Ahead a woman was hurrying down the drive to the Withern yard gate.

'Hell,' he said explosively. 'It's Alex's mother.'

He took hold of Hades, as the big dog sauntered past. 'Let's wait a bit until she's out of the way. I don't want to bump into her.'

'She is an awful woman,' Niri said. 'I'm sorry for Alex.'

'Alex,' Will said. 'What about Hugh? He's the one she's always got it in for.'

'Yes, I know, but...' She broke off.

From the farmyard there came the sound of a woman shouting. A gunshot rang out, and a woman began to scream.

The sound of the gunshot was clearly audible in the meadow above the farmyard. Lucy had reached the gate at the top of the hill when she heard it. She stopped abruptly, wondering if her senses were playing her false. The last time she had heard a shot up here she was falling into the nearby quarry. For a moment she felt faint, confused. Ben had come back to her, nudging her hand, and the feel of his smooth head cleared her mind.

She stared down the hill. The gunshot had come from the farmyard. It was too far away to have come from the storerooms, but Mike and Anna must have heard it too.

They had. Mike broke off in mid-sentence as Anna swung round in alarm.

'Mike!'

'Yes, come on.' He charged towards the door, where Adam stood as if stupefied, blocking the way out.

Anna bumped painfully into Mike's back as he stopped abruptly, flinging out an arm to restrain her. 'What…' she began. Then she saw it too.

The boring inoffensive student had changed. His round-shouldered body had straightened, become bulkier. His earnest face had taken on a hardness, making it sharper, more alert. And in his hand he held a revolver, its blunt nose pointing right at them.

'What the hell do you think you're doing?' Mike snarled.

In spite of her fear, Anna felt a stab of wild amusement. She had not really thought anybody would actually say that in these circumstances.

'It's not a time for play-acting,' Mike said. Anna felt guilty until she realised he was speaking to Adam.

'Oh, it's not a game, Mike,' the student said. 'Just do as I say and neither of you will get hurt. Back off, right against the far wall, and keep your hands where I can see them. Stay together,' he ordered sharply, as Mike moved back and away from Anna.

Watching them closely, one hand steady on the revolver, Adam edged out of the door and began to close it. Suddenly he staggered, the gun dropping from his hand. A whirlwind of black hair had struck him on the back, sending him forward off balance. Ben sprang round, his teeth bared close to Adam's throat as he stood over the fallen man.

Mike was already out of the door, grabbing the gun from the ground. Anna was right behind him. They looked up to see Lucy, her pointed face white with anger. 'Not again,' she said. 'Not more guns here.'

'The shot came from the farmyard,' Mike said. 'We'd better

get down there.'

'You go,' Anna said. 'Take the gun.'

Mike looked indecisive. 'You can use it, can't you?' she demanded, without taking her eyes off the man on the ground. Adam lay still, not watching Mike. His attention was riveted on the collie, who was crouched, teeth bared, ready to spring at him again.

'Of course I can,' Mike said crossly. 'But what about him?' He gestured towards Adam, and Anna flinched slightly as he used the hand with the gun.

'Don't wave it around,' she snapped. 'Hold it on him while I check he doesn't have another gun, or a knife.'

Mike began to expostulate, but Anna cut him off. 'Mike, if he tries anything I'll break his arm.' She glared at Adam. 'Don't think I won't. It'll be a pleasure.'

'That bloody self-defence course,' Mike said gruffly. 'I don't know why I ever forget you were the star student.'

'Oh, I've gone well beyond that,' Anna said. 'I got my judo black belt earlier this year.'

Mike choked, but said nothing as she ran her hands over Adam's pockets.

'Nothing,' she said, straightening up and standing back. 'Now you'd better give me the gun, Mike. And don't argue' she said sharply as Mike opened his mouth to protest. 'We can cope with Adam. Hugh must be in trouble. But don't go being a hero. The police aren't far away, they'll have heard the shot too.'

For a moment longer Mike hesitated. Abruptly he thrust the revolver into Anna's hand and set off at a run down the meadow towards the farmyard.

'Get one of those fence stakes, Lucy,' Anna instructed.

Lucy hesitated, staring after Mike, wondering who had been shot. She bit her lip. She had left Anna with a dead body once. She could not go off again, leaving her with a man who would harm her if he could. She moved obediently to fetch a stake, wondering how Anna meant to use it.

'Listen, you,' Anna said to Adam as Lucy returned with her stake. 'When I tell you, you're going to get up and keep your distance from us. You will walk slowly ahead of us downhill and into the farmyard. Try to run in any direction and Lucy will use the stake to trip you up, and we'll let Ben tear your throat out. If that doesn't stop you,' she said, 'I'll shoot you in the legs. Just give me the chance, it'll be a pleasure to use it.'

'I wondered if you'd work it out,' Maggie said. She glanced disparagingly at Alex. 'I was sure he'd break down and run bleating to you. No,' she said sharply to Hugh, 'don't try anything. I won't hesitate to kill you, don't think it.'

Looking into her hard eyes Hugh had no doubt that she would do exactly what she said. 'No one's moving,' he said calmly. 'But any shot will bring the police here in droves. They're still busy down by the river.'

'I know,' she said. 'But there is going to be a shot before they get here.' Her eyes studied him. 'It's a shame, but you already know too much. And you'd never pass money over to your brother. Who would?'

Alex flushed and shifted slightly.

She laughed, a harsh bark of sound. 'I need you alive,' she said to him, 'but I don't mind putting a bullet in you where it hurts. So keep still.'

She spoke to Hugh again. 'He won't talk, you know that. He'll tell the story we want, because he knows what will happen to him if he doesn't.'

'Is that why you killed Trone?' Hugh asked.

She smiled. It was not a pleasant sight. 'Clever,' she said. 'Yes, Hector was getting cold feet.' She sneered. 'He was happy to give us useful information about the people he met. In fact, he provided us with several sources of income for quite some time. Fortunate from his point of view, because he was a very unlucky gambler.'

'I'm sure,' Hugh said.

She smiled again. 'A stupid man. A very stupid man. If he'd played along with the latest game we wouldn't all be here now, and he'd be alive.'

'What wouldn't he do?'

'Broadcast to the world that you and he were lovers,' she said. 'The photos weren't enough to make you amenable, were they? Hector might have persuaded you to be reasonable. But,' she said, 'he wouldn't do it. He didn't think it would make any difference, and he was afraid his 'friends' in London would get to hear of it. Strange really,' she mused, 'how afraid he was of gossip when it was about himself.'

'What next?' Hugh asked. 'I don't think Alex will hide my murder, you know. And it won't benefit him. Everything I own goes to my wife.' He cursed silently, thinking fast. Had he put Lucy in danger? No, surely not. Will was her next of kin.

'Dear, dear,' Maggie said softly. 'You dealt in criminal cases, didn't you? Maybe you didn't study inheritance law? Or maybe you just don't remember.'

Hugh stared at her, his mind whirling, trying to think what she meant.

'If you die within thirty days of your uncles,' Maggie told him, 'their next heir comes in for it all.' She jerked her head towards Alex. 'He'll be a rich man. Rich enough to pay his debts and get us off his back.'

Hugh laughed. 'When you can still blackmail him about my murder? He wouldn't be stupid enough to let you get away with it.'

'Oh, I think he would,' she said softly.

'Look here,' Alex said angrily. 'I won't do it.'

'We'll see, won't we?' Maggie asked, unperturbed. 'It'll be your story against mine, and you've so much to gain, haven't you, by Hugh's death? You'd be a fool not to tell the police my version.'

She steadied the hand that held the gun. 'After all, I came out to find you both struggling with the gun. When you forced Hugh to drop it I picked it up and pointed it, to try to stop you fighting.

And sadly it went off when Hugh tried to grab it.'

'Why would we be fighting?' Hugh demanded, desperate to keep her talking. Surely someone would come soon.

'Why, you thought dear Alex was trying to blackmail you,' she said in mock surprise. 'You meant to give him a fright, that's all, but it got out of hand. And so,' her finger began to tighten on the trigger, 'it's goodbye, Hugh.'

'Alex!' It was a woman's voice, angry, strident, calling from the gateway into the farmyard.

Hugh knew it at once. So did Alex. But Maggie did not, and for an instant her attention wavered.

Hugh sprang forward, lunging for the hand with the gun. Alex moved at the same moment. The sound of the shot was loud, loud enough to cover Bel's scream.

The yard garden was chaotic. Bushes had been crushed, primroses and cyclamen squashed, while a pool of blood was growing around the body that lay very still on the ground. Nearby two people rolled backwards and forwards over the path, bumping into the body, tumbling over grass tussocks and under shrubs, oblivious to bruising and scratching. One person fought for their life, the other for escape as Bel ran screaming towards them.

She flung herself down beside them, her fingers reaching for Maggie's face. 'You've killed him,' she screamed. 'You bitch, I'll get you.'

Hugh had Maggie pinned now, although she writhed strenuously, forcing him to use all of his strength to restrain her. 'Get off, Bel,' he grunted. 'Don't get in the way.'

Maggie was stronger than he would have expected, and eventually he had to lie flat across her, half suffocating her before she stopped struggling. With one arm he fended off Bel, whose nails raked his hand as she tried to get to Maggie. 'For God's sake, you bloody stupid woman,' he yelled, shoving her away with his shoulder, 'see to Alex.'

She fell back off balance. 'Alex,' she mumbled, stumbling over to the body that lay so still. 'Yes, Alex, see to Alex, my baby.'

Maggie was limp now under Hugh's weight. But he hesitated to move, afraid she was shamming. Cautiously he lifted himself, braced for any movement from her. When it came it still caught him by surprise. She heaved her head up, catching him under the jaw.

As he slackened his hold in shock and pain, she rolled away and to her feet. Lunging forward, he grabbed her ankles and brought her down. She crashed through the branches of the witch hazel, hitting her head heavily on its terracotta pot and fell like a sack of potatoes.

Through the agony in his head, Hugh realised she was really out of action this time. He felt his jaw, wondering if it was broken. Hysterical crying drew him, half crawling, half stumbling, to Alex's side. Bel was crouched there, trying to lift him onto her lap, and stop the blood that dripped onto her hands and clothes, trickling into a pool on the ground.

'Don't move him,' Hugh managed to say, each word forced painfully out. He fumbled for Alex's wrist, searching for a pulse. 'He's alive,' he whispered in relief.

Ripping his brother's scarlet-stained shirt open he saw that Alex's chest was covered in blood, pouring from a wound high up on his shoulder. 'Not seriously hurt,' Hugh uttered. 'Get to the police. In the drive.'

The thundering sound he heard suddenly became more than the pounding in his head. Footsteps were racing towards the farmyard. Cautiously he turned his head, wincing at the pain it caused. Hades was bounding towards him and the empty gateway was suddenly crowded with people. Will was just in front, running full pelt, Mike and Niri were close behind. Inspector Elliot and Sergeant Peters brought up the rear with Josefina and a phalanx of uniformed officers.

They reached him together, clustering around the trio on the ground. Hugh's attention was drawn at once to the gun Mike was picking up out of a bleached grass tussock.

'What happened?' Mike gasped, shifting the gun from one hand to the other. 'We heard the shot.'

Elliot followed Hugh's transfixed gaze to the gun that Mike was waving as he spoke. The inspector stepped forward and took it smoothly out of Mike's grasp, passing it to Sergeant Peters.

'Don't tell me it was his mother,' he said quietly to Hugh, staring at Bel as a uniformed constable moved her aside to check Alex.

Hugh began to shake his head, stopping abruptly.

'Maggie. Blackmailing Alex. Sorry,' he stopped, indicating his jaw. 'Bit painful.'

Elliot bent over him, feeling it gently. 'Bruised, I think, not broken, but we'd better get you to hospital.'

'Me and Alex. He's worse. Been shot. Tried to stop her shooting me.'

'My God,' Mike said, stunned. 'Brotherly love where you'd least expect it.'

EIGHT

It was not yet dark outside although the sun was sinking in the west, casting rosy streaks across the far horizon. A male blackbird sat high on one of the oaks that lined the drive, his piercing song ringing out over the territory he claimed.

His clear notes were audible in Withern's silent sitting room. The lights were already on here, brightening the pale blue walls, deepening the clear blues and greens of the angular modern armchairs. The room radiated an air of calmness and peace that was not echoed by the people who had crowded into it.

The large standard lamp shone above Mike, who was sprawled across the sofa, leaving only a small gap for Anna, who sat next to him. She stuck her elbow out, poking him hard in the ribs, and he scowled at her, but moved up a fraction. 'Thanks, Mike,' she said sarcastically. 'If you take up much more space I'll need to sit on your lap.'

Mike's scowl was succeeded by a look of such horror that a laugh was jerked unwillingly from Will. The younger man lay across the rug in front of the fireplace, pulling gently at Hades' ears, while the big dog's eyes gradually drooped sleepily.

Hugh lay back in an armchair, his drawn face showing a new batch of cuts and bruises. His eyes were closed, purple stains of tiredness around their sockets. Since returning from the hospital he had changed into brown chinos and a cream shirt, but the fresh clothes just emphasised how exhausted he was.

Anna studied him with concern as she wriggled into a more comfortable position on the sofa. Her dark blue eyes flickered to Lucy, who sat stiffly upright in another armchair near the fireplace. Her head was bent forward over her tightly entwined fingers, and the long curtain of her chestnut bob hid her face. Ben lay at her feet, his eyes on her. He knows, Anna thought, that something's wrong.

The heavy silence that filled the room grew. Anna glanced round at the others. They must all know there was something wrong. Will was keeping his head down, no doubt hoping the problem would go away. Niri was curled on a floor cushion nearby, completely self-contained, as she glanced through a magazine, distancing herself from the atmosphere that was almost visible around Lucy.

Anna tried desperately to think of something light and amusing to say, anything really to break the tension. But her mind was blank, she could not think at all. She cast a look at Mike, wondering if he was aware of the strained feeling in the room.

Mike was looking at Lucy, his brows lowered in a heavy frown. Feeling Anna's eyes on him, he glanced sideways. 'What the hell is keeping Elliot so long?' he demanded. 'Why don't you go and hurry him up? Some of us have work to do.' He balled his fists and thumped his knees angrily. 'Especially as I've lost two of my students.'

'Two?' Anna said in surprise. 'Is the other one involved as well? The woman,' she struggled to remember the name, 'Laura.'

At the sound of footsteps in the hall Ben's head turned towards the door, just as Hades' eyelids rolled open as he looked to see who was coming.

Mike shrugged. 'Ask Elliot,' he advised gruffly, waving a hand towards the doorway, where the inspector was pausing, looking into the room.

Elliot's tall figure looked strange. He was still wearing some of Hugh's clothes, since his own suit was drying after his immersion in the river. But the jeans and shirt were rumpled now, so the inspector seemed even more different to the immaculately dressed person they were used to.

'Ask away,' he said, his grey eyes strained and tired as he looked around the room. 'But I can't guarantee answers.'

'I was wondering whether Laura was involved in all this,' Anna explained.

'We don't know,' he said frankly, moving into the room. 'But at the very least she can give us information about Adam's movements. I don't think we'll get much though, they didn't come down together or spend time with each other off the dig.' He glanced at Mike. 'We won't keep her any longer than we have to, but she's not all that lucid right now. She's in a state of shock,' he added with a note of warning, 'so she may not be of much use to you for a bit.'

'Work will be just what she needs,' Mike said dogmatically. 'I'll get her to concentrate on that. After all, she's going to have to do the work of two.'

Anna refused to be distracted. She was staring past Elliot at the woman who had followed him into the room.

Josefina was barely recognisable. It wasn't, Anna realised, a matter of clothes or hair. She was still wearing the faded dungarees. She still had the same knot of hair tied loosely on her neck. But now there was a quiet air of authority about her that altered her considerably.

Will stared at her, wondering why she was there. Niri looked quickly from Josefina to Inspector Elliot, who stood back slightly to let Josefina move in front of him. She moved a chair, sitting down in it to face the room. Elliot came to stand beside her. Everybody had watched this. Nobody had said a word.

The inspector's eyes ran over the faces that stared at him, resting for a brief second on Anna's puzzled expression. 'You all know Josefina,' he said, his voice seeming loud as it broke the silence. 'But now you're meeting her in her real incarnation, as Detective Inspector Tansfield of Special Branch.'

Will drew a deep breath, his thin face full of amazement as he sat up on the floor, his arms hugging his knees. 'Who were you following?' he demanded. 'That Flim man?'

'Partly,' Josefina replied.

Even her voice sounded different, Anna thought. There was no trace of an accent now, and a definite crispness to her words.

'It's a long story, but I'll make it as simple as possible.' She glanced at Hugh, whose eyes were open now and fixed on her. 'You were brought into it because your brother was in it. He was drawn into a gambling club that was one of many facets of an international crime organisation. I don't know yet why they bothered with him, he was very small beer for the barons running it. They normally focus on people with more money or important connections.'

'Like Hector Trone,' Lucy said suddenly. She was sitting back in her chair, her fingers still tightly clenched in her lap. 'Society secrets at his fingertips.'

Josefina nodded. 'Yes, he was in their clutches too. And they didn't plan to let him go, he was far too useful.'

'Yet he's dead,' Mike said abruptly. 'Are you saying it was an accident?'

'Oh no,' Josefina was adamant. 'But they pushed him too far and he was about to rebel. They couldn't risk him talking to Hugh or to the police.' She studied the others in the room for a moment. 'Some of this is guesswork as yet, it has to be nailed firmly into place with evidence.' She lifted her shoulders slightly, easing her stiff posture. 'Behind the gambling club is a slick and sophisticated blackmailing operation.' She sighed. 'It's the usual thing. Punters do well when they first visit the club, so they come back, then their 'luck' changes,' she said ironically. 'So they keep coming, expecting it to turn again, until they've run up massive debts. Money is always useful to the barons, they have plenty of ways of using it. But people who can't pay what they owe with money are invited to pay in kind. With information.'

Hugh had sat forward awkwardly, wincing with pain. He was

watching her closely.

'Information,' Josefina's cool voice carried on, 'that sometimes allows the barons to blackmail other people, and so the cycle continues indefinitely. Sometimes the information they acquire can be bought back by the people it incriminates, often in kind with other information. It is a very powerful set-up, one we've been watching for a long time.'

'What else do they do with the information?' Hugh asked with difficulty.

Josefina nodded. 'I think you've guessed. That's why I'm involved. Certain information isn't used as a lever. If it's the really vital stuff it's sold on to interested parties. Many of those parties have ordered it in the first place.'

'Military, security information?' Hugh demanded.

'Yes. Or information about people with useful positions. High-ranking military officers, government ministers, journalists, anybody in a position of power.'

'Bloody hell,' Mike said forcefully. 'Are you saying Alex was involved in this?'

'No,' Josefina said quickly. 'They wanted money from him. We've no indication that he's connected with anyone they want to pressurise. My hunch is that they misjudged his value to them. I believe they thought he had more financial prospects than he had.' She looked again at Hugh. 'That, I think, is how you became drawn into this. Alex no doubt tried to propitiate them with his prospective inheritance. Then later when the conditions of the first will were fully known he told them you'd let him access his share. But by then they knew that you came in for the majority of the money.'

Hugh was silent for a while, thinking this over. He shook his head at last. 'Even if they had an informant in the solicitor's office to give them details of the will, they were still here before Edward died, before the will came into effect,' Hugh pointed out. 'Maggie's cv came round at least four weeks ago.'

'And Adam must have signed up for the dig about then too,'

Mike put in. His eyes rolled as he did a rapid mental calculation. 'Definitely before Edward died.' He sat up with a jerk, making Anna slip sideways on the sofa. 'Dear God, they didn't kill him too?'

'We've no reason to think so,' Josefina said carefully. 'I think Hugh had already been identified as a potential source of funding for Alex to tap, and spies were put in place to watch the situation. And to add to the pressure on Alex if necessary.'

'Was that why you came down?' Anna asked. She was doing a calculation of her own. 'You must have answered Fran's advertisement about a month ago.'

'Yes,' Josefina admitted. 'We have had the whole quartet under surveillance for some time. Maggie, Adam, Trone and Alex. Maggie and Adam are major lieutenants in the organisation.' She frowned slightly. 'I don't really know why they were involved in something at this level. Unless,' her eyes narrowed, fastening on Hugh, 'you have some information they want.'

He began to shake his head, stopping quickly with a gasp of pain.

'Cool,' Will said. 'The hidden secret. What can it be?'

'It's possible that they wanted you on their side as a barrister,' Josefina said slowly, 'when the need arises. They would know of your past success, they could use a man of your skill.'

'Did Alex know about all this?' Anna asked.

'No, I'm sure he didn't,' Josefina replied. 'His main concern was to raise the money.' She looked thoughtfully at Hugh. 'In fact, I was beginning to think he hoped to secretly raise enough money to sneak off out of what he thought was their range. It would have probably been the end of him. The organisation is international in its range and totally ruthless about its victims.'

'Like Hector,' Anna said.

'Mmm.' Josefina nodded. 'He was put into place here at the last minute to get into Hugh's confidence, and he seemed to be succeeding.'

Anna looked quickly at Hugh. He was looking across at Lucy,

who had neither said a word nor met his gaze. She was watching Josefina, her pointed face quite impassive.

'And when Hugh proved recalcitrant as a blackmail victim, I suspect they planned to use Trone to up the stakes,' Josefina continued. 'But moving from photographs to a false public avowal of a homosexual relationship was more than Trone could bear.'

Anna stared at her, then lifted her eyes to where Inspector Elliot stood. Rob Elliot, she realised with a shock, had passed that information on to Josefina. So Rob had known all along what was happening.

She started as Hugh asked, 'Did Hector kill himself?'

'No.' It was Elliot who replied. 'The post-mortem showed he'd had a good thump on the head, and it doesn't seem possible from the angle that he would have got it falling overboard.'

'He'd probably decided to confess the whole thing to Hugh,' Josefina said. 'Or they thought he had. And when Maggie saw Alex buttonhole Hugh in the yard garden she thought he was going to do the same. We were just moving in when things came to a head. I'm sorry it ended so painfully for you, but we've had to let things run for a while. We've been dovetailing this operation with a number of others, to get as many of the operatives as we can.'

Lucy was staring at her. She spoke for the first time. 'So you've known all the time what was happening.'

'Pretty much,' Josefina agreed. 'We just needed enough evidence to make the case against them watertight. If we're particularly lucky they may spill a lot of beans. But,' she sounded philosophical, 'I'm not counting on it.'

'Did they kill James?' Lucy asked, one hand resting on Ben's hand as he pushed against her legs.

Josefina's face darkened. 'Yes. I'm afraid we missed the relevance of Maggie's other life as a gardener at Meryl Harper's house. She'd have found it easy enough to copy Ms Harper's front-door key. The dodgy catch played right into her hands, confusing the entry issue.'

Hugh's eyes widened. 'What?' he exclaimed. 'Was Maggie behind that too?'

'I'm afraid so,' Josefina said. 'We didn't know of the link between Meryl and your uncle James, or about the silver collections. I'm so sorry. But we think Adam was one of the men involved, minus that conspicuous wig and beard he sported. We're just checking his movements. And we'll find out who the other was.'

Anna was staring at Josefina in amazement. Before she could utter a word, Lucy asked in a cold voice, 'Why did they kill James? Surely they didn't have to?'

'Of course they didn't have to,' Josefina agreed. 'He'd have been easily overcome by the two of them.' She glanced at Hugh. 'I guess they knew how much he would leave to you. They certainly knew that if you inherited and died within a month of your uncles the money, all the money from both of them, would pass to your half-brother. That gave them two options – blackmail you, or kill you and blackmail Alex.' She shrugged. 'It may not even have been that. These people are killers, James's resistance may just have triggered their inclination to finish the job.'

'Was it the same two men who attacked me in the field after I left Hector's boat?' Hugh asked. He added resignedly, 'I suppose you were there when I needed you because you were watching them, rather than me.'

Josefina's teeth flashed in a grin. 'Yes, it was Adam and his mate. I knew they were out and about late at night. I'd hoped to dissuade Will and Niri from evening wanderings by telling them about the prowlers. I didn't,' the grin widened, 'know them very well, then.'

Will grinned back at her. 'I'd never have guessed what you are,' he said. 'You make a good farmer.'

She laughed. 'My mother is Bulgarian, I used her name when I replied to Fran's advertisement. And her parents have a farm in the Elhova region, where I used to spend a lot of my school holidays. So I'm not a complete fake.'

Anna sat bolt upright with a startled exclamation. 'What about Fran's farm?' she demanded. 'You won't be staying there now, will you?'

'I'm afraid not,' Josefina said ruefully. 'But I'll provide a replacement. Don't worry about it.'

'We can stay and help,' Will offered eagerly. 'Fran's only away for another two weeks.'

'Will,' Niri expostulated, 'we haven't even started our revision yet. You know we're supposed to be going back to the manor this evening to give us plenty of time to get on with it.'

'No need, Will, but thank you,' Josefina said. 'I've got some-body ready to step in. I didn't expect to be here for very long.' She looked apologetically at Anna. 'He's a colleague of mine who grew up on a farm, he's happy to spend a couple of weeks of his leave working on Fran's farm. It'll seem like a holiday after what he does in London.'

'Well,' Anna was clearly unhappy at the thought, 'I suppose I don't have much choice.'

'I'll make the arrangements straightaway,' Josefina said. 'He'll be here by evening. His name is Jono.' She turned to Inspector Elliot, who had stayed silent behind her. 'Now we must go. There is a great deal to sort out.'

Elliot glanced around the room. 'I'll keep you informed about what's happening,' he said. His eyes lingered briefly on Anna, whose gaze met his without her usual warmth.

'Fine,' Hugh said awkwardly. 'We'll see you.'

Nobody in the room moved to accompany the police to the front door. When it banged shut Mike got up and strode to the window, following their progress down the front garden to the police car that waited on the drive. The sound of the engine start-ing was clearly audible in the silent room. As it died away Mike announced with a sigh of relief, 'They've gone.'

'He must have known about this all along, mustn't he?' Anna demanded, her hands clenched on the knees of her trousers. 'Rob, I mean. He must have known what was happening here.'

'It's his patch,' Hugh said. 'Of course he had to know.'

'And he didn't warn us,' Anna said furiously.

'How could he?' Hugh said tiredly. 'He couldn't risk letting too many people in on the plan. Too much depended on keeping the police actions undercover until the last moment.'

'The bloke was only doing his job,' Mike said, sitting down heavily on the sofa next to Anna.

'Hugh could have died,' Anna pointed out, turning to glare at Mike. 'James did die. Rob's supposed to be a friend, why was he leaving us in danger without any help? He was hardly ever here either. Afraid of blowing Josefina's cover, I suppose. And,' she added, as a final thought struck her, 'I bet that's why he couldn't come to Fran's wedding.'

'He's a policeman,' Mike repeated gruffly. 'He was only doing his job.'

'And that mattered more than his friends,' Anna said. The anger in her blue eyes made Mike flinch as she leaned towards him.

Mike threw out his hands in exasperation. 'What do you expect?' he demanded. 'Anyway, what are you fussing about? Hugh's survived, hasn't he?'

'So friendship doesn't count. Right, at least I know where I am. And what am I supposed to do about the farm?' Anna demanded, her anger unappeased. 'It's all very well Josefina sending another farming policeman. How do I know if he's any good? And should I tell Fran about what's happened? I suppose I must,' she sighed. 'But I don't want her to come rushing back.'

'I'll keep an eye on things,' Will offered. 'Really, I won't let it interfere with revision. And maybe Alex will help too if he's still around.' He turned to Hugh, who was lying back in his chair, his eyes closed again. 'How is he?'

'Thinking a bullet hole isn't all that much to put up with,' Hugh said, opening his eyes. 'He's paid a high price for his stupidity, and he knows it, but he'll probably come out of it all quite lightly in the end. After all, he wasn't actually involved in anything illegal.'

'James is the one who paid the price,' Lucy said. Her voice was quiet, but everyone looked at her quickly, startled by its tone. 'And possibly Edward. You would have too, Hugh, if you hadn't been lucky. After all, they'd got your interests cleverly worked out, hadn't they? Work first, then good conversation. And they got to you through them.'

An awkward silence fell. Mike coughed, glaring at Anna, willing her to say something.

'Yes,' Hugh said with difficulty. 'I'm guilty on all counts. And I'm going to make life worse, Lucy. I am sorry, but I had to ask Bel and Alex to stay. After what happened here I couldn't insist they remain in the hotel. And they will have to be around for a week or so to answer questions.'

'Uh, maybe we should just check out Fran's farm,' Will said quickly, getting to his feet. Hades lifted his head enquiringly, then leaped up, watching his master. Will glanced meaningfully at Niri, who rose smoothly and joined him as he walked to the door. 'We'll just get our things, Lucy, they're all ready,' he said with an effort at nonchalance. 'Then we won't need to bother you on our way home.'

They left the room abruptly and disappeared from sight. The people left in the sitting room listened to the sound of their footsteps running up the stairs and fading away.

'Umm, I suppose you want to have a look at your storerooms, Mike,' Anna said.

'What?' he demanded, taken aback.

'You know,' she frowned at him, 'to see if you need more student help. I'll come with you and we can arrange a date for you to talk to me about the play I'm doing for Berhane. Remember I asked you about it?'

'Oh yes,' Mike said, with only a hint of reluctance, 'I've been thinking about that.'

'Not now, tell me as we go,' Anna diverted him, getting lightly to her feet.

'Well, aah, of course, I see.' Mike's square face was suddenly illuminated with understanding as she pulled a face, jerking her head very slightly towards Hugh and Lucy. Mike's eyes flickered between Hugh's troubled expression and Lucy's stony countenance, before fastening on Anna. 'Yes, let's go now.'

He heaved himself off the sofa and strode to the door, where he almost collided with Will. The younger man had dropped his rucksack in the hall, where Niri waited with her own.

'Lucy,' Will said eagerly, 'you can let me know at any time if there's a problem on Fran's farm. It won't take me long to get over there from home.'

'That's a nice idea, Will.' Lucy's eyes turned to him without pleasure. 'But I won't be here to do it.'

'What?' Mike demanded, alarmed. 'Isn't that...'

'Mike,' Anna tugged at his arm. 'Let Lucy explain.' She tried to pull him out of the room, but Will stood stock still in the doorway, staring at his sister.

'Oh, it's nothing to get excited about,' she said, with brittle lightness. 'I've got a new job, that's all, and it means that I'll be working in Hampshire for part of the week.'

She looked at Hugh, who was watching her, his face shuttered and still. 'I've been trying to tell you for a while, but somehow we never had time to talk to each other.'

Anna had succeeded in pushing Will and Mike out of the room. She shut the door firmly behind her.

'Anna already knows what your plans are, doesn't she?' Hugh asked.

'Yes, I told her all about it when we went out walking.'

'Lucy, I'm so sorry,' he said. 'I've been getting too tied up in my own affairs. Do you want to sit down now and tell me about it? What is the job?'

She looked at her watch. 'I'm afraid I don't have time to talk now. I've got to pack my things.'

'So soon?' He was startled. 'What's so urgent about it?'

'Nothing. The induction starts next week, and I want to be

there in time to look around the place.'

'I see.' Hugh felt a surge of anger, which he tried to subdue. 'So you must have known about this for a while. And you couldn't be bothered to tell me.'

'Would you have been interested?' Lucy demanded. 'I don't think so. You haven't really listened to what I've said about anything recently. When the vacancy at the seed bank came up, I wasn't sure of my own mind, there were other things I needed to discuss with you. But you didn't want to talk about them, and that left me in limbo. So the job seemed even more appealing and I applied for it.'

Hugh lost control of his anger. 'This is all about punishing me, isn't it? Because I'm not fussed that you can't have children. Because I don't want to adopt. Now you've seen my family dynamics,' he demanded, 'are you surprised?'

Lucy was coldly unfazed, her pointed face set and pale. 'Don't flatter yourself, Hugh,' she said sharply. 'You've got something of your own, the company you wanted to set up. I'm sure you'll make time for your photography later on, and be successful at that too. But now this is my chance to work for a short time in the real field I belong in. It's where I'd have been if Daddy hadn't died and left the manor in difficulties.'

'But you saved that for Will,' Hugh snapped. 'Then I suppose I came along and stopped you doing what you most wanted to do. But that doesn't matter now, you can swan off to do it, leaving me based in the back of beyond. I only agreed to stay down here because of you.'

'Come off it, Hugh. You said you could work anywhere. And it gives you chance to take the bird photos you want. So don't try to blame me for coming to Withern.'

He drew a deep breath and waited a moment, deliberately relaxing his muscles, forcing himself to calm down. 'Sorry, Lucy,' he said with an effort. 'It's been a hell of a few days, and this just seems like another blow.'

'I'm sure you'll manage just fine,' she said. 'You'll be busy with the company again now that Maggie's not around. Busier than ever, I mean.'

'Look, let's not keep sniping at each other,' he said. 'Tell me about what you're doing. Maybe time apart will do us some good.'

'Maybe,' she agreed, without much conviction. 'Anyway, it's only maternity leave cover. And only three days away.' At the moment, she thought. 'So I'll be here for part of the week, as well as weekends.'

'What about Ben? He'll miss you,' Hugh pointed out.

She stared at him in surprise. 'I wouldn't leave Ben,' she said. 'He's coming with me. I've got a flat at the botanic gardens, and he can come into the office with me. There'll be plenty of walking for him, he'll be alright.'

Hugh stared back at her. 'You've got it all sorted, haven't you? Without saying a word to me. I don't even know where you're going. But you'd better go and start packing, I wouldn't want you to waste time hanging around here.' He turned in his chair, looking out of the window without seeing the garden or the drive beyond.

Lucy looked at his back for a moment. 'Ben,' she called, turning to the door.

The collie, who had been lying in front of the hearth, looked anxiously at her, then at Hugh. He got up reluctantly, hesitating.

Lucy called again, and Hugh made no move. Ben walked with dragging paws to the door and out into the hall. Lucy shut the door with a quiet firmness that sounded louder than a slam.

MARY TANT's Rossington series

1 *The Rossington Inheritance*

Lucy Rossington has put a promising career on hold, so that she can keep the family home going for her young brother Will – not an easy task, when home is an Elizabethan manor that the family have lived in for generations.

When the taint of avarice and deceit from the past seems to stain the present, she had to know who she can trust, not only for her own happiness, but also for the safety of her family and friends. Will she find out in time?

2007   £6.99   PAPERBACK   ISBN 978–1–903152–21–8

2 *Death at the Priory*

Lucy Rossington doesn't need any more trouble just now. She's got plenty of that already at the family manor in an idyllic West Country valley.

So it's really the last straw when odd incidents plague the priory excavations, under the leadership of the mercurial Mike Shannon. Does the death of an archaeologist mean more than a temporary disturbance? Is Lucy imagining evil where none exists? She is soon to know.

2008   £7.99   ISBN 978–1–903152–17–1

3 *Friends... and a Foe*

Life looks promising for Lucy Rossington and her family – there is no way they could guess that in just a few days their happiness might be shattered for ever..

Old friends rejoin the family circle – one of them brings in their wake a secret that somebody would kill to keep. How could the Rossingtons know that this secret will cost them dearly?

2009   £7.99   ISBN 978–1–903152–22–5

4 Players and Betrayers

The play's the thing. It certainly is for Anna Evesleigh, with her first summer production at Rossington Manor. She needs to prove to herself – and irascible archaeologist Mike Shannon? – that she can succeed with this.

Since her own near brush with death earlier in the year, Lucy has slowly recovered. By the time she picks up the threads, the shadow of that master hand lays heavily over her family and friends, and Lucy inevitably finds herself in danger.

2010   £7.99   ISBN 978–1–903152–26–3

5 The Watcher on the Cliff

Who stalks the cliffs of the remote West Country, mysteriously swathed in cloak and hat? Is there a connection with Lucy Rossington's startling discovery?

Coincidence has brought many of the Rossington circle together again. They can't know that soon they will be drawn into the pageant of death that will stalk the cliffs. This time Lucy's instinct for evil doesn't plumb the full depth of the plot that threatens those she loves. If she can't unmask the villain, is there anyone who can?

2011   £7.99   ISBN 978-1-903152-27-0

6 Don't Come Back

Not everyone is pleased when Berhane comes back to the moor. She was first there as an adopted child, now she's back to stay. But her return is like a stone dropped into a quiet pool, creating ever-widening ripples.

As the snow comes down and the bells ring out the New Year, they unknowingly herald another death. And soon Lucy is drawn into danger again. Will she be able to save her friend? The odds seem to be against it.

2012   £7.99   ISBN 978-1-903152-30-0

MARY TANT'S WEBSITE

Find out more about Mary Tant's world by visiting her website

www.marytant.com

- ❏ Find out more about her plots
- ❏ See which authors' books she has in her library
- ❏ Explore the bookshops she finds
- ❏ Visit the teashops she enjoys
- ❏ Follow her regular nature blog
- ❏ Get the latest news of further Rossington titles.

The eighth novel in the Rossington series will be available in Spring 2014. Watch Mary's website for further details closer to publication: www.marytant.com.